DRAGON
COAST

OTHER BOOKS BY GREG VAN EEKHOUT

DRAGON COAST

Greg van Eekhout

A TOM DOHERTY ASSOCIATES BOOK

NEW YORK

DRAGON COAST

Copyright © 2015 by Greg van Eekhout

Edited by Patrick Nielsen Hayden

A Tor Book
Published by Tom Doherty Associates, LLC
175 Fifth Avenue
New York, NY 10010

www.tor-forge.com

Tor® is a registered trademark of Tom Doherty Associates, LLC.

Library of Congress Cataloging-in-Publication Data

Van Eekhout, Greg.
    Dragon coast / Greg van Eekhout.—First edition.
        pg. cm.
    ISBN 978-0-7653-2857-1 (hardcover)
    ISBN 978-1-4299-5143-2 (e-book)
    I. Title.
    PS3622.A585485D73 2015
    813'.6—dc23
                                                    2015019189

Our books may be purchased in bulk for promotional, educational, or business use. Please contact your local bookseller or the Macmillan Corporate and Premium Sales Department at (800) 221-7945, extension 5442, or by e-mail at MacmillanSpecialMarkets@macmillan.com.

First Edition: September 2015

Printed in the United States of America

0 9 8 7 6 5 4 3 2 1

*To my friend Tim Pratt, who was sad
that I hadn't yet dedicated a book to him*

DRAGON COAST

Sam lived in a world of bones. He found them throughout the dragon, wherever he walked, embedded in the tissues lining every artery, every organ, every cavity, like fossils in rock. The bones came from griffin and basilisk and garuda raptor and lesser dragons, from creatures of earth and fire and flight. The Pacific firedrake was a patchwork creature, constructed of bits and odds and ends from hundreds of other creatures, and Sam figured all the bones he found were leftover parts. He couldn't be sure. He was alone inside the dragon, without anyone to explain his world to him.

He spent most of his time in a cockpit built from various arm and leg bones and ribs. The cobblestone floor was mostly armored scales and spinal plates. The pilot seat was a weave of smaller bones, and it'd taken Sam a while before he figured out how to sit in it without jabbing himself in the ass.

And then there were the finicky controls. The pilot's yoke. The wing levers. The fire valve. These were made up of thousands of tiny bones, knitted together and threaded into each other like an intricate dry stone wall.

Most of the controls didn't do anything. Maybe the problem was that Sam had basically no idea how airplanes worked.

But he suspected there might be more to it. His relationship with the dragon had changed and gotten weirder over time. Last year, the dragon was a monster that existed outside of him, a creature he was trying to sabotage, because some awful people were going to use it as a weapon of mass destruction. So he'd leaped into the dragon's gestation tank to prevent that from happening and ended up losing his body and having his consciousness and magical essence absorbed into the dragon.

He'd been destroyed. He'd dissolved away, flesh and blood and sinew and bone, like a seltzer tablet in water.

But he wasn't dead.

He was in the dragon now.

He understood that he wasn't literally in the dragon. He wasn't literally kicking around inside a hundred-foot-long living bomber. He was no longer a physical being. Yet his back ached when he sat too long in the pilot's chair. And he still needed to pee and shit, which he did way down away from the cockpit in the base of the dragon's neck. He still needed to sleep, which he did in a hammock made from stringy bits of flesh he'd torn off from the inside of the dragon's cheek.

And he needed to eat.

He looked out through the dragon's eyes, his cockpit's windows. He could see craters in the dark part of the crescent moon. Every meteor trail was a brilliant firework. The stars would have been bright enough to read by if he had anything to read.

And, below, the ocean churned, and Sam saw whales. It was migration season for the California grays, making their journey from the frigid Bering Sea south to the warm bathwaters of Baja. The sea was black as ink, but he could make out white patches on the whales' backs and mottled skin, crusted with barnacles. He pulled on the stick and the dragon banked around. It usually didn't respond to Sam's touch, diving when Sam tried to climb, belching flame when he cranked the fire valves shut so tight he lost skin on his palms, but now it followed his command. The dragon was as hungry as Sam.

He flew in a broad circle, defining his kill zone. It contained three whales: a forty-foot cow with a one-year-old calf, and surfacing a few miles from her, a massive bull.

Sam focused his attention on the bull.

The bull dove and Sam pulled back on the stick. The dragon shot up hundreds of feet, its wings pushing air with the sound of rending thunder. At the apex of its climb, Sam thrust the stick forward and yanked on the wing levers. The dragon reversed direction in a tight loop, swept its wings back, and dropped.

Sam braced his legs against the control panel to keep from falling out of his seat. He didn't think he could crash through the dragon's eyes, but he wasn't terribly confident about that assumption. Really, he ought to get around to making seat belts.

The surface of the ocean rushed up at him. In seconds, the dragon hit the water with a monumental crash that stung Sam's cheeks. He descended into the depths, pursuing the whale.

The gray worked its massive tail, fleeing for its life, but it couldn't match the dragon's speed. Other whales answered its grunted alarm calls, not just the nearby female and her calf, but more whales from miles around. Sam didn't speak whale, but their voices saddened him. They sounded frightened. He didn't like feeding on them any more than he liked eating shark and grouper and marlin and seal and walrus. Before becoming part of the dragon, in the world he thought of as Past, when he'd been a seventeen-year-old guy walking on two legs, he'd been a vegetarian.

As the dragon's nose drilled through the cold depths, Sam sighted the whale, a great, dark column of muscle and flesh desperately heaving its tail and plunging yet deeper. Then, abruptly, the whale reversed course. With a grunt that reverberated in Sam's belly, it climbed through the water on a collision course with the dragon.

Whalers used to call grays "devil fish" for the violence they did against wooden ships and men hurling harpoons. But Sam was piloting a living weapon. The whale would be no match for the dragon's powerful rear legs or its curving talons the length of school buses. Sam leaned to his right and pulled on the pair of femur levers that controlled the firedrake's legs. The dragon's talons closed on the top of the whale's head. They ripped through hide and blubber.

The whale beat its flukes, not frantically, but with purpose. It rammed its forehead into the dragon's midsection, and the dragon coughed out a parcel of superheated air. A cloud of bubbles and boiling water and blood filled the cockpit windows. Sam's own air escaped with a *whoof*. His diaphragm spasmed as he tried to refill his emptied lungs.

Blinded and gasping, he took another hit from the whale with the impact of colliding moons. The firedrake's armored scales rang and clanked, and Sam doubled over in his seat, his mouth and eyes wide open in pain. He reached out, pawing the control panel for the talon levers, and when his hand landed on them, he pulled and pushed them, hoping to rake his talons down the whale's belly.

The water became blood and partially digested plankton and viscera. The whale gave a long, final deep moan, and the dragon sank its serrated teeth into blubber and flesh, tearing away giant slabs of meat and swallowing them whole. Sam caught his breath and felt his body filling with nutrition and energy. The tang of blood and the rich, sweet flavor of whale flooded his senses.

Sam was an osteomancer, and osteomancers gained magic

from the creatures they ate. The whale was not an osteomantic creature, not like the firedrake was, but Sam could still sense what it had been before he killed it. It had lived more than half a century and swam in the black, crushing pressure of fifty fathoms. It had seen shipwrecks, and squid longer than itself, and witnessed islands drowned by tsunamis. It had wondered at dolphins and at calving glaciers. It had mated and fathered a dozen offspring.

Sam was grateful, and he mourned.

Hours later the firedrake glided low over the Southern California Kingdom. The sun dawned across the desert, just peeking over the dark purple mountains on the eastern horizon. The dragon usually flew over land at night, the people down in the twinkling grid of city lights oblivious to its presence. But today it would be seen.

As soon as it set course, Sam wrestled with the stick. He tried to plunge back into the sea, or nose-dive into an empty parking lot, or climb above the clouds, all the way to the airless skies. Maybe the flame in the dragon's fire chambers would starve and go out. Maybe the dragon would suffocate and die.

Sam didn't want to die, but since he'd already sacrificed his life once to prevent the dragon from doing harm, he was willing to do it again. But the dragon was on self-pilot now.

It approached from the north, paralleling the shore and cliffs of Point Dume and soaring over the beach houses of the Malibu Colony. In seconds, it reached the Santa Monica Pier, where the roller-coaster cars still sat parked on the track and the Ferris wheel wasn't yet turning.

Sam pulled the stick right to steer back out to sea, but instead the dragon turned left, inland. It beat its wings, and dogs howled. Pigeons and rats cowered among the palm fronds.

It slowed over a Mid-City neighborhood. Low-slung buildings lined the main canals of Pico and Robertson—an assortment of shops, cafés, consignment furniture stores, a handful of synagogues and churches. Dingbat apartments and single-story houses clung to the side canals. There were no great powers here, just office workers and dental hygienists and drywall installers. Just people.

Sam made sure the fire control wheels were spun all the way left, firmly in the closed position. There was nothing else he could do. Whatever destruction the dragon wrought, how many lives it took, Sam wasn't responsible for it. These were the firedrake's crimes, and the crimes of Otis Roth and the osteomancers who'd built the dragon.

And yet, the dragon's previous targets were connected to Sam. He'd burned every last one of Otis Roth's warehouses. He'd burned Sister Tooth's church of bone. He'd burned the San Gabriel Grand Port and a gas station out on the northern shore of the Salton Sea. These were places associated with the people who'd built the dragon, or places Sam had been in the few days before his dive into the dragon's tank.

So, really, the idea that the dragon's path of destruction had nothing to do with him was just a thin fiction.

But he didn't have any particular ties to the neighborhood below. Maybe the dragon was expanding its range of targets. Or maybe Sam was becoming random in his cruelty.

A searchlight mounted on the roof of a liquor store pinned the dragon in an illuminated beam, and an instant later a siren revved up and wailed. Lights snapped on in windows, and Sam allowed himself a drop of hope. Maybe there'd be antiaircraft.

Maybe a shell at such close range would shatter the dragon's skull and end this.

But no artillery barrage came.

The dragon bellowed. Leaves shook from the trees, and panicked birds exploded from their perches. Cats darted under houses. Windows shattered, a noise no harsher to Sam inside the dragon than the impact of jacaranda petals floating free from the branches and landing on the surface of the canals. The dragon's call was an alarm clock. It wanted people awake when it visited horrors upon them. The spicy, sour tinge of terror floated up to him, and the dragon sucked it up, and Sam loved the smell.

The cockpit swung around on the end of the dragon's neck and pointed straight down. Sam fell forward, his ribs and knees crashing into the control panel. He looked out the dragon's eyes to see what the dragon would burn first.

No more than a hundred feet down was a little stucco house with maybe two or three bedrooms. The people who lived there had put in a nice garden. There were rows of tomatoes and peppers and a lime bush. Sam imagined weekend parties with homemade salsa and margaritas. Two boats were docked on the canal out front, which meant they were probably home.

The dragon exhaled, and the air danced in a heat mirage. Once again, Sam tried to tighten down the fire control wheels. They reminded him of oven knobs, made from chunks of gnawed vertebrae. He gripped them and turned with all his strength, fighting to make them budge even as skin tore loose from his palms.

Of course, it didn't help. It never did.

The dragon sent a massive ball of liquid flame onto the house. Burning with deep reds and purple-blacks and near-white yellows, the flame flowed down the sides of the roof like melting wax. The roof caught, tar shingles flaking and crumbling away. In only a moment, Sam could see burning rafters and insulation boiling with toxic smoke.

The dragon beat its wings, spreading a storm of glowing embers to the neighboring houses. More fires caught, but the dragon wasn't done.

It turned next to a two-story apartment building. Patio furniture and potted plants occupied the balconies. And on some of them, toys.

"Stop it," Sam screamed, his voice bouncing off the sharp angles inside the cockpit. "Just stop it."

The dragon shrieked fire down on the building. It caught even faster than the house.

By now the roar of flames and crackle of burning wood and plaster leached through the dragon's hide. Sam smelled the pleasant bitter odors of smoke, and he tried to suppress the satisfaction of having created more heat than he'd spent. Scrambling across the cockpit floor, he picked up a bone the size of a baseball bat. He'd been using it as source bone for various tools and hardware—screws, pins, handles, levers—all to devise new and better mechanisms to wrest control of the dragon. He wielded the bone as a club now, striking the cockpit windows. He wasn't sure what he was hoping to accomplish. But eyes were sensitive, weren't they? If he couldn't control the dragon, maybe he could hurt it from inside. Maybe he could turn its attention to him, away from more houses and buildings to burn. Maybe he could shatter the windows and crawl out the dragon's eyes.

And if he managed that, what would he be then? An escaped thought?

He bashed the windows a few more times, but the bone just bounced back as if he were hitting taut sheets of leather.

The dragon beat its wings, generating more wind and storms of embers. At least a dozen houses were in full conflagration now. Orange light danced behind windows. Roofs went up in whirlwinds of flame and sparks. People staggered on the sidewalks, or fled, barefoot. Some carried their most precious items or just whatever they could grab: photo albums, boxes of papers, crucifixes. One old man in nothing but his pajama bottoms clutched a fly-fishing rod.

Flames engulfed half the docked boats, and in the canal, a woman with three small kids threaded a skiff around burning debris. She kicked away flaming palm fronds falling on the boat and the water steamed around her.

The dragon swiveled its head toward her. It wheeled around in a lazy arc, flapping its wings just enough to hover above the little morsel. Terrified, the woman putted along as fast as the boat would go, and the dragon vented heat from its nostrils.

"Why are you doing this?" Sam screamed.

But that was the wrong question.

The purest expression of osteomancy wasn't just eating magical creatures, but becoming them. Somehow, in a way Sam didn't have the learning or experience to understand, he had become the firedrake.

The correct question, then, was why was *he* doing this?

He had no idea.

He climbed back into the pilot's seat. Grabbing the stick again, he tried to pull up, to lift the dragon into a climb. The stick moved, but the dragon didn't. Flames wavered on the edges of the windows.

There was no logic to this. No reason. This place, these

people, meant nothing to him. It was just a place where people lived, a neighborhood like hundreds of other neighborhoods in Los Angeles. He had nothing to gain from their loss.

Flames swirled before him, as if the dragon were sculpting death, just for the mother and her children in the boat below. Why was it toying with them? Or with Sam?

He squeezed the stick, driving the bone into his bleeding palms, grinding his teeth so tight he was sure they'd shatter. There was a crackling like dry straw, and the control stick splintered and snapped off in his hands.

The dragon raised its great wings, the tips smashing into the sides of houses and shattering roofs. It brought them down again, and the waves they generated almost capsized the woman's skiff. But the dragon began to climb. It rose through smoke into clear air, where Sam could see flames still spreading to other houses and people crawling on front lawns and families holding hands and running away. He caught sight of the woman in her skiff. She was stuck now in a clog of traffic of other people trying to get away in their boats.

Whatever he'd done differently this time seemed to have worked. Somehow, this time, he'd managed to exert some control over the dragon. Sam wasn't steering the dragon, but at least it was flying away without immolating the woman and her children in the skiff.

The dragon rumbled with a vocalization. To Sam, it sounded like laughter.

The water mage disliked water. At least he did now, when there was far too much of it, especially when it was water he didn't control.

He stood at the bow of the fifty-foot shrimp boat as it rode swells taller than three-story buildings. The deck rose and then dropped beneath his feet, and he gripped the rail and reminded himself that he could have delegated this work to someone else, if he didn't mind it being done wrong. Right now, Gabriel Argent wished he had a higher tolerance for things being done wrong. But he was a control freak. Other people said that like it was a bad thing.

Spray obscured the wheelhouse windows, but he could imagine the glares of contempt directed at him by the captain and radio operator. Sailors knew better than to be out in this weather. Only the privilege of Gabriel's high office shielded him from complaint. They might think nasty things at him, but they wouldn't say them out loud. There was only one person who told him to his face when he was being stupid.

The bright orange life jacket the captain insisted Gabriel wear did little to make him look rugged, nor did his constant and futile attempts to wipe water off his glasses. He entertained no illusions about his appearance. He was a man thinned by late hours and skipped meals, with a physique well suited to the strenuous exercise of lifting pens and bending over engineering diagrams and grimoires. He pocketed his glasses and squinted into the wet gloom.

Beneath the surface, the Pacific Ocean churned, 760 trillion pounds of water that made Gabriel Argent's own network of aqueducts and canals and sewers and pipes seem like a dribble.

And there were other powers lurking among shipwrecks and whale carcasses: the magically potent remains of kraken, and dragon turtle, and horse-serpents sleeping in the crushing depths.

The only thing that made Gabriel even more uneasy than the sea was the sky.

A voice crackled through the intercom speaker: "We have visual contact." It belonged to the pilot of the spotter plane, three thousand feet up and six miles downrange. He was probably hating the weather even more than Gabriel was.

Gabriel peered through the binoculars, but he could see nothing through the wadded low clouds.

"Max?"

Max leaned into the wind and lurched up the deck to stand beside him, water streaming from his oilskin hood and from the tip of his long, sharp nose. He gave Gabriel a deadpan glare of annoyance. Unlike Gabriel's other subordinates, Max wasn't afraid to call out Gabriel's mistakes, shortcomings, and bad ideas. That was only one reason Max was more than a subordinate. He was more of an equal who did what Gabriel told him.

"You think I can smell anything with all this water flying in my face?" he said over the storm.

"What's the point in having a great nose if you're not willing to use it?"

Max's grumbles were lost in the wind and wet. He drew in breath, closed his eyes, and analyzed the scents.

"I smell a heart pumping fire," he said.

From his pocket, Gabriel took a ball of glass about the size of a baby food jar. It was filled with strangely silver water, so pure it glowed with its own light. In his other hand, he held a tuning fork.

"Dragon's climbing," came the spotter pilot's voice. "I'm trying to keep it in range."

"Max, I need to know if it's the firedrake."

Gabriel knew what he was asking of his friend. The dragon, if it was a dragon, was thousands of feet in the air and miles away. Just to detect it at all, Max had to use every bit of concentration and sensitivity he could summon. And Max knew as well as Gabriel that they only had one chance to get this right. There was only enough water in the jar for one attempt.

Gabriel lifted the binoculars again and peered through the thinning low clouds. He saw a dot now. He couldn't be sure if it was the dragon or his plane or a pelican at lower altitude. This was the price for not using his resources to build a military force. Instead, he used them to deliver water and life through the realm.

"I smell the old Hierarch," Max said, at last.

This is what Gabriel expected. The Hierarch, of course, was long dead. Daniel Blackland had killed him in a duel, and instead of taking the old wizard's place as ruler of the Southern Californian realm, Blackland had gone running, devoting himself to keeping the Hierarch's legacy safe. That legacy was a boy living in an osteomantically generated duplicate of the Hierarch's body: Sam Blackland.

Unlike Daniel, Sam had acquired a tendency to run toward trouble instead of away from it, and in trying to prevent a cabal of Northern osteomancers from making a weapon of mass destruction in the form of the Pacific firedrake, Sam had ended up being absorbed by the dragon. Or fused with it. Or some other magical thing Gabriel didn't quite understand.

In any event, killing the dragon meant killing Sam Blackland. Not something Gabriel was eager to do.

The pilot's urgency cut through the radio crackle. "Dragon's still climbing. Please instruct."

"Is there anything else it could be, Max?"

Max held his head rigid, still sniffing. "It's the boy, Gabriel. You know it is."

Sam wasn't the Hierarch. He was a kid. A very decent one. A courageous one. Gabriel wished he could let Sam live.

But the dragon had been ravaging the kingdom. It had breathed fire down on neighborhoods from Sherman Oaks to Palm Springs, from Anaheim to San Juan Capistrano. Whenever the dragon turned inland, houses burned and hundreds died.

All Gabriel had to do was release the silvery water from the jar and strike the tuning fork. A simple procedure that had taken him a year of preparation and thousands of man-hours and millions of dollars. He'd dug deep wells for it. He'd gone back to Catalina to recover the last few extant drops of the dragon's amniotic fluid. At great expense, he'd built a team of osteomancers and hydromancers who linked the water to the dragon.

The water contained the compressed vibrations of a force equivalent to 25,000 tons of TNT. Release the water, strike the tuning fork, and the dragon would die. And Sam with it.

Gabriel felt the ticks of his watch in his wrist bones, or maybe it was just his pulse. Cold brine sprayed his face, and the deck rose and fell.

"Target climbing," the pilot reported.

Gabriel sensed Max watching him.

"Climbing fast."

"Gabriel?" Max reached for the jar, maybe thinking Gabriel had suffered paralysis, but Gabriel moved the jar out of his reach.

"Target above five thousand feet," came the pilot's voice.

According to Gabriel's calculations, the water would lose effectiveness at atmospheric pressures below twelve pounds per square inch.

"Go to the wheelhouse," he told Max. "Please have them radio the pilot to break off pursuit."

"Because you don't want to kill Sam?" Max said. "Because that would put you in Daniel's crosshairs?"

Gabriel didn't answer right away. He knew he'd just failed to do his job. "I didn't want to kill Sam because I didn't want to kill Sam. Because I wanted to be a good man, Max. But sometimes what I need to be is an awful man."

"I'm not sure it's possible to be both. I think you have to choose. I think you chose right."

Gabriel wiped seawater from his face. "Tell me that again the next time I have to walk through the dragon's ruins."

The next time came less than twenty-four hours later.

Rust-colored smoke smudged the morning sky. On the ground, all was charred wood, blackened and crumbling masonry, and the sodden remains of eight square blocks of Mid-City.

Gabriel toured the wreckage, taking toll. Forty-three houses, sixteen shops, a synagogue, a church, and eighty-nine lives. The fire department had done a good job of preventing the blaze from spreading beyond the neighborhood, and the minimally funded rescue workers had done as well as they could. The Council had done an efficient job of transporting the survivors out to care ships, where they would spend months or years in the dark, scrubbed-out holds of decommissioned oil tankers. Through no fault of their own, they'd languish in homeless prisons, because, well, it was Los Angeles, and Gabriel didn't yet rule the whole city, only the waterways running through the territories belonging to the great osteomancers.

In the backyard of what used to be a two-bedroom Spanish Revival, he came upon a swing set. The seats had been consumed, leaving chains dangling from the still-burning redwood frame. Beyond that was a swimming pool. Bougainvillea and jacaranda petals turned black and fell into the water, dissolving into ash.

Gabriel remembered another night of flowers and ashes. He remembered Hancock Park, the neighborhood where he lived in a Tudor mansion until the age of six with his mother and father. He remembered koi ponds and private gondolas and ordinances against noise and excess and anything that might jar the tranquility of affluence.

Gabriel's father was a real estate attorney. Sedate and successful and rich, he was the sort of person who fit in well there. His mother was an osteomancer, a niece of the Hierarch.

Both his parents' occupations were obscure to Gabriel. His father did things with stacks of paper and made a lot of phone calls. His mother went to an office where she stirred things, or something like that. He knew his mother didn't want him to be an osteomancer. Adults sometimes spoke around kids as though they were stupid or deaf, and once at some dinner party, while he was playing with building blocks under the grand piano with one of his cousins, someone asked his mother about Gabriel's future. And his mother said, "No, not Gabriel. Not the bone trade for him. Not ever."

Gabriel wanted to be a gondolier when he grew up. He went to private school where everyone told him he was very smart. His hobbies were digging for worms with a bucket and shovel in the backyard, climbing the apricot tree, and throwing rocks into the canal.

Then, one night, a pounding on the door. He shot upright in his bed and went to the bedroom door, but Liliana, Gabriel's nanny, blocked his way out into the hall.

"It's nothing," she said, preempting any questions. "Go to sleep."

Gabriel trusted Liliana. He trusted the strength of her arms to carry him when he fell off his bike. He trusted the coolness of her hand when he had a fever. When his parents argued, he trusted the steadiness of her voice to read to him and make him believe everything was okay.

But she was wrong now. It was not "nothing." He could see red and blue lights flashing behind the curtains, and the pounding downstairs continued. He could see with his own eyes and hear with his own ears that it was not "nothing."

He went to the window and saw four police boats docked in front of the house down on the canal. People in black uniforms were coming up the walkway with cleaver clubs drawn.

The impacts against the door gave way to cracking and splintering and there was screaming. Gabriel ran at Liliana and pushed past her, evading grasping hands that only wanted to protect him. He raced downstairs, turned the corner into the foyer, and then saw his mother truly for the first time.

She held one of the police officers by the throat and lifted him off the ground.

"Leave my house," she said.

She was a slight woman, with small, graceful hands that Gabriel liked to watch play piano or dance on the keyboard of her manual typewriter or color in his coloring books with him, using his crayons with quick, precise movements. And he had seen her angry, of course, when he threw a ball up to the ceiling fan in the kitchen, when he tracked mud over the pristine white sitting room carpet. But that wasn't real anger. Real anger was what he saw on her face now, her jaw tense, the veins in her thin arms bulging with the strength of her blood flow. And those fingers of hers penetrated the flesh of the man she hoisted up with one hand, and blood flowed between them.

Gabriel's father's face was even worse to look at. He was afraid for his wife, but he was also afraid of her. This was the first time Gabriel was aware of his ability to read people, not through any magical means, but just by observation and thought, even at the most horrible moments. He could witness pain and understand where it came from. It was almost like math. Later, he would understand that he had a useful skill, but now understanding horrible things only made them more horrible.

A man stepped to the front of the group of police officers wearing the wings-and-tusks emblem on his windbreaker. Gabriel learned at school that the wings-and-tusks was the symbol of the Hierarch. First they taught him cursive writing, and then they taught him how to sign his name, and then they showed him how to sign the Pledge of Allegiance, which was printed on a sheet of paper bearing the wings-and-tusks.

Gabriel's mother took a breath and closed her eyes, and the police officer she had by the neck made gargling sounds. All his flesh sloughed off. All his muscle and tendon. All of what he was splashed to the white carpet in a steaming puddle, and then his skeleton came apart and clattered into the mess.

Gabriel couldn't identify all the wave of stench that washed over him, the smells of the insides of a human being and the burning, gluey stink of basilisk venom. But he understood that he was smelling power and the consequences of power, and even as he gagged, he knew what he was feeling was a mix of revulsion and attraction and love for his mother and feelings that came more from his belly and heart than from his brain. Later, he would tag this stew of emotion as awe.

The man in the wings-and-tusks sheathed his cleaver club. "You can kill all of us, Madame Argent," he said. "But the Hierarch will send more. And this time, instead of just taking you, he will also take your husband. He will also take your son."

Things happened so quickly after that. There was the briefest of kisses exchanged by his mother and father. There was sorrow and love in his mother's eyes as her hand brushed Gabriel's cheek. And then she was placed in handcuffs that she could surely burn through if she wanted, and she went meekly with the police and the man in the wings-and-tusks.

They put his mother in a boat, and he never saw her again.

They did not hurt Gabriel or his father, but some of the police stayed behind and splashed cans of gasoline all over the house. They lit it with a candle they found on the piano, and Gabriel and his father were made to stand across the street and watch while their house caught fire and burned to ashes.

Through all the smells of the fire, bitter wood, and plastic and chemicals and upholstery, the scents of his mother's power cut through. The smell was so strong, but her power had not been enough to save Gabriel from his loss.

There was a lesson in that. Decades later, Gabriel was still trying to work it out.

Gabriel."
    Soot smudged Max's fingers and pant cuffs. He'd been sniffing through the ruins.

"Don't sneak up on me like that, Max. It's rude."

"I've been standing behind you for at least half a minute."

"Well, next time cough or something, so I know you're there."

"How is coughing preferable to saying your actual name?"

"Don't change the subject," Gabriel said. "Tell the fire captain that we've got a hotspot here."

"Already did. She's sending her people over. You should stop reminiscing and get out of their way."

"Reminiscing?"

"You always reminisce after a fire. You can't burn toast without getting that faraway look."

"Change the subject, Max."

Max tilted his magnificent, invaluable nose to the air. Powerful people had made Gabriel extravagant offers for that nose, and the analytical brain that came attached to it. Money, favors, promises to kill this or that of his enemies and support him against this or that osteomancer.

Gabriel's answer was always the same: "You wouldn't like Max. He bites."

Gabriel slogged through a soup of burned and soaked timbers and roofing shingles and furniture fabric and plaster, out to the sidewalk. The remains of people's lives stuck to his shoes. Most of the houses on this block were just foundations and chimneys now. A few survivors picked through wreckage, searching for heirlooms. A man clutched a ruined book to his chest. A photo album, a corpse of memories.

Witnesses said the attack came in the predawn dark. It was fire from above, with no sounds of explosions, no shaking, and it left behind no craters or shrapnel.

"Do you want to know what caused the fire?" Max said.

But Gabriel already knew.

THREE

Seven miles south of downtown Los Angeles sprawled an Assyrian palace. Concrete sphinxes looked out atop the walls. Bas-relief griffins decorated towers and buttresses, all modeled on the citadel of King Sargon the Second. The building had served as a tire factory, a shopping center, and was now the stronghold of an industrious osteomancer named Isaac Slough.

Daniel Blackland followed Slough down the catwalk overlooking the factory floor. Daniel liked what he saw. Technicians in white coats and gloves handled glassware that came sparkling out of autoclaves. Their worktables gleamed with cleanliness. In a soft tweed jacket and steel-rimmed glasses, Slough himself looked prosperous and professorial.

"I'm surprised you came to me," he said, taking Daniel down a spiral staircase to the floor. "I'm not the only person in the realm doing this kind of work."

"But you're the only one who was trained in the Ossuary. You're the only one who isn't running a slop-and-chop shop."

Daniel peered through the pancake-sized portholes in the stainless-steel tanks hooked to complex nests of pipes and hoses. Some contained tendrilled things that resembled mandrake roots. Other golems, farther along in gestation, had grown faces. One looked to be a boy of ten or eleven. Golems didn't grow like fetuses. They were more like vegetables, or mushrooms, or mineral formations. They grew according to a different set of natural laws.

Slough led Daniel into his office and shut the door. Bay windows flooded the place with bright sunlight and showed views of industrial surroundings—welding yards and machine shops—creating the sense that this was an exalted oasis in an ugly world.

"The first thing to consider," said Slough, settling into one of the sleek leather chairs arranged around a sleek glass coffee table, "is the quality of your source."

Daniel took the other chair. He felt as though he'd voluntarily lowered himself into the cup of a slingshot primed to launch him through the window. And what kind of paranoid had he become that now he even distrusted furniture?

"This is the source," he said, handing Slough a small glass jar. It contained a single strand of brown hair.

Slough held it up to the light. He squinted and pursed his lips in judgment. "Generally I prefer to work with more material."

Daniel had a second strand, but he couldn't afford to give it to Slough. He needed it for something else. "There's more there than it looks like. The source's magic is strong."

That was an understatement. Sam was possibly the most powerful osteomancer in both the Californian realms. A decent osteomancer should be able to extract more magic from a strand of Sam's hair than you'd find in the entire corpses of any ten other osteomancers.

Slough set the jar on the table with a sharp tap of glass on glass. "Okay. I've worked with less."

"I have some questions," Daniel said.

Slough smiled. "I would imagine so."

"What about age?"

"Aging can be retarded, if it's long life you're looking for. It's our most common request."

"I want the opposite. Can you accelerate aging to a specific point, and then reset the clock so the golem ages normally after that?"

Slough nodded. "That's more difficult, rarer, and more expensive. But, yes, I can do it. The magic from unicorn bones imparts immortality, or at least long life. I can prepare the bone to do the opposite. Rapid aging. If administered correctly, I can fine-tune the degree."

Slough presented himself as confident but not boastful. He seemed to know what he was talking about. And he didn't answer in riddles, with the cryptic affect so many sorcerers put on.

Daniel moved on. "Will he be . . . okay?"

"You mean, will he be functional and healthy? Both mentally and physically? Will he retain the magic and intelligence and memories of the donor? That's what you're asking?"

"That's what I'm asking."

Slough leaned back in his chair. It was identical to Daniel's, but Slough seemed absolutely comfortable in his. "The golem will be alive," he said, "with functioning organs and physiological systems."

"But will he be the person he was?"

"It would be irresponsible of me to make that guarantee. About half the time, the golem is a perfect duplicate of the donor in every way. I'm oversimplifying, but it's like rebinding a book. The content doesn't change. Yet it's not the most exact art. Many times things go wrong, and we have to start over."

"What happens to the ones that go wrong?"

Slough said nothing. He'd probably learned that most clients didn't actually want an answer to that one. Daniel decided not to be like most clients.

"Can the ones that . . . go wrong . . . be recovered?"

"With a great deal of effort and time, a failed golem can sometimes achieve trained response to simulation. Even a chicken can learn to play the piano."

"What about making a golem intentionally blank?"

Slough frowned. "I'm not sure what you mean."

"I mean," Daniel said, "a mentally blank golem. One with all the parts, all the systems, everything functioning, but the mind not turned on. Can you make a golem like that?"

Slough eyed him, clearly repulsed. It was a repulsive thing that Daniel was asking.

"I've never done it."

"That wasn't my question. Can you do it?"

"Of course," Slough said. "But at this point, I have to tell you, what I *can* do isn't the most important question. It's what I am willing to do."

"I can't pay you. Not anything like what you're used to."

Slough smiled again, his thin lips and sharp eyes giving him a snake-like aspect. "I wasn't aware this was just an informational interview."

"It's not. I'm convinced you're the best person for the job. The best person available, anyway. And I need you. I need you to make a golem from the magic in this hair, and I need the golem gestated to the physical age of a seventeen-year-old, and I need it to be mentally blank."

Leather creaked as Slough shifted in his chair. "And for this difficult, time-consuming, resource-costly work, you expect to pay . . . nothing."

"Let me answer that with one more question, Dr. Slough."

Slough flicked his hand in a gesture both impatient and indulgent. "Ask."

"Do you know who I am?"

"Of course I do. From before you walked into my factory. I employ very good hounds."

Daniel had presented himself in his customary fashion: thin, rumpled, and overdue for a haircut. He didn't arrive like a king, and because he didn't look or act like one, even people who knew his history forgot that all he had to do to claim a throne was remove a few dozen other osteomancers, a talent that he'd amply demonstrated a decade ago when he killed the most fearsome osteomancer of them all.

Slough was cool, self-possessed, in control of himself. But Daniel's nose was as keen as Slough's hounds, and he smelled a wisp of fear.

Daniel stood. "How would you like to make a friendly gesture toward the man who ate the Hierarch's heart?"

"I see," said Slough. He took up the jar, and without being summoned, an assistant arrived with a metal case about the size of a lunch box. Slough delicately set the jar inside the foam-padded interior.

"I hope you understand this isn't an overnight job."

"I have some necessary travel. You'll do a good job while I'm away."

"I will," said Slough. "And not for your offer of friendship, or for the threat implied in it. I'll do my best work because I'm a craftsman, and craft means something to me."

Slough escorted him back out across the laboratory and into the reception hall.

"Normally I have clients sign a contract, but I have a hunch you'd prefer a handshake deal."

"You haven't asked who the donor is. Who you're building a duplicate of."

"I think I know. Back when you were a thief, what would you have called him? The goods? The score? The booty? We called him the Kingdom's Treasure."

"You have a son of your own," Daniel said. "He likes music. Plays the clarinet. I understand he's good. Some kids, you have to force them to practice. But you have to force yours to stop so he'll eat dinner and use the bathroom. His teacher says he might be good enough to play professionally someday."

"If you're threatening me—" Slough said with real, incautious anger.

"I'm not. I don't threaten children. Ever. Yes, the source is what you call the Kingdom's Treasure. He's the Hierarch's golem. But I call him Sam. He's important to me, the way your son is to you. Do we understand each other?"

A moment passed while Slough assessed him.

"I'll do my very best, Mr. Blackland."

"I know you will. And let me give you a word of advice, one father to another: Don't bring your boy into the family business. Let him be a musician."

"That's my hope, Mr. Blackland. That's why I work so hard. And what about your son? Did you bring him into the family business?"

"I'm still trying to get him out of it."

Daniel made his way around the tombs and grave markers of Hollywood Cemetery. Palm trees stood in black silhouette against the flat coppery light from the sodium-vapor lamps lining Van Ness Canal. Some of the tombs were equipped with their own spotlights, little Greek temples built to honor entertainment lawyers and record executives. He passed a gravestone with a sexy, bare-shouldered woman carved in granite. She was falling out of her dress and clutching the grave marker with inconsolable grief. Other stones were less melodramatic, film clapboards and likenesses of the deceased depicted playing electric guitar or swinging a baseball bat. One gravestone was shaped like a grand piano. Install some holes in the lawn and the cemetery would make a fine miniature golf course.

Dead osteomancers were generally not interred. Usually, their bodies were digested.

He found the tomb he was looking for, another one of the Greek jobs with white fluted columns surrounding a solid block of white stone. The door was an imposing barrier of green patinated metal. For a thief like Daniel, the lock was a joke and it fell apart after nine seconds of work.

He pushed the door open just a crack and tossed three brittle pellets of gorgon bone inside. He waited and listened to shuffling, scrabbling noises, like the sounds of panicked rats. When the noises subsided, he pushed the door open wider and slipped inside.

Two guards stood stiff as stone, their guns fallen to the ground through their unfeeling fingers. The flesh of their faces and hands was cement gray, their open eyes as brittle as eggshells. The gorgon bone would wear off in an hour or so, but for them it would be a long and rather horrific hour.

As for himself, Daniel wasn't looking forward to the next few minutes. This was not the first grave he'd ever robbed, and he'd had some unpleasant experiences.

He slipped a screw jack beneath the sarcophagus lid, threaded in the crank, and jacked the lid up several inches. With a second screw jack, he performed the same operation on the wooden coffin inside. Please just let it be a mummy, he thought, clicking on his flashlight. He saw glossy black hair, a pink cheek, blue-gray fabric. Not a mummy.

He jacked both lids higher and shined his flashlight over the body to examine it more thoroughly.

She'd been young when she died, maybe nineteen or twenty, a birdlike girl with hands that looked like they should belong to a stronger person crossing over her chest. Her dress was a sober thing, long sleeves and a skirt down to her ankles, with a little bit of lace on the sleeve cuffs and the high collar. Was she wearing a maid's outfit? Daniel wouldn't put it past a rich old osteomancer to lay a favorite servant to rest in the same uniform she wore when waiting hand and foot on her master. It was probably supposed to be some kind of compliment.

She was perfectly preserved, no gruesome wrinkling, no odd tightness in her face or hands. He smelled no putrefaction. Yet neither did he smell embalming oil or osteomantic substances.

Unlike the girl, the padding of her coffin did show wear. The black velvet looked dull in the light and was dry to the touch.

He continued his flashlight search of the body, hoping he wouldn't have to touch it to find the bone he'd come here for. He wasn't squeamish about corpses, but touching what looked like a sleeping girl would feel like a violation.

He patted her down, tentatively at first, then, gritting his teeth, more thoroughly. Nothing. He pressed his thumbs into her jaw and hinged open her mouth. A glossy black disc about the size of a quarter rested on her tongue. Conscious of his breath on the girl's face, he leaned in closer. The disc was odorless, but he could see cellular striations of bone.

The body belonged to her maid, but the tomb was bought and paid for by one Angelica Chasterlain, heiress to a great Los

Angeles oil fortune. Some people kept their greatest treasures in bank vaults. Chasterlain used her maid's tomb to store a sliver of bone said to come from a creature at the center of the earth, the *axis mundi* dragon.

It had taken Daniel seven months of hard footwork to discover where such bones could be found. The largest fragment was on the other side of the world in the vaults of the Chinese government. Another was in the Northern Kingdom. And the third, the least of them all, was here.

"Sorry about this," he whispered, plucking the bone from the girl's mouth.

The corpse drew a great, ragged breath. Her eyes opened slowly, her lids resisting decades of being shut. She reached out and clutched Daniel's shirt. He stepped back, but she held tight, and when he saw the confusion and fear in her face, instead of prying her hand off him, he just covered it with his own.

"It's okay," he said. "It's okay. You're not alone."

Her hand was already growing cold. He didn't know if it would be a kindness to put the *axis mundi* bone back into her mouth, to return her to sleeping death inside her tomb, or if it was better to let her finally pass. But it wasn't uncertainty that made him pocket the bone. He needed it for Sam. So he would keep it, and she would die, and kindness would not be a factor.

She worked her mouth, trying to say something, but she could only manage a weak garble.

"It's okay," he said, over and over, trying to reassure her as her hand withered and the bones grew sharper under his warm palm.

He should leave now. But he stayed and looked into her frightened eyes and said meaningless things to her as her flesh grew brittle and shrank away to little more than a thin wrapper around her skeleton. He looked into her eyes until they yellowed like fossil ivory and broke into thin cracks and flaked away like ash into the recesses of her eye sockets. Even after the girl was bones and skin and hair shrouded in a blue-gray dress, he murmured assurances that she would be all right.

For Sam, he told himself.

FOUR

D aniel searched the sky for the dragon. Binoculars to his face, he paced a circle over jumbled granite and snow, not having any idea from which direction the dragon might come. At least the skies were clear, offering hundreds of miles of visibility. He stood on the peak of Mount Whitney, the tallest mountain between Alaska and Mexico. Far down below, in the east, the desolate sprawl of Death Valley turned shades of purple and copper in the setting sun. To the north and south rose 14,000-foot crags of stone.

Wind found its way past his scarf and balaclava and bit his skin through layers of wool and cotton. His head hurt and his lungs couldn't get enough oxygen from the thin air. He was in Sam's world now, one of sky and clouds and a view so vast Daniel's dull eyes couldn't encompass it. Except for the hair left with Isaac Slough, any remaining spark of Sam dwelled in the form of a flying god, and Daniel found himself a little envious of him.

He tucked his chin against the wind and headed to the storm shelter. The Hierarch's mountain brigade had built the stone-and-mortar hut a century earlier, and some genius had outfitted it with a corrugated-metal roof that served as a pretty effective magnet for lightning. But at least it supplied a break from the wind and it was free of vermin. Not that the construction deserved any credit for that; the only animals that ever made it up here were itinerant butterflies and a masochistic species of finch.

Inside, Moth and Em were setting up the harpoon gun. Em did most of the work, adjusting small screws and swiping at Moth's hands when he tried to help.

Daniel pulled down his balaclava and warmed himself by the camp stove. "How's it coming?"

"The sight got jostled on the hike up," Em said, taking another swat at Moth. "But I think I can fix it if you tell Moth to stop trying to futz."

"Moth, stop futzing," Daniel said. "Em's allowed to futz. You don't futz."

Moth drew himself up to his full, proud height. "This is a finesse job, I get that. But I'm a finesse guy. Tell her, Daniel. Tell her how good I am at piano."

Actually, Moth could be quite a delicate tinkler on the keys.

"Come help with the projectile, Moth."

Daniel pulled his balaclava back up over his mouth and nose, lifted one of the bags they'd hauled up the mountain, and went back outside.

"Out there?" Moth wailed behind him. "It's all windy-howly out there."

But Moth followed, as he had always done, through forest and river and city and suburb and desert, crisscrossing the realm in search of the dragon. Daniel and Moth and Em had spent weeks on a hired fishing boat and months in a string of motor-court motels and even more months sleeping in a van, and now that Slough was cultivating a body for Sam, and Daniel had possession of the *axis mundi* bone, there was only one thing left to do: bring the dragon down.

Things felt right tonight. For starters, Daniel had a good feeling about the eyewitnesses he'd interviewed, from the fugitive inmate camping outside Lone Pine to the smuggler moving hippogriff bone by pack mule down Hogback Road. They described shapes in the sky and a noise that rolled through the valleys like high-pitched thunder.

And there was a smell here. It reminded him of Sam. Or maybe that was wishful thinking.

Daniel had hoped Moth and Em would be home by now. But their homes had moved on without them. Em's golem sisters had abandoned their Mojave ranch hideout a few months back and hadn't contacted her with their new address, which either meant their communications network wasn't secure, or worse. And Moth's boyfriend had sold Moth's restaurant in Crumville, told Moth he could pick up half the money in cash at the Crumville bank, and headed out for more secure pastures.

Daniel's fault. And even though Em and Moth both insisted they were with him by choice, that they'd made their sacrifices willingly, how hard had Daniel really tried to convince them they had no further obligation to him or Sam?

Not very hard.

For Daniel, things hadn't changed much. He'd been living like this for a decade.

Tugging his gloves off with his teeth, he set up his osteomancer's torch on a rock. He moved quickly, trying to get the job done before the cold stiffened his fingers. Once he had it lit, he passed his hands over the heat of the flame before putting his gloves back on. Next, he removed a thermos bottle from his pack.

Moth stepped back, wary.

"Don't worry, this stuff's not dangerous," Daniel said. "It's just a scent to draw the dragon."

"What's in it?" The thin, whistling air weakened Moth's voice.

"Essences he'll find familiar. Me, mostly."

Moth's balaclava exposed only his eyes and the chapped bridge of his nose, but Daniel didn't need to see the rest of Moth's face to read his expression. They'd been friends for twenty years, and Moth's mix of bewilderment, mockery, and concern was as familiar as a favorite pair of shoes.

"Okay, Moth, what's your problem?"

"You're using yourself as bait."

"If you know of a better way to draw out a dragon—"

"Not my area of expertise."

"Not mine, either," Daniel admitted. He poured the liquefied magic into a blue-speckled kettle set on a tripod over the torch. "It'll take a while to vaporize at this altitude, so let's get the rest set up."

Moth helped Em lug the gas-powered harpoon launcher from the hut, and together, with a fair bit of squabbling, they assembled the whole apparatus. The last piece to go on was the harpoon itself, a five-foot-long missile tipped with a bulb of alp dust.

The alp came from the kitchens of Mother Cauldron, the most brilliant mixer of osteomantic materials Daniel knew, and it hadn't come cheap. He'd spent a full month of the last year breaking into vaults and warehouses and strongholds, stealing entire fortunes of bones for her. But she assured Daniel her alp mixture could tranquilize even a Pacific firedrake, and if she was telling the truth, the month of thieving would be a small price to pay.

Smoke boiled from the kettle and threaded through the air.

"Now we wait," said Daniel. "You two should go back in the hut."

Moth looked appalled. "But what about s'mores?"

"Yeah," Em said, reaching inside her parka. "I brought s'mores." She proudly displayed a box of graham crackers, a bag of marshmallows, and a giant chocolate bar.

"You guys want to make s'mores in the flames of my torch? My osteomancer's torch, an instrument with more moving parts than a Swiss watch?"

"We figured it'd make really good s'mores," Em said.

Daniel eyed the kettle. It had stopped smoking and releasing Daniel's scents. He took the kettle off the torch. "Okay. S'mores."

Moth rubbed his hands in delight, and then a great noise ripped through the sky, like the crack of a sequoia-sized whip.

"Position the gun," Daniel snapped. He looked to the sky. Nothing north, south, or east. But in the west, a shape came out of the sun: a sharp silhouette standing out against the red sky, with a slim serpentine body, sail-like wings, a long neck and undulating tail. Through the binoculars, Daniel could make out the shingles of its belly armor and licks of flame from its snout.

"Em . . . ?"

Em peered through the gun sight. "I've got him but he's not in range."

Moth stood behind her. "You guys never told me how close he has to get."

"Yeah, we kinda hid that from you," Em said. "A hundred meters."

Moth sputtered. "Are you kidding me? We're supposed to stand a hundred meters from a Pacific firedrake? I could throw the harpoon that far."

Em turned the crank to tilt the gun up. "I worked out the weight of the harpoon, its aerodynamics, and your arm strength. We're using the gun."

Moth shook his head and planted his feet, as if readying himself for a body blow.

The dragon climbed ever higher, just a dark smudge against a lilac band of sky pricked with the evening's first stars. It froze there a moment, then dove.

A shockwave of heat preceded the dragon, and the air swam with mirage. It spread out its wings, enflamed sky glowing behind translucent membranes. Every beat of its wings pummeled the air, and it hovered, its sleek, canoe-shaped head level with the mountain summit.

Its eyes fixed upon Daniel, pupils like black fissures in burning orange irises.

Daniel stared right back.

He'd eaten dragon, and he felt his own flame rising up in his lungs, felt his fingertips crackle with lightning. He was an osteomancer, and the way to deal with power was to consume it. He wanted to flay the dragon of its flesh, and pry off its armor plates, gut it and scrape and shovel away meat until its fine, rich bones were exposed. Eat the firedrake's bones, and Daniel would have its power to add to his own.

A crushing pressure took his shoulder. It was Moth's hand. "Daniel," Moth said, low and gentle. "Em's waiting for the order."

"God," Daniel whispered, horrified. "It's Sam."

"Yeah," Moth said. "I'm sure he smells like a big banquet, but Em's waiting."

Daniel looked at Em and nodded.

She fired. The gun launched the harpoon with a bang, and the harpoon hit true, dead center in the cruciform of the dragon's body and outspread wings. The bulb at its tip crumbled to chalky powder.

The dragon roared with a fury that rippled Daniel's pant legs and punched his heart like a battering ram.

He and Moth and Em raced for the granite shelter, hoping to escape a torrent of dragon flame if the alp didn't work like Mother Cauldron had promised.

Once they reached the shelter, Daniel pushed Em and Moth through the open door. Before heading in himself, he turned to look at the dragon.

Despite beating its wings harder, it was losing altitude. Its eyes had lost some of their gleam.

The alp was doing its job.

"Sleep," Daniel whispered. "Just go to sleep, Sam. It'll be better when you wake up. I promise you."

The dragon struggled to stay aloft. The claws of one of its hind legs touched earth and gouged deep runnels in the solid rock. It let out a strangled roar, both frightful and pitiful. Exhalations of searing heat warped its face behind the disturbed air.

One wing scraped against the summit's ledge, dislodging tons of stone and earth in an avalanche. The ground jolted with the crash of boulders tumbling, the world coming undone.

Then, an eerie quiet, only the clatter of smaller rocks and gravel and sifting sand.

Daniel rushed to the crumbling ledge and peered over. The dragon had slid to a stop about three hundred feet below, its body sprawled across a shallow part of the slope, head resting on an outcropping.

Em ran over with climbing gear and helped Daniel get into his harness. She tugged on the straps, making sure they were secure.

"He fell a long way," she said. "Is he okay?"

"That's not a long way for a fully armored firedrake," Daniel said, affecting his most reassuring tone.

She wasn't having it. "But what about Sam?"

Daniel aimed his flashlight down the slope. The dragon's scales changed color in the light, swirling with deep reds and blues and greens, as much a creature of the sea as it was of fire. Its body was a treasure horde of nearly unimaginable value, its bones and teeth and claws fairly crackling with magic. It seemed as durable as the mountain itself. But the essence of Sam, somewhere beneath the iridescent outer plating, was an ephemeral wisp.

"We'll see," Daniel said, reaching into his pocket to make sure the case containing the *axis mundi* bone was still there.

Em anchored the free end of the rope in a nest of boulders, checked her knots three times, and gave everything several violent tugs before deeming it worthy of her thumbs-up.

With Moth belaying, Daniel brought his heels to the ledge and crouched.

He paused there.

There was always a moment when a job went to shit. Daniel's instinct and experience told him such a moment was at hand.

Moth gave him a questioning look, and then they both heard it: a low drone.

"There," Em said, pointing southward.

Three airships approached.

Daniel came away from the ledge and unclipped the rope. Em unzipped her duffel and removed the components of a rifle and began screwing them together. Moth cracked his knuckles.

The bows of the ships rose above the south ledge like whale shadows, blotting out a good part of the sky. No longer muffled by the mountain, the propeller engines buzzed an insectile baritone.

Who in Southern California had airships? There used to be a few freight companies that used them to get around Gabriel Argent's canal tolls, but Argent put a stop to that.

Daniel reached for the oldest, deepest magic in his bones, the first osteomantic substance he'd ever consumed, from a beach far away, when his father held his hand and began crafting him into a bone sorcerer. Electricity seared his nerve endings, building painfully till he could feel it in his eyes and in his gums. He longed to release it.

"Hit the deck," Daniel shouted. Moth and Em dropped, and Daniel unleashed bolts of blue-white kraken lightning, guiding them down the length of his arm.

He targeted the main body of the leading ship, hoping to burn through the envelope and rupture its gas cells. Instead, the bolts were drawn to a spar protruding from the bow like a narwhal's tusk. The arcs branched off from the rod, conducted down webs of wire running the length of the ship and away along trailing fronds. The ship continued to rise, revealing a gondola. The forward window was shuttered, leaving small portholes for the pilot. The only other openings were slits.

With the noise of stuttering gunfire, the boulders at Daniel's feet exploded in chips and powder. Moth crawled toward Em to protect her with his own body. He cried out, bullets tearing through his back and shoulders. Em scrambled over to him and deftly wrapped a length of rope through his armpits and around his torso to make a tow line. Only a quarter of his size, she dragged him to a cluster of boulders, bullets cratering the rocks around her.

This was no longer a job going to shit. This was a job going fatal.

All three ships had risen above the summit now, their great bulks passing fifty feet overhead. Daniel breathed fire at the nearest one, engulfing the gondola in a storm of blue flame, but it continued on, unaffected. The heated metal gave off unfamiliar aromas, the osteomancy of creatures Daniel didn't recognize. These weren't freight ships, but warships, equipped with magic Daniel had never encountered.

An apple-sized thing fell from the gondola, and there was a flash of light and noise and then an echoing susurration, like waves in a sea cave. A cruel ache gripped Daniel's head, and something gouged his spine. He'd fallen on his back against the jagged rocks. Through blurred vision, he watched lines unspool from the airships. Black-clad human figures slid down the lines. Daniel tried to stand but got only halfway up before he lost balance and crashed back to the ground. Then, like magic, he was in the air, floating.

More gunshots and a grunt and hot blood splashing his face.

He wasn't floating. Moth was carrying him. The blood was Moth's, from more bullets tearing through his body. Yet Moth ran, with Em alongside, firing shots at people in black fatigues. As Daniel's vision cleared, he saw now that they were soldiers, armed and armored. Whose soldiers, he didn't know.

A blow struck his hip and he screamed out in pain.

Moth got him to the shelter, collapsing to the ground as soon as they were past the threshold. Moth was in horrible shape, more blood than visible skin, and as soon as he dropped Daniel, he rolled onto his back and moaned. But he would heal. Moth always did. He had as much eocorn horn and hydra regenerative in his system as he had chili grease, and he would heal. But it would take hours. Maybe days.

Em took up position, huddled to the side of the open doorway and dared a few shots when she could.

Daniel checked his hip where the bullet had struck, using his knife to cut through the thick fabric of his insulated pants.

There was no blood. The bullet hadn't penetrated his flesh. It was worse than that. It had struck the case containing the *axis mundi* bone, flattening it.

With dread, Daniel pried the deformed lid open. He gasped with relief. The little coin-sized bone remained intact.

Still a chance to save Sam.

"I can't hold them off," Em said.

Daniel crawled over to her. "I just need a second."

He took a few breaths and thought of the black sea bottom, and crushing pressure, and the scent of whale blood. He forced more kraken magic from his cells until the charge coursed through his arms and blue sparks flared beneath his fingertips.

The airships were equipped to deal with lightning. But what about the soldiers?

At a break in the gunfire, he rolled into the doorway, rose to a kneeling position, and let lightning surge indiscriminately from his fingers. He brought down three soldiers. A few others scrambled for cover in the rocks, but the summit was emptier than it had been just moments ago. Where had most of the soldiers gone?

The airships loomed overhead and lowered more soldiers, but instead of landing on the summit, they came down off the western ledge where the dragon had fallen. When one of the airships lowered a massive bundle of cargo netting and chains, Daniel finally got it.

This was a heist. Someone was stealing the dragon.

He charged out of the storm shelter into the howling wind, sending forks of lightning upward and outward. Renewed gunfire answered him, not from the soldiers on the ground, but from the airships themselves. Darting from boulder to boulder, Daniel made his way to the western ledge and peered over. Below him, dozens of soldiers clambered over the dragon as if it were terrain to be conquered. Two of them operated a hydraulic hoist to lift the dragon's tail and position cargo netting underneath it. Another pair connected the netting to chains dangling from one of the airships.

Daniel reached back to sense memories of a Colombian dragon, the sensation of wind whipping past smooth, scaled cheeks, the sight of mastodons stampeding in fright. Sam was a Pacific firedrake, and Daniel's fire wouldn't hurt him. But Daniel would burn these motherfuckers.

He vomited blue flames.

The flames fell short, the soldiers beyond his range. There was one thing to do about that. Without rope and harness, he edged himself to the ledge and began picking his way down.

Digging his fingers into loose earth, he rested one foot on a pancake-sized protrusion of rock. Pain exploded in his calf. Blood ran down his leg. A single gunshot. He held on, the gloved fingers of one hand gripping rock, the other squeezing the *axis mundi* bone.

More shots. One grazed his arm, and he squeezed the bone tighter. Another went through the back of his hand, and he screamed in agony and in frustration. He knew without looking. He could feel it. He could smell it.

The *axis mundi* bone was powder, shrieking away in the high-altitude wind.

Daniel's foot slipped off the rock and he fell. He glanced off a knuckle of stone with rib-cracking impact, slid down gravel, and came to rest with his feet toward the summit and his head hanging over thousands of feet of nothing. He couldn't breathe. Blood from his leg and arm and hand ran down the slope, pooling near his head.

He was supposed to be a mighty sorcerer, and he wasn't going to lose Sam again from a bullet and a fall.

But it wasn't just a bullet and a fall. It was a well-armed and -equipped squadron of quality fighters. It was three airships and lifting gear. It was osteomancy from creatures he didn't know. This wasn't Los Angeles. It had to be the Northern Kingdom.

He tried to move and slipped another inch down the slope. His head hung even farther over the abyss, and only by pressing the palm of his uninjured hand hard against the ground did he keep himself from going over. Helpless, he watched the three airships dip below the mountain, engines straining, carrying Sam away.

Cassandra Morales dug a hole. It didn't have to be a deep hole, because down in this dry gully on the borders of Los Angeles and Riverside counties it didn't take much work to hide things. There wasn't a human settlement for twenty miles, just brown hills and dusty chaparral. Suburban enclaves with names like Quail Valley and Rainbow and Home Gardens had become ghost towns after Gabriel Argent decided bringing water out here was unsustainable and irresponsible, and once he shut off the spigots, the communities got handed back to coyotes and mountain lions.

Now, here, it was just her and Otis Roth.

"You remember the first words you ever said to me, Otis? I only remember them because you said the same exact thing to all the kids you took in. And you took in a lot of us. 'I won't harm you. I won't beat you. I won't rape you. Neither will anyone else who works for me. I'm Otis Roth, and nobody will dare.' I guess some of us were comforted by that. In certain circumstances, it could sound kind of nice. But I heard it differently. I heard it more like, 'I won't harm you unless I want to. Nobody else will harm you, because you belong to me. I'm Otis Roth, and I own you.'"

Her shovel bit into earth.

Otis had taken Cassandra in because her parents owed him money they couldn't pay back, and Cassandra was collateral. Her first night in his warehouse, in her bed with new, stiff sheets, she shoved her face into her pillow and cried as softly as she could. This was her life now. Her parents weren't picking her up tomorrow. She knew how much money they owed, and how much money they usually made on jobs, because she often pretended to be asleep while they talked money and schemes. They would never be able to pay off their debt unless they took on bigger and riskier jobs. They'd probably die trying.

She could run away, but then Otis would have them killed.

As it turned out, they managed to die without Otis's help, only a few months later. It wasn't even a big job, just a payroll robbery that turned into a shootout. The take wouldn't have even made a dent in their debt to Otis.

And it was Otis who came to tell her.

"You tried to lay it on me gently," Cassandra said, wiping sweat off the back of her neck. She'd probably dug her hole deep enough, but she didn't want animals undoing her work, so she kept tossing up shovelfuls of dirt. "And I think I took it pretty well, considering. No hysterics. No tantrums. There were some of your guys waiting outside my room in case I flipped out and attacked you. But all I did was ask if you were going to set me free now that my parents were dead. I didn't want revenge. I wanted my mom and dad back. But you know me, always the realist. I wasn't going to get what I wanted. So I was willing to settle for my freedom. And you told me, just seconds after I learned my parents were shot up and their bodies being hauled to the city furnaces, that the terms of the contract meant I would remain in your care until the debt was paid or my eighteenth birthday. I think that's when I started crying. But not too much.

Remember what you said to comfort me? I'll never forget your kindness. You said, 'Be patient, Cassandra. It's just until you're eighteen. And you're almost fourteen now.' "

Cassandra was not patient. She was industrious. True to his word, Otis gave her an education. Not in subjects like history and algebra, but his henchminions tutored her in marksmanship and nose-breaking and pickpocketing and, eventually, safe-cracking. She was a good pupil.

Otis had his own reasons for giving her skills—there was no point in using someone if she wasn't useful. She had her own reasons for accepting his tutelage. Once she turned eighteen, she'd need to make her own way in the world.

A bee landed on the taped-tight bundle of plastic sheeting on the edge of her hole. She shooed it away and kept digging.

Along with marketable skills, she'd also found a bit of higher purpose in Otis's warehouse. Some of the other little thieves Otis took in weren't as self-sufficient as she was. They'd eat sugar three meals a day if you'd let them, or they'd get stupid and try to filch little nuggets of the osteomancy Otis trafficked. They needed a big sister, and Cassandra accepted that as her job. Without anyone to take care of her, she found she was good at taking care of others.

There was one boy in particular who needed her more than most. He was a dark and quiet kid who never spoke at communal dinners up at the big kitchen table. The rumor was that he was the son of some big, high-level osteomancer who worked with the Hierarch himself and grew so powerful that the Hierarch had him killed. In the more sensational version of the story, the Hierarch dined on the boy's father.

As Cassandra later found out, the stories were true.

"That was Daniel, of course. And what a weird, damaged kid. But you know what? He was also sweet. And it turned out we had the same way of dealing with not having anyone to take care of us. We took care of the ones who needed it most. Me and Daniel, and then Moth, and Punch. We took care of each other. We became a little family. And you liked that, Otis. You encouraged it. You teamed us up on jobs, and you made sure we had skills or magic that complemented each other, and we became a really tight crew of thieves. You made an awful lot of money with us."

Standing shoulder-deep in the hole, she threw her shovel over the top and lifted herself out. It was now a couple of hours past noon, and she'd still have to hike about a mile back to her car, and then a few more hours to the park-and-ride, and depending on traffic, more hours navigating the L.A. canals back home.

"I don't hate you, Otis. And I'm not scared of you. You're not my boogeyman. And as far as my business concerns go, I don't even see you as a rival. In fact, I'm grateful to you. That's how big of a person I am. I can set the immensely shitty things you've done aside and see the things you gave me. You gave me skills, a family, and a purpose. I take care of my own. I do things for my friends that they can't do for themselves. Or won't do, because they're too decent. Daniel should have killed you years ago. You sold him to the Hierarch. You're the reason he lost Sam. If you'd done that to me, I would have killed you without hesitation. But that's Daniel. Anyway. Hey, you remember what you gave my parents when they handed me over to you?"

She picked up her shovel and slid the blade under the plastic-wrapped bundle. With some care, she leveraged Otis's body into the grave.

"You gave them a receipt."

She threw in the first of many shovelfuls of dirt.

SIX

Sam journeyed to the firedrake's belly. He crawled on his hands and knees through moist tunnels and followed twisting passages and descended ladders made of bony ridges embedded in red tissue. He'd never studied dragon anatomy, much less dragon architecture, so all he had for guidance was intuition. But he knew the belly was important.

Trying to control the dragon from the cockpit was useless. All the levers and wheels and knobs and valves did nothing. He couldn't land the dragon, or crash it, or get it to stop burning things, and if this kept up, the death toll would reach into the tens of thousands.

So, Sam decided to give up on piloting the dragon. But maybe he could sabotage it before it hurt someone else he cared about, or even a total stranger. Sabotage was just breaking things with purpose. Sam knew how to break things.

His boots squelched on the soft floor of a down-sloping passage. Like the other parts of the dragon he'd explored, it was littered with bones and fragments of bones. He picked up a triangular shard that came to a terribly sharp point. A strange urge took hold of him, and he scraped his name into the side of the tunnel. Ancient cave paintings, prison-wall scrawls, graffiti on the sides of buses, and names gouged in the internal tissues of monsters: Sam was now part of a very old tradition of defacing surfaces for reasons that were hard to articulate. He understood the human need to communicate, but communication required an audience.

"Well, I just tagged a dragon," he said. And then he regretted opening his mouth. He hadn't spoken out loud in a long time, and his own voice unsettled him. It sounded like that of a stranger he ought to know, or a person familiar to him who ought to be a stranger.

He continued his descent, marking his way with more slashes in the dragon's tissues. He didn't want to get lost inside here.

The sound of pumping blood grew stronger, humming behind the tissue walls. The scent of pyrogenic fuel grew stronger.

It was also getting hotter, the air cooking his skin, his eyes, his gums. Sweat rained down his face and the back of his neck. He felt like soup. Osteomancers should strive not to sweat, bleed, or weep. Osteomancers liked to keep their magic essences contained inside their bodies until needed. Daniel taught him this when Sam was seven years old and they were camping in the Inyo Forest, on the run from a leech gang. Sam had tripped on a sapling and cut his knee open. He bit his lip to cry silently, and Daniel told him how an osteomancer was a vessel of precious magic, and that the vessel had to remain whole, and even then Sam could tell that Daniel himself thought this was a ridiculous thing to say to a child with a bleeding knee.

Sam sponged his face with his sleeve and kept going.

He arrived at a vast chamber where the walls bent inward and soared to a pink ceiling some fifty feet high. A gigantic fleshy sack hung from tubes the color of raw beef.

There was a smell here. Old, deep osteomancy, like refined

bone simmering for days on the back burner, breaking down into pure, rich magic. Lights wavered like flames behind the translucent skin of the bag. This must be the source of the dragon's flames.

He craned his neck to peer into the murky air above. The fuel likely passed through the tubes, and from there to the lungs, then to the air pipe, and out the mouth. So, what if Sam climbed the bag and severed the tubes?

They were the width of wine barrels, so he'd need to craft a good saw.

Not to mention climbing gear.

Some climbing skills might be useful as well.

He walked around the sack, pushing through searing heat. If he cut through the tubes or the sack, the fuel might gush out, but not without burning or drowning him or maybe both.

He missed Em. She was pretty good at things like climbing and running around. She had all those commando and saboteur skills that Sam found sexy.

She was also good with ideas. And she could make Sam feel like the fate of the world didn't rest solely on his narrow shoulders. He wished they'd had more than just a few days together. He'd never even gotten to kiss her.

"Who the hell are you?" A girl jumped out at him as he rounded the curve of the bag. Rosy-cheeked, she wore a high-necked white blouse and a plaid skirt, with a matching ribbon in her curly black hair. She gripped a femur of some creature like a ball bat, and the way she was holding it made Sam think she was very close to tee-balling his head.

Sam gathered his composure. He didn't know what was going on, who or what this girl was, what kind of threat she presented, but instead of fear, his overwhelming emotion was one of relief.

He wasn't alone.

"Hi. My name's Sam," he said.

"Sam. Well, you scared the hell out of me, Sam. You must be the one banging around upstairs." She didn't lower her club.

"How long have you been . . . here?" he asked.

"Let's get out of the fire belly before we talk. It's hotter than the devil's crotch in here."

Sam was only too happy to. She made him lead the way back out to the passageway, far enough from the chamber until the heat was more bearable.

She considered him a moment, then lowered her club.

"Annabel Stokes," she said, wiping her hand on her skirt and offering it for a shake.

The feel of her calloused palm startled him.

It felt real. It felt like a hand.

It was too much for Sam. "Am I dreaming you?"

Annabel Stokes frowned. "You have vivid dreams, do you? Been practicing dreaming things into life? Working hard at it?"

"No."

"Then what makes you think you suddenly got a brain that can dream a whole person into life?"

"Sorry," Sam said. "It's just that, I don't really understand how things work in here. I figured I was sort of dreaming myself, maybe, and now you're here, so maybe you're a manifestation of some other compartment of my consciousness."

Annabel didn't seem to think much of Sam's explanation.

"Well, anyway, I'm glad I finally found someone. How long have you been in here?" he asked again.

She gave him a guarded look, as if trying to decide if she should answer him or crack him over the head.

"I don't know," she said. "Days, weeks, years . . . there's no day or night here, no chronometer. And I'm pretty sure my sleep cycle's glitched. The last day I clearly remember was Monday, June fifth. I was in the Ossuary, getting my work station ready—"

"The Ossuary?" Sam interrupted.

"I work for the Council. I'm an osteomancer."

Only high-level osteomancers actually worked in the Ossuary, and if she worked there, that meant she'd worked close to the Hierarch himself.

Sam concentrated on keeping his face neutral. "Sorry, go on."

"I'd been having such a good day, too. Nice bones to work with, my mixtures were coming out right . . . I was working with hydra regenerative."

Sam played dumb. "Regenerative?"

"Yeah. It's a healing agent. We extract it from hydra bones. The job is teasing the most essence out of the least possible amount of raw bone, which is really important when you're trying to spread it across four dozen frontline field hospitals." She paused. "I'm talking too much. I'm so used to babbling to myself, I forgot there's actually a poor sap stuck here listening to me."

"I don't mind," Sam said. "I haven't had anybody babble at me in a long time."

Her mention of the front line, and of field hospitals, and the way she was dressed, all added up to make Sam think the Monday she remembered happened a very long time ago. Maybe more than half a century past.

"A runner came up to me with a note. An invitation." She seemed reluctant to continue.

"An invitation," Sam prompted.

"An invitation to dinner. From the Hierarch."

"Oh," Sam said, fully understanding. "Oh."

"Right. So, I did what any sensible gal would do. I went to

the ladies' room and tried to escape out the window. Didn't get far." Her hand drifted to her belly. "That's the last thing I remember before finding myself here."

Sam had a feeling she remembered more, but he didn't push. Everything that came after the Hierarch's dinner invitation wasn't anything Sam needed to hear about.

"So, what about you, Sam? What's your story?"

Daniel would have warned Sam to reveal nothing because Daniel's world was one of enemies. And what would Annabel think about him once she found out he was the golem of the man who ate her?

On the other hand, Sam was lonely, and he had to tell her something that was true.

"I'm late of Los Angeles, the Salton Sea, and just about everywhere else in Southern California. The thing we're in, the firedrake . . . it was a project of the Northern realm, with help from some jerks in Southern California. I was trying to sabotage it. But it didn't work out the way I hoped, and here I am. I came down to the belly hoping to disable the dragon's ability to make fire." He glanced back toward the chamber housing the fire bag. "I figure the big sack is part of its fire-generation system."

"Yeah. But why do you want to disable it?"

"Don't you know what the dragon's been up to?"

"Raising hell, from the sounds of it."

"It just annihilated a whole neighborhood," Sam said. "There must be hundreds dead."

"And that wasn't your aim? To burn everything down?"

"No," Sam said, outraged. "Why would I want that?"

"Hm. My mistake. I thought it was you piloting. Who's up in the cockpit, then?"

"Well, me, usually. But I'm not in control."

She puffed out air. "This train's a runaway volcano, that's for sure. Well, mind if I have a look upstairs? I've been dying to know what's up there."

"Why didn't you just come up?"

"I tried to find it a few dozen times. Always got turned around and lost. How long did it take you to make your way down here?"

"I don't know. Not very long, I don't think." The journey from the cockpit to the fire belly seemed like a half hour or so, but without a way to keep time, he couldn't be sure. He'd heard of people being trapped in coal mines for weeks and thinking only a few days had passed.

This wasn't fun to think about. If he ever managed to get out of here, would Em and Daniel still be around? Maybe they'd be long dead and crumbled to dust.

"Well," Sam said, "come see my part of the world."

The earth was in shadow and the sun hung on the far western horizon, bathing the sky with purples and pinks and golds. Granite ridges dusted with snow loomed ahead. Pine trees fringed the base of the mountain, and beyond them sprawled a valley of dry, fissured desert.

Annabel cast her gaze over Sam's control panel, clucking and humming in a way that could mean she was impressed with what she saw, or else just the opposite. She squinted at the view outside the dragon's eyes.

"What are we doing over the Sierras?"

"The dragon roosts here sometimes," Sam said.

Annabel took this in, knowing and worried, like an old mariner witnessing the early warnings of a typhoon. "You ever read Yang's treatise on the transitive essences of dragon species?"

"That one must have been checked out of the library."

"Where were you schooled, anyway? You're not an academy brat?"

"No. I learned from . . ." He almost said Daniel's name. Probably not a good idea. "I had a private tutor. What about you?"

"I'm self-taught. No money in my family for academies. But I found an old osteomancer's library and workshop in a locked-up building my grandfather used to rent out, and that was enough to get me started."

"That must have been a hell of a good library," he said.

She shrugged. "Came with everything I needed."

Sam would bet her education was a little more complicated than that. A lot of osteomancers began their careers by feeding on other osteomancers. Finding yourself a nice, old, juicy sorcerer to eat could give you a good leg up.

"So what does Yang say about dragons?"

"Firedrakes like mountaintops," Annabel said. "Even the ocean-born. They like to perch on high and search out suitable prey."

"It can't be hungry again already. We just ate a gray whale."

"Food's not the only thing dragons hunt."

Just as Sam began to wonder what else the dragon might be after, a blast of air rushed into the cockpit, strong enough to flap Sam's pant legs.

"It's scenting," Annabel said, and her face looked grave. "It wants something bad." She took three sharp sniffs. "You smell that? That's some strong osteomancy."

Sam did. Not just magic, but a magic as familiar to him as his own. He'd grown up with that smell, and it brought a mix of emotions: comfort, and fear, and resentment, and love.

There was no other osteomancy quite like this. There was no osteomancer quite like its source.

He was smelling Daniel.

The firedrake climbed a few hundred feet and wheeled around, aiming for a stony peak shaped like a weathered flint ax.

"Ah, that's Mount Whitney," Annabel said with warm appreciation. "Tallest peak in the Southern realm. A very fine place for dragon."

Sam leaned over the controls. Even in the fading light, he made out three human forms, bundled up against the howling cold.

Daniel was looking back at him through binoculars.

Daniel had done it.

He'd found Sam. He'd crossed the kingdom, he'd figured out a place where the firedrake might show, he'd baited the air with his own scent, and he'd climbed more than fourteen thousand feet to find Sam. And of course Moth was with him, his ridiculous, giant shadow. And Em, not because she was loyal to Daniel, but because she was loyal to Sam.

Sam raised his hand in a greeting he knew none of them could see.

"You know those folks?" Annabel asked.

"Friends of mine," Sam said.

"Looks like two of your friends are fixing to fire a harpoon at us."

Sam smiled. He'd wondered what Daniel was planning to do once he tracked down the dragon. He bet Daniel had gone through quite a bit of trouble to obtain whatever bone was on the end of the harpoon.

Sam wanted the firedrake to hover there and take whatever was coming to it. He only wished he could find a way to let Daniel know it was okay, because if things went wrong and Daniel ended up killing him, Sam didn't want Daniel to spend the rest of his life moping around with guilt.

The harpoon flew at the dragon. There was not so much as a bump, a shudder, or even a noise when it struck the dragon's belly. But Sam could tell right away something was happening. The dragon's wing beats slowed.

Annabel sniffed the air. "That smell like alp to you?"

"No. What's alp?"

"It's a shape changer. Doesn't even have a native form. But you can cook it into a powerful tranquilizer."

"Powerful enough to put the firedrake to sleep?"

"Not unless it's mixed by a phenomenally good osteomancer. Are your friends phenomenally good osteomancers?"

"One of them is," Sam said as the dragon lost altitude. It reached out with a talon, tearing loose tons of rock, and kept sinking. The floor pitched, and Sam and Annabel grabbed on to the pilot's chair for balance.

"I think your friends might actually manage to put the dragon to sleep. What do you think they have planned for us next? You think they can kill us?"

The dragon's wings stopped beating. It fell, crashing against the mountainside. Boulders shattered into shrapnel. The dragon dragged massive parcels of rock and dirt in its wake as it slid down the slope to a precarious rest on a ledge.

"They're not going to kill us," Sam said, trying not to hope too much. "I think they're going to save us."

"How?"

"I don't know. But Daniel will." Annabel's life was in as much jeopardy as Sam's. She had a right to know Daniel's name. She had a right not to have secrets kept from her.

Annabel made a skeptical noise. "I don't think those airships are part of his plan."

Sam looked out the dragon's eye where she was pointing. Three enormous airships cruised in from the west across the desert.

They weren't from the Southern realm. They were from the North.

SEVEN

Gabriel lived in a windowed perch above the Mulholland Locks. His views spanned the San Gabriel Mountains to the towers of downtown, all the way out to the sea. On clear nights it was as if an entire skyful of stars had fallen and shattered across the Los Angeles basin.

He came home after an eighteen-hour workday to find Daniel Blackland enjoying the view from his living room couch.

Gabriel set down his briefcase and hung his coat. "Can I get you something to drink?"

Daniel lifted a bottle of wine to him. "No need."

"Is that the ninety-three Wolfskill cabernet?"

"I didn't read the label. It tastes like smog."

"The ninety-seven, then. You look beat." Daniel always looked a little beat: thin, unshaven, hair cropped by a box cutter. One of his hands was bundled with a comically large bandage. "What happened to you?"

"Where's your hound?" Daniel said, ignoring the question because he always seemed to get a kick from evading questions put to him by authority figures, and despite the frightening power that resided in his bones, he considered Gabriel an authority figure.

"By 'hound' I think you're referring to the assistant director of the Department of Water and Power?"

"Wow, you're starchy today. Isn't that what I said?"

"Not even close. To what do I owe this visit, Daniel?"

Daniel took a swig of Gabriel's wine. "I suppose you know where I've just come back from."

"Well, I know you hired Isaac Slough to grow a new body for Sam. But I'm not actually spying on you. However, your face is pretty chapped, even though we've had wet weather the last two weeks. Out to sea? Mountaintop?"

Daniel raised the bottle at "mountaintop."

"Mount Whitney. I found Sam there. Then lost him."

"Lost him to whom?"

"The Northern realm." Daniel took a swig.

Gabriel lowered himself into the opposite chair. He relieved Daniel of the bottle and took a long pull. "Tell me what happened on the mountain."

Daniel told him about the airships and the Northern soldiers, and how he watched them carry the dragon away. He told him about his visit to Hollywood Cemetery, and how he obtained a small piece of the *axis mundi* dragon. Gabriel pretended he didn't know what that was.

"Basically," Daniel said, "it's like a soul magnet. I hoped to use it to draw Sam's consciousness from the firedrake, store it in the bone, and then put his consciousness inside Slough's golem." Daniel let out a small, bitter laugh. "It sounds so straightforward when I say it like that."

"Maybe not straightforward in execution, but certainly in concept." Gabriel liked it. It was neat, with clear objectives and mileposts. "So, the only thing that's changed is now instead of drawing the firedrake to a mountaintop, you have to find it in the Northern realm."

"Right, that's all there is to it. Oh, except for I lost the *axis mundi* bone in all the high-altitude fisticuffs, and the only other known fragments are in China and the Northern realm. You have any friends in China?"

"Where in the Northern realm, exactly?"

"In the stronghold of one of their most powerful osteomancers. He's very close to the Northern Hierarch. Or at least he was."

Gabriel realized Daniel was setting him up for some bad news. "What happened to him?" Gabriel asked, playing the straight man.

"I killed him."

Daniel reached for the bottle. Gabriel took an extra-long swig before handing it back.

"Paul Sigilo had the bone. Your golem-brother."

"My golem-brother, the osteomancer who built the Pacific firedrake. Who I killed on Catalina."

"You don't make things easy, do you, Blackland?"

"Nothing's easy. That's why I've come to you. I can't do this by myself. Too many moving parts, and none of them close to hand. By myself, I could maybe find the firedrake in the North. By myself, I could maybe find a way to get the *axis mundi* bone from Paul's house."

These were big, ambitious, conspicuous capers they were talking about.

"I'm skeptical about even a 'maybe,'" Gabriel said. "I take it you're proposing we join forces in this unlikely endeavor?"

"What could be better, Gabriel? We worked together to off the Hierarch, now we can work together to save my kid."

"But you know I've been working to do just the opposite. I've been working to destroy the Pacific firedrake."

Daniel put down the bottle. "I do know that. And now you're going to stop doing that."

Some osteomancers spent magic on letting their power show. Mother Cauldron used hers to grow herself monstrously large and to sprout extra arms. Alex Vermilion used his to glow in the dark. Daniel had never spent one iota of magic to impress. He always let himself look like something left out in the rain. And knowing the power that resided in his bones, Gabriel found him all the more frightening.

Outside the window, the valley lights twinkled. Billions of gallons of water flowed through city waterworks, as much a part of Gabriel as the blood coursing through his veins. Gabriel's power was far-reaching and immense, but he had absolutely no desire to test it against Daniel Blackland's magic.

"I'm waiting for you to articulate the reason I'm going to help you, Daniel."

Daniel stood. "Because otherwise, at long last, after more than ten years of avoidance, you and I will be at war."

He went to the door, poised to put a period on this dramatic parting.

Gabriel hated drama.

"Show up to my office at eight," he said. "We'll start discussing a plan."

"Will there be doughnuts?" Daniel asked, hand on the doorknob.

"Will we be at war if there aren't?"

Daniel smiled.

"I'll make sure we have doughnuts."

Jo Alverado threw her arms around Daniel's neck and planted a wet kiss on his cheek. Daniel didn't even get to say hello before she tugged him by the arm into her apartment, steered him to a chair in her kitchen, and filled a teacup from a kettle still exhaling the last of a whistle.

She waved off his attempted apologies at not having looked her up sooner when he came back to Los Angeles, and instead kept him busy fielding questions about how he was doing, about his health, about his bandaged hand, whether he'd looked in on Cassandra, and if he had anyone special in his life right now. And so on.

Daniel went through two cups of tea before she deemed him sufficiently debriefed and allowed him to get to business.

He'd just been through two long days of planning with Gabriel Argent. Argent was smart and efficient, and it was amazing how quickly he'd put things in motion. But there were some things for which he still had to rely on his friends.

"I need a new face," he said.

"I've been telling you that for years. What for?"

"It's part of trying to get Sam back. I lost him on Catalina Island. 'Lost' is maybe not the right word. He—"

"I know what's been going on," she said with gentleness. "You've been scarce, but I still hear from Moth."

In the old days, Daniel was the glue that held his group of friends together. They were a band of thieves, and he was their mastermind. It startled him to think of Moth being the center now.

"Whose face do you need?"

"I just want some alterations to my own. I've got some good chimera bone to make me pliable, but I'm not a sculptor like you."

"I've never changed anyone else's face but my own."

"I know your talents, Jo. There's nobody else I'd come to for something like this."

The flattery touched her, and Daniel felt ashamed of himself.

He could no longer justify telling someone just what she needed to hear as anything other than manipulation.

"Whatever I can do to help, D. You know that, right? Anything, any time?"

She touched his good hand, and he wrapped his fingers around hers and felt even more ashamed. "Thank you. You really are the best."

Jo took him into her bathroom. She had a whole Hollywood makeup thing going, complete with lightbulbs rimming the mirror. She was still a professional thief, posing as people who had a right to walk into places and wouldn't be suspected of walking out with a few Rolexes in their pockets. She used to be an actress. Still was, actually, just on different stages.

She sat Daniel in front of the mirror and adjusted the height of his chair. "Okay, so what kind of effect are we trying to achieve here?"

"Let's start with my nose. Can you make it look like it hasn't been broken five times?"

"How long ago did you take that chimera?"

"About an hour."

"Then you should be good and squishy. Okay, let's have a go."

She pressed down on the prominent bump rising from the bridge of Daniel's nose.

"That . . . hey, that hurts. A lot."

"*Pobrecito*. Changing your shape hurts, sweetie."

"But you do it all the time."

"And I'm a badass so I don't complain."

"Well, I'm not a badass. Can you be more gentle?"

"Yes. But it's still going to hurt."

She pressed her fingertips to Daniel's nose and straightened it. He yelped, but when she was done, his nose looked right.

"That's perfect, Jo."

"I liked it better before. Next?"

"This scar through my eyebrow . . . can you shift stuff around to fix it?"

"It's going to hurt."

"I'm getting that."

Daniel flinched and carried on like a baby as Jo worked over his face.

The pain was worth it. After fifteen minutes, Daniel stared in the mirror and the face of his golem-brother, Paul, looked back at him. It was a good face, a less broken face. Or maybe just broken in different ways.

"I look better this way. I should have done this a long time ago."

"Then you wouldn't be Daniel, and that would be a loss."

"That's funny to hear, coming from you."

"Why?"

"Because, you're a shape-shifter. I'd think you'd be telling me that what you are, who you are, doesn't change just because your outer form is different."

"That may be true of some people," Jo said. "Maybe it's even true of me. But not you. You are your scars. You remember them, and you lug them around like chains. You without your scars? Not Daniel."

"That's okay, I guess. I need to not be me for a while."

She started trying to tame his tousled hair with a comb. She wasn't gentle, but he let her, because Paul was better groomed than he was.

"I know who you're trying to be," she said, working a tangle, "and I don't like it. There's no reason to go North as Paul that isn't incredibly dangerous, and I wish you wouldn't."

He looked at her reflection in the mirror, then turned to look at her properly. "I don't have much choice, Jo."

"I know. You're doing it for Sam. But still."

"How much do you know?"

"As much as Moth knows. He keeps in touch with his friends, unlike you." She hit his head with the comb.

"Any professional acting advice for me?"

She resumed the tug-of-war between Daniel's hair and her comb. "You can't be Paul. But you have to get as close to being him as you can. The new look will help. Actors rely on costume and makeup all the time. But to convince anyone, you'll have to really get inside his head."

"I don't know if I can do that. Paul was a weird guy."

"You're a weird guy."

"I mean different weird."

"How so?"

Daniel thought back to Catalina, to the single hour he'd spent with Paul before he killed him. Paul had a slow, distracted manner of speaking, as if he had to concentrate on being in the same room as others because the most important part of him was somewhere else. It reminded Daniel so much of his father.

And with that realization, he knew how to play his brother.

It wouldn't even be the hardest part of this job.

The hardest part would be Daniel's mother.

Daniel looked around the bleak, ten-by-twelve storage unit and felt like a heel. He put on a sunny smile anyway. "Okay, so, you've got a fridge stocked with goodies and a microwave."

"And a cot," Em said. "And a strip of canvas stretched between some aluminum rods, which I suspect is some kind of chair. I've got magazines. Books. Plus a radio and a chemical toilet. I'm all set."

"We're aiming to be back from the North in six days, but if something goes wrong . . ."

"It could be longer. It could be never. I know, Daniel. I was at the meetings."

A mechanical hum and the soft gurgle of osteomantic fluid bled through the wooden crate that filled most of the space. Inside the crate was a gleaming steel tank, and inside the tank was the gestating golem Isaac Slough had grown from a single strand of Sam's hair.

"I hate to leave you here by yourself. It's just that—"

"You don't trust anyone enough but me to guard Sam's new body," Em said. "Neither do I. I'll be here when you get back, no matter how long it takes. I'll keep him safe."

"There could be hounds. Thieves. Other osteomancers. Even without a consciousness, the body contains Sam's osteomantic essence. The golem is probably the richest trove of osteomancy in the realm."

Em sank into the camp chair and rested her rifle across her lap. Nearby, she'd placed ammo boxes full of explosive ruhk eggs. She cracked open a paperback.

"Bring me a beer when you get back," she said.

"You don't drink beer."

"I know, but it's the kind of thing you and Moth say to each other. I thought you'd know it means go away, do your job, and let me do mine."

"Okay, Em." He lifted the roll gate, letting in the last sunshine Em would see for quite some time. "Seriously, tell me what I can bring you back."

She set down her book and looked thoughtful. "You're going to San Francisco. They make chocolate there. Better than ours. You're a cook with an osteomancer's nose, so you should know what good chocolate is. Bring it to me. Bring me the best."

She returned to her book, this young Emma with a gun on her lap, guarding a crate containing half the key to the job's success.

"The best ever," Daniel said, shutting her in.

Cassandra registered no surprise when she found Daniel on the front porch of her Mar Vista stucco cottage. She gave him a tired smile, a quick hug, and let him inside.

"You changed your face."

"How'd you know it was me?"

"Give me a break."

He stood in the middle of her living room, taking in her mismatched but harmonious thrift-shop furniture and her small selection of perfectly chosen vases and candlesticks and knickknacks. Cassandra almost never stayed anywhere more than a few months, but she'd developed the art of making a temporary place look like a home she'd lived in for years.

"Sorry to drop in on you like this, Cass. I was hoping you might help me with some—"

"You need papers." She handed him a file folder. "It's all there."

There were Northern California internal travel passes, identification, and work licenses for the team. Everything Daniel had come here planning to ask her for. And everything looked authentic. Cassandra had been supporting herself by smuggling bone from Northern California, and she knew how to get Northern papers.

"Moth told you?"

She brought Daniel into the kitchen and poured him a cup of coffee. "He figured to save us a long, awkward conversation in which you'd ask me for something while trying not to ask me."

"I liked it better when I was the mastermind and he was the muscle."

Cassandra touched her mug against his and they sat at her kitchen table. "I think you actually like it this way more than you realize."

"I guess it is nice to have a second brain, even if it's Moth's." He flexed his bandaged hand. It was almost healed, a few days' treatment with hydra regenerative knitting bones and tendons and muscle tissue back together.

"So, elephant in the room," he said.

"Which one? We have so many."

"I'm talking about Otis. I'm still not comfortable with you keeping him captive. He's a disease. He's poison. And as long as you're holding him, you've got a target on your back."

Cassandra dropped a couple of sugar cubes in her coffee and stirred. There was something she didn't want to tell him, and she was stalling for time. She clinked her spoon sharply on the edge of her cup. "Otis is dead. I shot him and buried him outside Riverside."

Mute, Daniel could only stare at her.

"You disapprove?" she said.

"Approval doesn't come into it. Just . . . why, Cass?"

"The question is why not."

He knew Cassandra well enough to see past her flat affect. She was practical. But she wasn't cold.

"This isn't like you. I mean . . . we've both done things we wish we didn't have—"

"We've both killed."

"But it's always been in the middle of things. With people shooting at us. With chaos and . . . did you drive him all the

way out to the desert and then shoot him, or did you shoot him
and . . . I don't even know why I'm asking. I don't even know
what difference it makes."

Now he saw some anger in her eyes. With Cassandra, anger
was always the surface layer of pain.

"It makes all the difference. Everything about it makes a difference. Every second of it makes a difference. I killed Otis. Of
course it makes a difference."

"Oh, Cass. Why?"

She set the mug down hard. "Because he took me as collateral
on a defaulted loan. Because he sold you to the Hierarch. Because Sam. Because Moth. Because Jo, and because Punch. Because alive, he would find a way to screw us over again. Because
alive, he'd find a way to make sure you never get Sam back.
Because he deserved to die. Because you wouldn't kill him, so
I had to."

Daniel set his own cup down, very carefully. "You didn't do
this for me."

"Of course I did it for you. I did it for all of us. Because you
didn't."

"I won't thank you for it."

"I don't want you to. And you're welcome. You always come
to me, not asking, but hoping—*knowing*—I'll give you the
things you're afraid to ask for."

"Maybe you're too generous sometimes."

Cassandra shook her head with impatience. "You're misun-
derstanding. I didn't kill Otis as a personal favor to you. I killed
him for the same reason you ripped the Hierarch's heart from
his chest."

"I killed the Hierarch because he was trying to kill me."

"Exactly," Cassandra said. "Survival. Otis never stood to
your face and shot lightning at you, but he's been doing us harm

since we were children. You were about to give him another chance when you knew you shouldn't. I took the chance away from him. For me, for you, for everyone. And now you're here asking for papers. Goddamn papers, Daniel. Because you need me to do something else, and you won't ask, but you know I'm joining you on the job. You came here knowing that. You need help to get the *axis mundi* bone. That's Moth. You need someone to watch over Sam's golem. That's Em. And you need someone to make sure Gabriel Argent doesn't screw you."

She drank down her coffee, and he drank his, both of them using the pause in conversation to recalibrate.

"Ask me," she said.

He traced a finger along the wood grain of the table.

"Cass, will you be on Gabriel's team, to make sure he doesn't screw me?"

"My bag's already packed, you idiot."

He laughed, and this was almost a nice moment they'd landed on, and he wished he could just ride it out like a gentle wave. But there was another elephant in the room, and he knew Cassie wouldn't let it sit there, so he preempted her.

"My mom will be in the North."

"Yes," she said. "And some decisions will have to be made about how to deal with her. Hopefully by you."

EIGHT

Gabriel needed to drown himself.

He had Max drive him to the East Los Angeles Interchange along the banks of the Los Angeles River where the Golden State, San Bernardino/Santa Monica, Pomona, and Hollywood flumeways converged. This was not the geographical center of Los Angeles, but it was the focus of the mandala of canals begun by Abbot Kinney and William Mulholland and continued by Gabriel. For a water mage there was no more powerful place in the entire kingdom.

Max docked at a utility inlet, and they climbed out onto a narrow pier.

"It's down here," Gabriel said over the roar of water and boat traffic. He led the way through the ivy barrier and down a spiral staircase, to a platform beneath the giant nest of flumeway overpasses. The ground was sparsely littered with some shattered glass, a few cigarette butts, fast food wrappers, and a toaster, the kind of random objects that inevitably turned up in uninviting places like this.

This wasn't a secret place, but it was hidden away, and no one but Gabriel knew there was a reason to come here.

He kicked away a scattering of dead leaves to clear a manhole cover. The ring of soot and plant dust around the perimeter indicated it hadn't been disturbed since the last time Gabriel came by to check on it. The weld was still in place.

"I'm going to lift it," he said.

Max leaned his tall frame over it. "How? We didn't bring one of those hook-wrench things."

"It's called a lift key," Gabriel said, producing a metal hook from his jacket pocket. "And you know it's called a lift key. But you insist on not using my jargon. Why, Max?"

"Because your exasperation hormones smell like humility."

"Are you saying I need humility?"

"I am. You've agreed to embark on an operation behind enemy lines with Daniel Blackland and his cohorts, and you seem to have forgotten you are an unathletic bureaucrat, not a commando."

"I'm actually one of the great magical powers of the Southern Kingdom, Max."

Max just looked at him.

"Okay. I know. It's not a lack of humility. It's a lack of better options."

"You have other hydromancers. You could assign it to one of them."

"I have people who can move water around. And I trust them. To a degree. But not enough to put them near a weapon like the firedrake. I trust only two people for that: me and you."

"Well," Max said, "I trust half that many."

Even after all these years, Gabriel couldn't always tell when Max was kidding.

He turned back to the manhole cover. "Anyway, it's called a lift key. And it'll take more than a lift key to pop this top."

He dug a small vial of water from his jacket and held it up before his face. It was clear, and when he swirled it, no sediments floated in suspension. It appeared unremarkable.

He poured it around the weld. There was a sizzle. Threads of smoke unwound in air and the scar of metal boiled away. With the lift key, he pried the cover up and dragged it aside with a lot of grunting. He wished he'd asked Max to do this part, since Max sometimes exercised and was unfairly gifted with physical fitness, but he didn't want to risk some sort of comedic and unpredictable mishap resulting in Max falling down the hole.

Gabriel looked down into impenetrable blackness. He could hear the whirlpool roaring louder than any dragon, like an ocean forced through a tight conduit. The vibrations rumbled through his feet, through his entire body.

"If I don't come up, don't go in after me," Gabriel said over the noise.

"If you don't . . . wait. You're going *in* there?"

Gabriel unknotted his tie, pulled it free, and handed it to Max. He took off his jacket, then his belt, and unbuttoned his shirt.

"Why am I being made to watch you disrobe?" Max asked, accepting each item of clothing from Gabriel as it came off.

"I'm serious about not going in the well, no matter what. If I don't pop back up after, say, twenty minutes, just put the cover back over the hole, go back to your office, and look in your pencil tray."

"Why, what's in there?"

"Cash, travel papers, dirty secrets on anyone you might need to extort for favors, keys to my house—"

"I don't need keys to get in your house."

"—all you need to live a comfortable life."

"I had no idea a comfortable life was so near to my grasp. Why don't you stop talking and jump in?"

Gabriel peeled out of his boxers and laid them on top of the expensive, tailored fabrics now piled in Max's arms. The socks went last, and a deep chill leeched into the bottoms of his feet.

"Oh, hold this for me, too." He dug out a steel flask from his inner jacket pocket.

Max shook it. "It's empty."

"Last time, Max. Don't go in the water. Strict orders."

"I know how to stay," Max said. "Why am I even here?"

Max's face tended not to betray his feelings, seldom straying from a look of weary concentration. He'd been made into a magic sniffer at a young age. Nobody was interested in his feelings. He was just supposed to smell osteomancy. But he'd been the closest thing Gabriel had to a friend for over a decade now, and Gabriel could tell when Max was angry or frightened, both of which were rare for him, and both of which he was revealing in his level gaze.

"Max, I'd hate to die alone."

Max opened his mouth, said nothing, closed it again. Finally, he said, "I'll be right here, Gabriel."

"Thank you, Max."

And before he could change his mind, Gabriel stepped over the edge of the hole and let himself fall.

He hit the water, and the water hit him back, twisting his body like a piece of string in a hurricane. Everything was black and unfathomably loud, and the whirlpool consumed him and drew him down.

It was an extraordinary relief not to feel as though he were drowning. He'd done research on drowning, having calculated a 63 percent chance that drowning would, indeed, be his eventual fate, and he'd lost sleep dreading the agonizing pressure on his lungs, and the spikes of pain generated by oxygen-starved brain cells, and the horror of watching his last-ever breath abandon him in a cascade of bubbles.

So, yes, it was good not to drown. He never wanted to be one of those about whom people said, "That guy? Yeah, he did okay until he decided to take a swim in the well at the heart of the mandala. What made him think that could possibly be a good idea?"

That was the kind of thing a sorcerer did, and even though Gabriel was the kingdom's most powerful water mage, he never considered himself a sorcerer. He'd started out as an administrator and was proud of being a good one. By necessity, he became an engineer, learning everything about how water worked, how to design canals and flumeways and how to channel and control its magic. But to conquer the dragon, he'd have to conquer Daniel Blackland. And Daniel Blackland was a sorcerer, and a great one. Gabriel simply needed more direct access to his own power.

A horrible necessity, and it went against Gabriel's nature. His mother was an osteomancer, but she'd never raised him to be one. He asked her why enough times that she finally ran out of deflections and told him her truth: Magic is painful. She didn't want her son to live by pain. At the time, he resented being denied gifts of power. But later in life he realized that magic sometimes made one great, but it almost never made one good.

All his mother's power, and she ended up on the Hierarch's dinner table. All the Hierarch's power, and Daniel Blackland tore his heart from his chest with his bare hands. All William Mulholland's power, and Max shot him in the head.

The water had a voice.

In fact, it had many voices. The voices of all the boats traversing the canals. The voices of the water coursing through the kingdom's plumbing, from its sewer mains to the capillaries threading behind its walls. The voices of every creature that drank and eliminated and swam in the kingdom's waters.

And there were voices from deeper waters, from below the city's bedrock, and farther down, from below the earth's crust.

Gabriel had studied water, and though he was no osteomancer, he had studied osteomancy. He knew all forms of magic were linked, and that the voices of the deepest osteomantic creatures could be captured in hydromantic medium.

To gain the power he needed, Gabriel would have to make himself the temporary medium for one of the deepest voices of all.

He opened his mouth and let the water rush in.

Gabriel's head broke the surface. Sunlight bored in through the manhole, searing his eyes. A hand emerged from the light, reaching for him, and Gabriel clasped it and surrendered to it as it lifted him up to the heavens.

It was not a god who met him.

It was only Max.

Gabriel coughed and his stomach convulsed, trying to vomit, but his body refused to surrender its water.

Max rolled him onto his back beside the manhole, and now he did feel as though he was drowning. His depleted lungs blazed and the air he drew in gasps provided nothing. Terrible pain seized every part of his body. Surely his bones were shattered. Surely the current had torn his flesh away.

He reached out his hand, and somehow Max knew what he wanted. He handed Gabriel the steel flask.

Gabriel vomited. Murky water came out in a tight, high-pressure jet, just enough to fill about half the flask. He capped it and clutched it to his chest.

"Forty minutes," said Max.

After a while, when the pain subsided enough and he could speak, Gabriel croaked, "What?"

"You were in there for forty minutes."

"That's a long time."

"I know. How do you feel?"

In the water, in the storm and the dark, he had felt like himself. On land, he was dying.

"It's awful, Max. I think I may have made a mistake."

Frowning, Max knelt at his side and sniffed him.

"Do I smell different?"

Max nodded, and with the stiff, professional tone of an uncomfortable doctor pronouncing a terminal diagnosis, he said, "You smell like magic."

NINE

Daniel and Moth landed ashore at San Simeon Harbor in broad daylight. Tan grass hills overlooked the broad stretch of coastline. Atop the hill rose twin white towers, like a cathedral against the bright blue sky. Spotters used to look for migrating gray whales from the heights and send men out with harpoons to kill them, and it was virtually impossible to arrive here undetected. As Moth and Daniel dragged their boat onto the beach, a dozen armed guards sped down the hill in all-terrain carts to meet them.

"I suggest a change of plan," Moth said. "You burn them all, and we dump the bodies and go have a vacation."

"Rejected. Get in character."

"Scowl," Moth said. "Scowl, glower, frown." Moth proceeded to do so beneath the nylon hood of his windbreaker.

A nervous minute passed while Daniel and Moth waited passively for the guards to reach them.

The carts came to a stop and the guards spilled out.

"This is private property," said one of them, leveling a rifle at Daniel's chest. She had two white stripes on her sleeve, one more than the others. They all wore black body armor and combat helmets, and their guns looked like the kind that fired big bullets rapidly. There were a lot of fingers curled around triggers. People took property rights seriously around here.

Daniel pulled his hood back. "I'm Paul Sigilo," he said.

He stared into the guard captain's eyes through the clear lens of her helmet's visor.

She redirected the muzzle of her gun away from him. "Stand down," she ordered, and the others did the same.

"My apologies, Baron Sigilo," she said. "Welcome home."

Home was a white Mediterranean castle surrounded by fountains and plazas and splashes of colorful flowers. Every surface was carved with some filigree or naked Greek, and Daniel saw money in every chisel mark. The newspaper tycoon William Randolph Hearst had built it, and its opulence was famous even in the Southern realm. When Hearst died, the Northern Hierarch took possession of it, and the fact that it had been let out to Paul gave Daniel a real sense of how high in the regime his damaged golem-twin had climbed.

Gardeners stopped clipping hedges at the sight of Daniel and Moth and the procession of guards escorting them across the plaza. Daniel tried to read their expressions. How did Paul's people feel about his return? No radiant smiles broke out. Nobody wiped tears of joy. So it wasn't love. But he didn't see fear, either. More a sort of curiosity, as if he were some kind of zoo animal. Maybe a little caution. So, they viewed him as a possibly dangerous exotic creature. Daniel could work with that.

A pace behind Daniel, Moth was in his full, towering gloom, the embodiment of potential violence, muscles in his forearms like steel cables, his shoulders like boulders, his chest like stone slabs. Daniel would work with that as well.

They went through a pair of massive wooden doors that must have been taken off an ancient European church and were met in an entry hall. Daniel nearly staggered. The scents of a hundred or more osteomantic creatures filled the air. Daniel scanned the assemblage for their source. Butlers and maids and cooks and tradesworkers and dozens of other members of Paul's household staff waited with stiff postures.

Of them all, one woman stood out, with striking cheekbones, eyes like pools of black ink, and black hair falling like a curtain to her knees. It wasn't only her appearance that attracted Daniel's attention. She didn't regard Daniel with nervous uncertainty, nor with the curiosity of the others. Locking eyes with him, she gave him a look he couldn't read.

A man in a neat suit with neat silver hair and a precise mustache stepped up. His eyes watered, and he regarded Daniel with the surprise and delight of someone who'd just found a live baby unicorn in his sock drawer. Some nicely dressed functionaries flanked him, throwing him glances for behavioral cues. Chief of staff? Majordomo? Something like that.

"My lord," Weepy Mustache said with a bow. "I can scarcely believe my eyes. We thought you dead."

Daniel responded with one of Paul's enigmatic blank looks. Weepy Mustache took it like a cattle prod.

"Not that I ever lost hope," he added hastily, putting the emphasis on *I* to make sure there was no possibility he could be confused with one of those disloyal, benighted idiots who presumed Paul dead, even though he'd identified himself as such fewer than three seconds ago. "It's just . . . I don't . . . How is this even possible, my lord?"

"Magic?" Daniel said.

No, that wasn't quite Paul's tone. Less sarcasm, next time. More flat-line.

"Of course, my lord, of course." Weepy fell just short of hitting himself. "Forgive my question. I did not mean to trespass. This is such a happy occasion, an overwhelmingly happy occasion, to have you back. The realm shall be flooded with tears of joy. I dare say, the Hierarch herself shall weep. To say nothing of your mother—"

Daniel twitched a nod, and Moth's bass cut Weepy off and filled the space.

"His lord is fatigued from his travels. News of his return will be withheld pending his lord's order."

Daniel winced. The Northerners' manner of speech would take some time to master. Passing themselves off as high-class wasn't something Moth or Daniel had much practice in. Still, Moth's presence alone conveyed authority, and as he trained his menacing glare on Weepy and the guards and the rest of the assemblage, he got the message across: If someone leaked Baron Paul Sigilo's presence, there would be broken bones.

Daniel waved his hand vaguely in Moth's direction. "This is Mr. Matthew, my steward."

Weepy went ashen. Daniel had probably just introduced him to his replacement.

The old steward gave Moth a jittery little bow. "I am your . . . I am the previous . . . I am Abram Gorov. If I may—"

"I'd like to go to my apartments now," Daniel announced.

Weepy's body threatened to divide in two as he struggled over whether to rush into action or step back and let Moth take charge.

"Lead the way, Gorov," Moth told him.

Good move, since neither Daniel nor Moth had any idea where Paul's private quarters were.

With maximum solicitation, Gorov took them up a staircase. Daniel gave a last glimpse at the crowd. The woman with the black hair turned and left the room, and with her went the scent of a hundred kinds of magic.

You are so unbelievably rich," Moth said, once Gorov left them alone in Paul's chambers. The wall behind Paul's canopied bed was lined with wooden panels painted with saints and martyrs. The carpet was posh enough to have been hung on a museum wall, and there wasn't a single surface in Daniel's eyeshot that wasn't adorned by something expensive.

Moth walked around the room, inspecting all the gold candlesticks and the lamp shades with gold tassels. "You think Gorov is going to be a problem?"

"He might be," Daniel said. "Don't be fooled by him. He acts like an abused waiter, but he stinks of griffin."

"And you very publicly gave me his job."

"Sorry, buddy. There was no way I could pass you off as my special friend with special access to me without making enemies in Paul's staff. At least this way, it's out in the open."

Moth picked up a pearl-and-gold box and pulled out a tissue. "Yeah, don't worry, I can manage him. But what about the spooky chick?"

"You noticed her, too? She stinks of all the magic."

"You want me to ask about her?"

"That's basically what I need you to do. Make a peace offering with Gorov, tell him he still runs the house, and you're just here to help me with my convalescence and get me back on my feet. Nose around, get into the dirt, talk to the housekeepers, bring back intel on who's who."

"You want me to be charming or terrifying?"

"Your usual combination of both will probably be good."

"And what are you doing while I'm making friends and victims?"

Daniel approached a bookcase and sniffed. He ran his fingers along the spines of leather-bound volumes and smelled his finger. It smelled of Paul. The scent was faint, because Paul hadn't been here in over a year, and the more efficient an osteomancer, the less magic he wasted on aroma. Paul was a very efficient osteomancer, and Daniel doubted many other noses could pick up his residue. But Paul was made of Daniel's own magic, and that gave him an advantage.

He pulled a bloodred book from the shelf, and the bookcase slid aside, revealing a black door. There was no knob, no visible lock or hardware of any kind, just smooth, matte-black wood.

Daniel rapped his knuckles against it. "Me? I'm going to work on this."

"I'll start with the kitchen staff, then," Moth said.

"Bring back milk and cookies," Daniel called after him.

He went back to sniffing, moving his nose around the edges of the door. He detected no sphinx or nhang lock, no familiar magic barriers, but Daniel was certain Paul's workshops were on the other side of the door: his stores of osteomantic bones, his equipment. And, most important, the *axis mundi* bone.

He began work on a key.

He'd performed magic in alleys, behind dumpsters, crammed into air vents, sitting on toilets in bus station rest rooms. But Paul had a lovely writing desk of wood so rich Daniel was tempted to lick it. Might as well work in comfort, he thought.

He got out his osteomancy kit and rummaged inside for the powdered bone of three different breath-stealing creatures. He sprinkled the powder into a glass vial and held the vial to the flame of his torch. Drawing in air from the room—air that

Paul had inhaled and exhaled—the powder turned from fog-gray to chalk-white, eventually crumbling into finer grains and dissolving. A small quantity of clear fluid rested at the bottom of the vial.

With a Q-tip, he swabbed his dead brother's condensed breath on the door and it swung open, letting him into Paul's world.

TEN

The plane rocked and dipped in the air like a barrel in the rapids. Rain shot out of the darkness and splattered against the windshield. Gabriel sat next to the pilot, a man with a lumberjack build and a blond beard cascading down his chest. The pilot peered at his gauges through gold-rimmed aviators, rarely bothering to look up from his instrument panel. Granite mountain crags and javelin points of fur trees allegedly lurked below, but Gabriel couldn't see anything.

"So you're comfortable with everything that's going on?" he asked over the headset.

The pilot's eyes crinkled, but Gabriel couldn't tell if he was smiling or grimacing below his bushy mustache. "This is the most dreadful weather I've ever pushed a plane through, sir. To tell you the truth, I'm pretty scared."

The plane shuddered and jumped like the EKG of a troubled heart.

"I thought pilots were supposed to be stoic and reassuring. I was led to believe this. I was *promised* this."

"Is this your first time flying, sir?"

"Yes."

"I hope it doesn't leave you with a bad impression."

The plane jolted, and Gabriel bit his lip to suppress a gasp.

"Sorry, sir. It'll all be over soon."

"What do you mean, 'over'?"

"I mean, we're almost there."

"I thought you meant we were going to crash."

The pilot's lack of response was not encouraging.

Gabriel twisted around in his seat. In the rear compartment, Max shifted as if readying to kick out a window and jump, choosing the time and manner of his own death. Cassandra tightened her boot laces. She made a twirly finger gesture at Gabriel and mouthed, "Turn around."

The plane hit. Gabriel's teeth clacked together, and he felt the impact in the small of his back. Not until water splashed across the windshield and the pilot nodded contentedly did he realize they hadn't crashed. They'd merely made the water landing. The pontoons kicked up rooster tails as the plane skidded to a stop.

"Well, I got you here," the pilot said. "Hope that was the most dangerous part of whatever it is you folks are doing."

"Wouldn't that be great?" Gabriel said, unbuckling. "Have a good flight back."

A howl of wind brought fresh salvos of driving rain.

Securing his backpack, he followed Max and Cassandra, leaping from the rear compartment hatch to a tiny wooden fishing pier. The pilot gave them a two-fingered wave through the cockpit window, and a few minutes later, he was back in the air, leaving them in enemy territory.

The way from the shore to the tree line was a muddy slog, but it would have been worse without the magic Daniel had cooked into the treads of their hiking boots. There'd be miles to go before reaching the Hetch Hetchy dam, and they needed to get there before daylight.

They hunkered among the trees on a sodden carpet of leaves and pine needles. Rain streamed from the upper limbs.

"Smell anything, Max?" Cassandra whispered.

Max sniffed the air. "I smell millions of things."

"Okay," Cassandra said, wiping water from her face with both hands. "When I ask you a question, you need to answer it."

"Do what she says, Max," Gabriel said.

Max sniffed in Cassandra's direction and averted his face, his version of giving her the middle finger. "If I picked up something scary I would have brought it to your attention without you having to ask. Just because we're on a suicide mission doesn't mean I want to die."

Cassandra stepped briskly off into the rain. "Let's move out. Gabriel, keep up with me."

Gabriel huffed, jogging to catch up. "Things starting off a little tense, aren't they?"

"I don't want you interceding between me and Max. When I give an instruction to either of you, follow it. Do it for the good of the job, and do it to stay alive. You're not in Los Angeles anymore."

"I don't normally resort to saying this kind of thing, but you are talking to a very powerful person right now."

"There's snot running out of your nose, grand mage."

Gabriel opened his mouth to respond but then stumbled over a tree root. He would have gone face-forward into the mud had Cassandra not caught him by the arm. Declarations of one's power were much less impressive after demonstrating one wasn't even very good at walking.

"Max and I have been close for a long time," he said, recovering. "We bonded when people were trying to kill us. That kind of thing tends to solidify a friendship, and we rely on each other."

"He's still your dog, and you're his master. He'll have to take directions from me and not expect a biscuit."

Despite the chilling rain, heat rose to Gabriel's face.

"He's not a dog. He's a man. And he's my friend."

"All right. That was . . . yeah, I'm sorry." They trudged on a few more steps in the muck. "Just the same, do whatever you have to do to keep him in line without undermining my authority."

Gabriel might have said something else if he hadn't tripped over another root. This time, Cassandra let him fall, and he tasted wet, frigid earth.

Dawn cast an amber glow over O'Shaughnessy Dam, a four-hundred-foot wall of concrete holding back the Hetch Hetchy Reservoir. Perched on a granite ledge above one end of the span, Gabriel felt the thundering power of the water in his belly. It blasted from the dam's eleven jet-flows, some into the Tuolumne River, but most of it diverted into an aqueduct that filled toilets and water glasses over 180 miles away in San Francisco.

In the early light, the water glinted with iridescent blues and pinks. The spire of Kolana Rock and the 2,400-foot Hetch Hetchy Dome stood as monumental grave markers for the valley that had been here millions of years before the construction of the dam. Submerged beneath the reservoir were what John

Muir called the "rarest and most precious mountain temples," a place where eagles had soared, where bobcats and bears hid from the shrieks of wyvern echoing through the valley. Water killed worlds.

Max inhaled sharply and squinted, his head darting back and forth like a pigeon's until he fixed on something. "Problem," he said. "Smells predatory."

They huddled behind a fallen pine tree and waited until a large, gray dog came into view, climbing the cliff face toward them. Deep-bellied and lean, the dog passed its gigantic nostrils over the ground, vacuuming up air and scents. It was a garm hound, the kind of dog Max was osteomantically altered to emulate. In the Southern Kingdom, they were used to sniff out contraband magic. Here in the North, for all Gabriel knew, they were trained to kill anyone who possessed it.

"Max?" Gabriel said, and Max unholstered his gun.

"No," Cassandra said. "I got this."

She unpacked a pair of tubes and screwed them together, forming a blowgun. Max returned his gun to its holster and seemed relieved.

With a puff of air, she sent a dart flying into the garm's neck. It let out one sharp whine and climbed a few more feet, but then its rear legs got wobbly, and it lay down on its belly, its big head resting on its front paws. Gabriel couldn't tell from this distance if it was still breathing.

"Dead?" he asked.

"Sleeping," Cassandra said. She turned to Max. "I hope that's okay with you."

"I can't object to sparing the life of a hound."

Max never smiled, but he came about as close to it as he ever did, and Cassandra returned his non-smile with half a grin.

Something passed between them—an understanding, or an appreciation. Gabriel should have been happy about it, but for some reason it made him feel uneasy.

"Clear now?" Cassandra asked Max.

He grunted, and Cassandra took the lead down the cliff face to the valley floor.

Despite Gabriel's osteomantically treated boot treads, the terrain was crumbly and treacherous, and after his third slip, it occurred to him that he could simply bring down the dam and create a cataclysmic flood that would rip sequoias from the ground, push over buildings and send them smashing into bridges, deliver a cargo of cars and bloated livestock carcasses and human corpses hundreds of miles below to San Francisco, and Gabriel could arrive behind the flood, like a general walking through the gates of a conquered city.

But he didn't want to be that kind of water mage, so he continued to slip and struggle down the cliff side.

Eventually they made it to the canyon power tunnel, a conduit that conducted water ten and a half miles to a power station downriver.

Kneeling in the crawlway maintenance shaft above the tunnel, Cassandra worked the bolts of an access hatch. Meanwhile, Gabriel assembled a maze of copper pipes, each barely wider than a drinking straw. Using the wrench he'd found among his predecessor's tools, an object he'd named the Wrench of All Purpose, he tightened fittings: S-curves and U-curves and corkscrews, funnels that concentrated water flow to laser-fine jets inside copper skin. Max crouched beside him, impatient, searching out aromas.

"Done," Cassandra announced, dragging the hatch cover off to the side. Down the hole, fewer than three feet below them, the water roared.

Gabriel threaded a valve wheel into place. A long straight pipe fed into one side of the configuration, and another fed out the other side: an intake and an outtake. He maneuvered the two pipes into the water.

Cassandra gave him a skeptical frown. "How's the crazy-straw work?"

Gabriel fed more pipe into the water. "Water magic comes from patterns. Signs, mandalas, even the letters of the alphabet, they all conduct power. Flow and current and eddies and whorls and hydrokinetic energy. Physics, engineering, and," he said, turning the valve, "sorcery."

He slowly brought his hands away from his sigil of copper knots and watched the contraption, ready to grab it should it begin to tip over. But it remained in place, as if planted in secure ground.

The quality of sound changed, less a roar of water now than the wet breath of a giant through a deep chasm. The copper tubes vibrated, and a profoundly deep bass note reverberated through the rock, through the water, through every cell of his body. His skin chilled.

The water blasted off to the sides of the tunnel like the Red Sea parted by Moses, leaving a walkable path in the middle.

"We can go in now."

He went down first, descending a chain-link ladder to the tunnel floor. Only a few inches of water remained on the tunnel floor, flowing over cobblestones that sloped downward toward distant turbines.

Gabriel wasn't surprised by his success. In his decade as water mage he'd spent many thousands of hours studying hydromantic texts, questioning the older water mages on his staff, experimenting with sigil shapes and mandalas. Of course, magic wasn't just pipes and valves. Magic demanded sacrifice.

And Gabriel had sacrificed himself. He lived alone. He had no children. He hadn't been on a date in more than ten years. He didn't take hikes on sunny days, his bike was rusting in his garage, and he hadn't read a book for pleasure or switched on his stereo in longer than he could remember. He didn't even have a cat.

But he could work water.

Max and Cassandra joined him down the ladder.

"You sure all this water's not going to come crashing down on us when we're halfway through the tunnel?" Cassandra said over the roar.

"Sure enough that I'm in here. If my magic fails, I'll be as drowned as the rest of you."

"Water mages can drown?"

"You'd be surprised. It usually starts with a squabble between rival mages, and before you know it, someone's facedown in a swimming pool."

Cassandra surprised him by allowing a little bit of humor in her eyes. "I love it when wizards die ironically. Please lead the way."

"I cheerfully obey," he said.

Laden with their heavy packs and trying not to twist ankles on the slippery cobblestones, they moved through the tunnel at the fastest pace the slowest of them could handle. That was Gabriel. He'd designed his water sigil to stand for five hours before its seals burst and it collapsed like a tower of straw, and then there'd be no spell to keep the water from falling away from the tunnel walls and drowning them. Gabriel checked his watch and began taking longer strides. He didn't want to die, and he didn't want to be the reason anyone else died.

Cassandra walked beside him. He expected her to snarl at him for slowing the group down, but instead, she struck up a conversation: "Daniel tells me you and he have some things in common."

Cassandra was a challenge. Her manner was grim, reserved, even cold, with flashes of anger and violence that made him think of land mines under thin, frosted earth. But Gabriel had been in her house. He'd seen her cheerful rooms, decorated with handcrafted chicken figurines and furniture piled with blankets and pillows that invited lingering over mugs of tea and naps. He'd seen her cat.

"Daniel and I do have some things in common," Gabriel answered. "His dad, my mom, both killed in the Third Correction. I was a few years older than Daniel when that happened, and I wasn't hunted, but I imagine Daniel and I could sit down over a few beers and trade war stories."

"I don't know about that. Your differences seem bigger than your commonalities."

"Daniel's afraid of power."

Cassandra laughed a little, obviously knowing that Gabriel had gotten it wrong. "He's not afraid of power. He just doesn't like the kind of people who seek it out."

"That's because he's never had to go looking for it. He was born with it in his bones."

"And you were the Hierarch's nephew."

"Grand-nephew, and the advantage of the family relation was questionable after he ate my mom. Listen, you want to know why I seized power? People either assume the answer's obvious, or else they're afraid to ask me."

"Shouldn't I be afraid?" Cassandra made a circular motion with her finger, pointing out the tube of open air Gabriel's magic had created.

Gabriel shrugged an acknowledgment. "When Daniel slew his monster, he created a power vacuum. He didn't step in to fill it, so other monsters did. Is the Southern realm better off now than it was eleven years ago? It is not."

"And when you killed the old water mage, you became the next monster," Cassandra said.

"But unlike him, I don't knock down dams and kill hundreds of people just to make a point. I may be a monster, but I'm a monster who's trying to make things a little better. That's why I'm in power. It's the only reason."

"Mm," was Cassandra's only answer.

"You're chattier than I expected," Gabriel said after a few minutes of sloshing. "What's this conversation really about?"

"There's a military aspect to this operation, but I'm not a soldier. If it ends up I have to risk my life to save yours, I'd like to think there's something likable about you."

"Max, tell Cassandra something likable about me. Lie if you have to. My life may depend on it."

Max stopped dead in his tracks. He held out his arms and turned a slow circle, sniffing. Cassandra started to say something, but Gabriel cut her off with a raised hand.

"Let him work."

Max stopped turning and peered into the dark. "We're not alone."

Cassandra unsnapped her holster. "What is it?"

"Osteomantic. Predatory. Not a hound, I don't think." He shook his head. His vision was good, his hearing, better, and his sense of smell, magical. He didn't like it when his tools failed him. "I'm not sure what it is. The magic is different here. I don't know all the smells."

"Can you tell how far off?"

"No. But it's ahead of us. Waiting for us, maybe."

Cassandra took only a few seconds to consider. She drew her gun. Taking the lead, she moved forward, deeper into the unknown.

ELEVEN

By their second day in the castle Moth had menaced the staff enough to know the lay of the land.

"Basically, they all hate you," he said, tearing into a roast chicken in Daniel's private dining room.

"What'd I do to them?" Daniel found himself feeling bad, even though it was Paul they hated, not him. How could they hate him? They didn't even know him. They didn't know what a swell guy he was.

"You've been gone for more than a year, doing your big, important osteomancer stuff. Meanwhile, they've been mowing your lawns and dusting your chandeliers and feeding your zebras."

"I have zebras? Why do I have zebras?"

"To keep the yaks and the ostriches company. And your staff has been taking care of your menagerie without pay."

"Why without pay?"

"Because you're a control freak and you're the only one authorized to unlock the vaults for payroll. But your staff can't leave for greener pastures because you made them sign lifetime employment contracts. It takes three years of nonpayment before it's considered dissolved."

Daniel stole a drumstick off Moth's plate. "Wow. I hate me, too."

"Then it's unanimous. But labor problems aren't your biggest worry. I learned some things about the Northern sorcerers' chain of command. It involves the spooky woman you saw in the entry when we arrived. The one with the hair. God, this chicken is magnificent. You ought to be ashamed of yourself, not paying a cook this good."

"I'm a bad man. Apparently. So, tell me."

"The top osteomancer in the realm is the Hierarch, of course. Beneath her is the High Grand Osteomancer, her second in matters of magic. That person was a woman named Gloria Bai."

"'Was'?"

"She died fourteen months ago of natural causes. I'm assuming 'natural' is loosely defined around here."

"Fourteen months. That's when Paul was on Catalina, constructing the Pacific firedrake."

"Exactly. Which complicated things. There were four candidates to succeed to her office." Moth produced four framed photographs and set them on the table.

"Where did you get those?"

"They were sitting on a shelf in the snooker room."

"And you just took them?"

"You don't have to say 'took' like that. I didn't steal them. I appropriated them in my capacity as your steward."

"What else have you appropriated?"

"Nothing," Moth said, wounded. "Nothing that they'll miss right away. Anyway, there's you." He set aside a photo of Paul. It was like looking in the mirror at a better-fed version of himself. "Then there's this guy, Nathaniel Cormorant." The photo was of an older man, high forehead, huge nose, sharp eyes hooded by a thick, white-fringed brow. He looked exactly like the kind of man who deserved a title like High Grand Os-teomancer. "You and him have some kind of teacher-student relationship. He's highly respected, even admired among the staff."

"So he might not hate me."

"Or he might hate you intensely. I wasn't able to find out. On the other hand, this next guy hates you so much you could wring him out and make a paste for loathing soup. Meet Baron Allaster Doring." The man in the photo was about Daniel's age—Paul's age—and was arrogantly handsome in a blond, blue-eyed Nazi sort of way. "He's head of the kingdom's shock troops, or some organization like that. Scary and much feared. But not as feared as her." Moth tapped the final photograph, the long-haired woman who smelled of a hundred kinds of magic.

"What do we know about her?"

"We know her name is Cynara Doring, and that she's Al-laster's older sister. Other than that, nothing. People clam up when you mention her, and I don't have enough charm or psycho-face to pry anything out of them."

"What's she doing here, in my house?"

"Again, don't know, but she's been here a couple of months now. She stays in one of your guest cottages. And, by the way, this guest cottage is like twenty-three hundred square feet with twenty-two-karat gold-leaf ceilings. Me, I'm staying in the Ce-lestial Suite, which is pretty plush, but it's also right under the bell towers. Morning wake-up is like getting sledgehammered from the inside out."

"Well, I'm not getting any sleep at all. Paul's bed is crazy." The bed was an ornately carved thing of lustrous black wal-nut, outfitted with gold-fringed blankets.

"That was Cardinal Richelieu's bed," Moth said. "You're too delicate for Cardinal Richelieu's bed?"

"I'm a musketeer and my spine requires a firm mattress. Stop judging me and brief me, please."

Moth fanned the photos out like playing cards. "So, these are your rivals. The Hierarch held the office open, pending Paul's hoped-for return."

"She didn't know Paul was dead?"

Daniel's plan was for Paul to make a comeback and demonstrate that reports of his death were somewhat exaggerated.

"I don't know what the Hierarch thought. But next week she was going to officially give up on you and pick a successor. Your coming home is not making many people happy."

"Maybe I should just preemptively turn down the office."

"Not a bad idea. Step aside from palace intrigue, let the other gunslingers shoot it out among themselves."

Moth put down his fork and took a last sip of Paul's excellent pinot noir. Sighing happily, he patted his lips with a linen napkin. "Anything else?"

"Just keep digging. I'm going to go back to exploring Paul's workshop. His gear is impressive, but I haven't found his notes yet, not to mention any bone from the dragon at the center of the world. Oh, how are you getting along with Gorov?"

"He's forgiven me now that he knows he still gets to boss the maids around. Giving him his back pay didn't hurt, either."

"I thought nobody was getting paid."

"Oh, yeah, forgot to tell you. I forged your signature and freed up payroll."

"So why does everyone still hate me?"

Moth dropped his napkin on the table and stood. "I'm honestly not sure. But I know this: A lot of people are loaded for bear and you smell like grizzly. There've been assassination attempts on Paul in the past. We thought the dangerous part of this would be the risk of you being exposed as Daniel. But being taken for Paul might not be all that safe, either."

It took clever magic to get into Paul's workshop, and under normal circumstances, Daniel would have been content with his progress. The room was at least fifty feet long. Thousands of books and scrolls lined the walls, more extensive than any osteomantic library Daniel had ever heard of. Copper tubes came down from the ceiling like the pipes of a crazy organ, delivering flame and a dazzling array of gas mixtures with the turn of a dial. In ceiling-to-floor cabinets of honey-toned wood, Paul kept a collection of osteomantic bone that rivaled the Southern Hierarch's Ossuary.

But Daniel suspected he hadn't gotten to the good stuff yet. A vault was set inside one of the walls, and so far he hadn't managed to pry it open.

He wished Cassandra were here. She was good at cracking boxes. And he didn't like having her on this job but away from him, with Gabriel Argent and his hound. He hadn't heard from her yet, not through the "water radio" Argent had configured, nor through the osteomantic method Daniel had cooked up because he didn't want to be dependent on Argent for communication.

He turned back to the lock. He'd tried swabbing it with more of Paul's condensed breath, and he'd employed the most sinuous sphinx riddle oils, and he'd lifted Paul's fingerprints from his furnishings and impressed them into shape-shifting bone keys, but all was still failure and sadness. The one thing left he hadn't tried was the only thing he thought had a good chance of working. It was also the one thing he least wanted to do.

Daniel couldn't just act like Paul. He had to *consume* him.

He settled himself in a leather wingback chair by the fireplace and unstoppered the vial of Paul's condensed breath. "Down the hatch, brother," he said, letting the drops fall on his tongue.

Pausing a moment to reconsider, he swallowed his brother's breath.

He fell through the soft leather chair and the thick Persian rug and the hardwood floor. Like a cannonball through feathers, he crashed through the lower floors and the basement and subbasements and the castle's stone foundations, through soil and sandstone and shale, through fossilized mammoth and whale and oceanic crust and mantle, to the molten core where the planet's first dragons formed. He was seeing things that Paul had seen, but he did not understand them the way Paul did.

Paul's memories flashed by, and Daniel tried to capture them, like plucking flying splinters in a tornado.

It was the first time Paul set eyes on Daniel. They were in the safe house, the place Daniel went after the Hierarch killed his father. Paul was frightened and confused by a face he'd only ever seen before in a mirror. He was still suffering from errors in his creation. He struggled with speech. He processed information slowly.

And then he was with Daniel's mother—his own mother—near the border of the Southern and Northern realms. They'd been running away but were caught, and now they were in trouble.

His mother was put in a car with border guards while he was left alone with others. An older guard said kind, soothing things to him while Paul knelt in a strawberry field with the man's gun to his head.

"You like baseball?" the man asked, and Paul nodded, even though he didn't know if he liked baseball and actually didn't know what baseball was, and the man told him to close his eyes and imagine a gorgeous blue sky and green field at Candlestick Park, and the smell of hot buttered popcorn, and the sound of the crowd, like the rush of a river, and he told Paul to think of that as he curled his finger around the trigger, and Paul had never experienced these things except for blue sky, so he looked at the sky now.

Lightning shattered the world. Blinding white daggers stabbed Paul's eyes, skewered his ears, and he pawed the tilled earth and sobbed for minutes until he could see again.

He was not burned.

The kind man with the gun lay several yards away, smoke rising from the top of his head. The other guards were dead, too. Lightning had entered through the eye of one of them and blown out the back of his head, splashing curly red chunks of brain over the brown soil. Another lay facedown, his nylon jacket smoldering and stinking of melting plastic. But the most pervasive smell was cold ocean mud and salt. It wasn't just in the air. It was coming off Paul. It was coming *out* of him. He somehow knew this was the scent of kraken magic, and that it resided in his own bones. He somehow knew this was the result of having been created from Daniel's essence.

His brother Daniel had saved him, and he loved him for it.

Other, later memories came, less distinct, because they were further removed from Paul's creation out of Daniel's substance. Paul walked alone down hundreds of miles of highway toward San Francisco, where he found a cage and more guards and osteomancers who drew blood and stuck needles so far into his body they scraped bone. His meals came through a slot in a steel door. He wept for his mother, and she didn't come, and he wept for Daniel, and he didn't come. He shivered and woke in darkness, until one day, the door to his cell opened and the dim light of the hallway outside blazed like a sun. His mother stood in the light like an eclipse surrounded by a corona.

After that, there were many homes, starting with a small house, and school dormitories, and makeshift cots in libraries and workshops when he couldn't be bothered to stop studying and go home, and houses of his own and mansions and finally, this place, his castle.

Daniel rose back up through the layers and returned to his own body. He was still in the chair by the fire. He sat there for a few minutes, dizzy and out of breath, weighted down by his own body, and yet feeling like stretched taffy, as if he were also thousands of miles away.

He stood, and when he was reasonably sure he could walk without keeling over, he went to the vault door. He breathed on it, and he was enough Paul that hidden mechanisms moved within the lock. Pushing on the door with a little pressure was enough to swing it open. He stepped into another room.

He'd expected it to be chilled like a mausoleum, a place untouched by human presence for more than a year. But it was warm with rich, osteomantic aromas.

His gaze landed on a tall, slim figure, silhouetted by sunlight filtered through a stained-glass window. The magic smells were dense from that part of the room, and as the figure stepped forward, the smells came along with it.

Coming away from the diffused light, the figure's features revealed themselves, the curve of her hips, the movement of her legs beneath a long, tight skirt.

She stopped and looked down at Daniel, mere inches away.

Her magic pushed into his nostrils, pounded his sinuses, and overwhelmed his taste buds. She was the strongest osteomancer he'd met since Paul, or maybe Sam, or maybe even the Southern Hierarch himself.

He felt himself swaying, and it took effort to steady himself.

"Cynara Doring," he said.

"Paul," she said. And then she leaned forward and kissed him.

Daniel drew in her scents and tasted her tongue. Her body blazed with essences of sabertooth cat and mastodon and river dolphin and species of griffin and other creatures different from the Southern Kingdom's varieties. She pressed against him, imparting the flavors of her magic.

Hardening, losing breath, skin tingling, Daniel forced himself to pull back.

"Uh," he said.

Her eyes narrowed in a frown, and the way the skin between her eyebrows wrinkled was perfectly ordinary and Daniel was utterly captivated by it. By sheer force of will, he recovered from the kiss and the flood of sensation from her magic and remembered that Cynara was Paul's rival, maybe his enemy, and that she'd been waiting for him in a room Daniel had entered only by drinking his dead brother's breath.

He looked at her more critically, trying to see her in that light.

"What's wrong with you?" she said.

There were so many ways to answer that question. He decided to go with his cover story, even though it might make him look like easy prey.

"I'm not quite myself yet. My injuries on Catalina were nontrivial. But," he added with a bit of warning, "I'm strong enough."

"Strong enough for what?"

Was that confusion in her tone, or challenge, or hurt feelings?

"For whatever comes next."

She stared at him a long time, and he began to think he was right about her hurt feelings.

"You've been gone for more than a year. I thought you were dead for more than a year. I've been on my own, fighting battles you started for more than a year. By all means, let's brush all that aside and talk about what's next."

Apologize? Beg forgiveness for whatever offense he'd committed? Play the amnesia card? Breathe fire and summon an earthquake and slink away while the castle collapsed around him?

"I am sorry," he said. "Things have been difficult. But maybe it would be best to discuss the future. The past is unchangeable."

She saddened. "Does that mean you want to change it?"

I don't know, do I? Daniel wanted to scream. Had Paul done some awful thing that he should wish to change if he could? Daniel wasn't good at these kind of fraught exchanges when he was being himself, let alone trying to pass himself off as someone's lover. And he found himself actually feeling bad for upsetting her. Maybe ingesting Paul's breath gave him more than memories and some magical essence. Maybe he was metabolizing Paul's emotions.

Cynara put her hand lightly on Daniel's shoulder. "I'm sorry, Paul. I'm being selfish. I'm pushing. It's just you stand here, smelling of new magic, looking as physically strong as ever." She glanced down at the pup tent in his crotch. "I mistook you for whole, but of course you're not."

"Thank you. I just need some time." Time to ransack Paul's library and workshop and find the *axis mundi* bone and then get far away from this castle, because it turned out Paul's domestic situation was more complicated than Daniel had anticipated.

Cynara slid her hand down to Daniel's hip and let it rest there, comfortable and intimate. "Time is not something you have in abundance, my love. My brother was so close to the prize, and you coming back just in time to snatch it away . . . You know what he's like."

Other than the fact that he looked like an Aryan fascist, Daniel really had no idea what Allaster Doring was like.

"What will his first move be?"

"He's already requested audience with the Hierarch. She'll see him tomorrow. He'll try to plant seeds of doubt in her mind. He'll tell her you're untrustworthy after your absence, an unknown quantity, and absolutely not suited to be High Grand Osteomancer."

"I'm not sure he's wrong."

That got a bit of a smile from her. It felt good to make her smile.

"The Hierarch knows Allaster's not my biggest fan," he said. No, that sounded too much like himself, not like Paul. He changed tack. "Let him have his audience. That gives us another day to prepare for him."

Cynara nodded, satisfied. At least for now. "As you say, more time." She kissed him again, softly, and Daniel felt a pang of loss when she pulled away and turned to the vault door. "Come by after eight," she said.

That sounded like the most wonderful and awful idea Daniel had ever heard.

"Cynara," he said, with true regret, "I have a lot of matters to catch up on. Perhaps tomorrow—"

"Tonight," she said, displaying steel that must be at least part of the reason she was reportedly feared throughout the realm. "You'll see Ethelinda. If this has been hard on you, imagine how hard it's been on her. She thought her father was dead."

Paul had a kid.

Oh, shit.

Paul had a *kid*.

"Yes," Daniel said numbly. "I'll come by tonight."

A form stepped out of the fog and blocked the narrow path from the castle to Cynara's guest house. He was tall and blond in a snug white dress shirt. His longish, tousled hair, and the way he wore his shirt open at the collar, and the way he kept his hands in his pockets, all contributed to an effortless insouciance that must have required practice. He made Daniel feel as he often did in the presence of beauty—grubby. Perhaps a bit snail-like. Even the buzz of kraken magic Daniel summoned to his hands brought him little comfort, because Allaster Doring smelled of even richer magic than his sister.

"Why are you hiding among my olive trees, Allaster?"

"I'm not hiding. I'm poaching. You grow fantastic olives." From his pocket, he produced a greenish, roundish thing that Daniel supposed was a rare and valuable olive.

"Don't let my steward catch you."

"Would that be your old steward, or the new one you brought from wherever the hell you've been?" Allaster sniffed the air. "And what's that magic you're summoning? I don't recognize the scent. Something you picked up on your travels?"

"I'd be happy to show it to you."

Allaster rolled the olive around with his his fingers, examining it with a keen eye. "Threats? That's not like you."

It wasn't? Threats were part of the way Daniel conducted business. They often saved him from having to burn people. Maybe Paul burned fewer people. Or maybe he just burned them without warning.

Daniel refrained from squeezing the bridge of his nose. He'd barely slept since leaving Los Angeles, and squeezing his nose was what he did whenever he had a stress headache, and maybe Paul never had stress headaches.

"Say what you came to say, Allaster."

Allaster maintained his tight, smug smile, but Daniel saw that, for just a brief moment, it took effort. "I came to see you, Paul. You've been gone. I thought you dead." Daniel said nothing to this, and Allaster's smile grew tighter and smugger and less convincing. "You look healthy enough. On the outside, anyway."

Now, was that a threat, the distinction between outside and inside? How many times had Daniel threatened to turn someone inside out, to soak up their magic with a sponge, to pick his teeth with their ribs?

"I feel fine. Thank you."

"I suppose you know I have an audience with our Hierarch tomorrow."

"I've heard you plan to impress upon her how unfit I am for the office of High Grand Osteomancer."

"That's the case I'm going to make. But first I wanted to make it to you."

"Generally, when I receive visitors, I don't do it in the dark of my gardens."

"I wanted to talk to you before you see my sister. Cynara can be . . . persuasive."

Through all this, Daniel's kraken magic sizzled and popped inside his finger bones.

"Make your case, Allaster. And make it brief."

"You're making my case for me, crackling with foreign magic, reappeared from the dead after a disastrous mission in enemy territory. And why there? Why did the great, mysterious weapon you supposedly crafted for our Hierarch have to be built in the waters of the Southern Kingdom?"

"I needed the resources there. They had the osteomantic materials I couldn't get anywhere else. And I needed to be free of obstructions. I didn't want anyone poaching my olives. So, your argument is that I'm using strange magic and it makes you nervous and you think I'm a traitor. Do you have anything else?"

Allaster dropped the smile entirely. He took two slow steps forward, eyes locked on Daniel's, and Daniel wondered if he'd realized Daniel wasn't Paul. Allaster smelled of molten rock, and chitinous armor, and the musk and manure of large cats.

Daniel readied himself.

"We used to be such good friends," Allaster said. He looked so sad. "What happened, Paul?"

Daniel had no idea what happened. He had no idea that Paul and Allaster were friends.

"Things change. People change."

Allaster nodded.

He dropped the olive in the dirt and turned down the path.

Daniel arrived at Cynara's guest house fifteen minutes early. Showing up before he was expected might lend him a little advantage of surprise, but the truer reason was that he was dreading this meeting and wanted to get it over with.

He kept his hands at his sides when Cynara answered the door, resisting the urge to touch her without invitation. But when she leaned forward and kissed him, he returned her kiss and brushed his fingers through her hair, cool silk in his hand.

She drew him into the house.

"Go see her," Cynara said. She picked up on Daniel's hesitation and uncertainty and added, "I put her to bed."

"The northwest bedroom?" Daniel had learned the floor plan from Moth so he could pretend a familiarity with the layout.

"You know she doesn't like the garden shadows in that room. She's in the eastern room."

"Right. I thought she might have grown out of it."

He found Ethelinda nearly buried under a white mountain of cotton blankets in bed. At its summit lay a fabric bunny with black button eyes.

Daniel remained rooted in the doorway, his heart cleaved in two. He knew her face so well. It was his mother's face, and his father's face, and his own face, blended together in a four-year-old child.

No, he reminded himself. She didn't look like him. She looked like Paul.

What nicknames did Paul have for her? What were their little jokes? What was her favorite book? Did he even read to her? What was the damn bunny's name?

Cynara nudged him into the room.

He came over and sat on her bed. Ethelinda looked at him suspiciously. He didn't know how Cynara was looking at him, because he flatly refused to turn his head in her direction. It would only make him more nervous.

"Hello."

"Hi, Daddy," she said in barely more than a whisper, sitting up. She was on the verge of tears.

Was she afraid of him? Did she know he was an impostor?

Or was she just overwhelmed by his return after his absence? After his death.

"I'm sorry I was gone for so long," he said. "I missed you. I would have come back sooner if I could."

Her lip trembled, her face crumpled, and she held in her sobs and turned her face as the tears started to fall.

Was she not allowed to cry? What kind of parents didn't let a four-year-old cry?

"I feel like crying, too. It's all a bit much, isn't it?"

More tears and quivers. She nodded.

"How about you just tell me what you did today?"

She cocked her head at him like a confused puppy.

"I just want to hear the whole story, from when you woke up till when you went to bed. Because I'm nosy."

He pulled out a tissue from her bed stand, ready to help her blow her nose, but she handled it herself.

"Boris told me about chrysalis spells," she began, sniffling.

Daniel had no idea who Boris was, nor what a chrysalis spell did, and he sat there with her, listening to her tell him about more unfamiliar names and places and books he'd never heard of and songs he didn't know, until she ran out of steam and sagged back in her bed.

He grew furious with Paul. Congratulations, brother, you made a Pacific firedrake and deprived your daughter of a dad.

No, that wasn't right. Paul hadn't deprived her of a father. Daniel had.

He took the wet tissue from her and tucked her blankets securely over her shoulders, but she pushed them off with sleepy irritation.

When he stood, Ethelinda reached out with her small brown fingers and put them in his calloused hand. Daniel gave them a gentle squeeze and touched them to his lips.

Cynara's face was unreadable as she turned out the light and led Daniel from Ethelinda's room. At the front door, she stood on one side of the threshold, in the warm, lit house, and Daniel stood outside in the damp night.

"She's what you almost gave up," Cynara said.

"I'm glad I didn't."

She nodded. "Tomorrow, we'll talk about putting me in power."

She shut the door with a soft click, followed by the heavier sounds of bolts and locks.

Daniel stood on a bluff overlooking the beach a few miles south of Paul's castle. The sun burned off the morning fog to reveal massive lumps of light brown flesh sprawled across the sand. They might have been easily mistaken for driftwood tree trunks until one of the bull elephant seals reared up, elevating its head eight feet from the ground, and let out a great, snuffling roar. Another bull rose up and roared a return.

"Are they going to fight?"

Daniel reached out with a restraining hand when Ethelinda moved closer to the cliff edge, her eyes full of solemn wonder.

"I hope not," he said.

The beasts weighed three tons or more, and their battles were brutal and ugly and deadly. A lot of their pups got crushed to death as collateral damage.

It had been Daniel's idea to take Ethelinda off the palace grounds. The household needed to see their lord doing more than hiding in the dark with books. And, more important, Cynara needed to believe he was Ethelinda's father. Also, he thought Ethelinda might enjoy it.

He found her gaze uncomfortably probing, so he looked away, out to the open sea.

"Mother said you were hurt," she said.

"I had an accident. It took a long time to get better. That's why I was away for so long."

"Were you burned? From the dragon?"

Daniel had killed Paul by vomiting poisonous magic in his face.

"Something like that."

"Did it hurt?"

He was sure it did. It must have been agonizing.

"A little bit."

They walked along the edge of the cliff. The waves crashed and the seals coughed and snuffled. A few lumbered into the water and became dark islands beyond the surf.

"I got hurt once," Ethelinda said. "There was a spider woman on my ceiling. When Mother killed her, she fell on me and her elbow hit me in the mouth."

Ethelinda skipped ahead to chase a foraging seagull, leaving Daniel behind, breathless.

He caught up to her. "What did your . . . what did Mother say about the spider?"

"That she was a maid at the house, but only so she could get close to me, and someone fed her spider magic to turn her into a spider. She tried to assa . . . assassa . . ."

She screwed her face into a frown, struggling with the word.

"Assassinate?"

"Assassinate me." She smiled with triumph, but only briefly, like a glint of sun on a black sea.

Daniel reached out for her hand and she took it.

"What did Mother do with the spider?"

"She cooked it and made magic for herself. When I'm old

enough, I get to have some. And she made all the maids go away."

Daniel didn't ask where they went. Out on the streets, or prison, or Cynara's cauldron. He didn't want to hear it in the girl's soft, serious voice.

"Did it hurt? When the spider hit you with her elbow?"

She tightened her grip on his fingers. "Yes. But I'm better now."

A t least half the books in Paul's library were locked with osteomantic devices, and each lock added minutes to the task of simply opening the cover. Many of the texts themselves were written in languages and scripts Daniel wasn't fluent in. Even the ones written in English employed nonstandardized spellings and unnecessarily baroque typefaces.

Moth came in, smelling of virgin honey soap. Daniel looked up from the book he'd been studying, winced from his stiff neck, and rubbed his eyes.

"Don't like your breakfast?" Moth asked, noticing the plate of morels and quail eggs with pickled ramp sauce and gorgeous, rare lamb medallions, untouched at his elbow. Daniel's wineglass contained a Sonoma coast pinot noir, jewel red when held to the morning light streaming through the windows. Daniel had not even sipped it.

"That was my dinner."

"Not hungry?"

"Not for poison," Daniel said, stretching his back and hearing an alarming pop.

Moth barked an incredulous laugh. "They tried to poison an osteomancer? One with your finicky nose? Do you want me to round up and club the usual suspects? Or club someone who can tell me who the usual suspects are?"

"No. We don't have time for that."

"When you've got bigger fish to fry than your own staff try-ing to kill you, you've been fishing in some shitty oceans. How about I send up a bagel and coffee and demote your head cook to food taster?"

"Bagel. Coffee. Please. Thank you." And then something oc-curred to him. "Who cooks for Cynara and Ethelinda?"

"Cynara has her own staff, including a cook. The ingredi-ents are brought in separately, just for her, and they're prepared in the cottage. Cynara's cook wouldn't have any contact with your food."

"No, that's not why I'm asking. Find out about this cook, will you? And everyone else who has contact with Ethelinda."

Moth frowned. "What's this about?"

Daniel told him of the attempt on Ethelinda's life. Moth was interested but didn't seem concerned. Ethelinda's welfare wasn't part of the job.

Daniel opened another book and began turning pages. It was a catalog of some kind, with ink and watercolor drawings of rings and pendants and bracelets. The notations were in a Lat-inate cypher, a script often used by seventeenth-century osteo-mancers that Daniel struggled to remember from his father's tutelage. He'd pulled sixteen other books just like this one down from the shelves, and the shelves still contained at least another sixty.

"You're going to ruin your eyes, you keep reading in this dim light." Moth said. "I can have your electricians install something brighter. I've got them working in the wine cellars, but I can pull them off that. You should see that place, by the way. Total fire hazard. Really, the whole house needs rewiring. And we've got termite damage under the rugs in the formal dining room. Talk about headaches."

"You are doing a very good job running the house, Moth. The toilets even flush on time. You do realize we're not going to spend one damn second here longer than necessary? As soon as I find the *axis mundi* bone, we're gone." That came out with more heat than Daniel had intended.

Moth didn't move, but he seemed to grow, his muscled body looming and building in menace. Daniel figured he managed it by flexing some muscle Daniel didn't even possess.

"Are you pissed at me?" Moth's voice was mild and frightening.

"No. No, I'm not," Daniel said with a sigh. "Sorry. I'm pissed at Paul. I'm pissed at him for being the kind of guy who gets himself entwined in byzantine power plays. I'm pissed that I can't tell the difference between his friends and lovers and enemies. I'm pissed he built a dragon that took Sam from me. I'm pissed he abandoned his four-year-old daughter."

"So, basically, you're really pissed at yourself."

"Yeah."

Moth relaxed, a storm cloud passing.

"Look, you didn't do to Ethelinda what the Hierarch did to you. It's not the same thing at all. Paul tried to kill you first. It was either you or him. You chose you. I'm glad you did. Stop blaming yourself."

"Even if the Hierarch had killed my dad in self-defense, I don't think I'd be shrugging and going, 'Oh, well, can't fault the guy for that, you do what you gotta do.' I think I'd still hate him enough to pull his heart out of his chest and eat it."

"Sorry, buddy. Killing sucks. Dying sucks. I know. I've died several times myself."

"The difference is, you always come back. I can't bring Paul back."

"We're not here for Paul. Or Ethelinda. We're here to bring Sam back. We can still do that."

Daniel turned more pages, looking at more jewelry and more crabby little script. Maybe he should send Moth to the kitchen for a plate of cookies. One cookie per page might be enough motivation to keep him going through the day.

He turned the page to an ink and watercolor drawing of a scepter consisting of a rod topped by a blue orb, banded in jewel-encrusted gold, and above that, a silver dagger. At the base of the silver dagger, in a bezeled setting, was a small, irregularly shaped black stone.

Daniel squinted at the script, concentrating so much to translate it that he didn't notice at first that the hand it was written in was as familiar as his own.

"This is Paul's writing," he said.

Moth came over to look. "The ink looks pretty fresh. Scribbling in old books, very naughty."

Daniel hadn't found Paul's writing in any of the other volumes. Something about this particular page of this particular book must have been important to him.

"Scepter of Bein," he read aloud. "Crafted by Rurik of St. Petersburg. Gold and platinum, hatted by . . . no, wait, not hatted . . . *crowned* by a sapphire orb . . . set with rubies and diamonds, and a lifted stick . . . no, that's wrong . . . a raised blade from the armory of Chagha'an the Cleaver . . ." Daniel smiled, reading the rest of the description. "And inset with a piece of the *axis mundi*."

"That's it, right?" Moth said. "That's the bone."

"It's got to be," Daniel agreed.

"Aces. So it's here somewhere. We just gotta start ripping

walls out." Moth rubbed his hands together, anxious for some simple, physical labor.

"Oh. Ugh," Daniel said.

"No, no 'ugh.' I don't like 'ugh.' Why 'ugh?' "

"I don't think it's in the house, Moth. Our intel must be a little off."

He showed Moth the book's title: *Crown Jewels of the Hierarch*.

"Maybe she gave him the bone as a gift?"

"A basket of muffins is a gift. An engraved watch. Okay, maybe even a piece of jewelry. But you don't give away crown jewels."

"Ugh," Moth said.

A knock at the door, and Daniel snapped the book shut.

Moth opened it to find Gorov, wringing his hands. The deposed steward tried to peer around Moth to see into the room, but Moth leaned to block his view.

"His lordship has a visitor," Gorov announced, with high, querulous pomp. He must be feeling a little important with a message for his boss's boss.

"His lordship is busy and doesn't feel well."

"Oh, dear, I'm distressed to hear that. Perhaps his lordship might like a cup of tea?" Gorov managed to sneak a look under Moth's arm and made brief eye contact with Daniel.

"Are you trying to poison him?"

"Why would I . . . no, of course not," Gorov said.

"Because someone is, and the only reason I'm not using the rotisserie to question the kitchen staff is because his lordship is kind and merciful."

"You *should* use the rotisserie," Gorov said, taking umbrage. "This sort of thing never happened when I was in charge."

"Are you questioning my leadership?"

"Yes," Gorov snapped. "Yes, that is absolutely what I am doing. Prior to taking care of his lordship, I ran this household for Lady Freedmont, and, before her, Baron Hearst. I have served at San Simeon for half a century, and in that time, no one—not head of household, nor family, nor a guest—has ever tasted so much as an undercooked piece of meat. The kitchens of San Simeon are the pride of the realm. Poison! This shame undoes decades of reputation—"

"Who's the visitor?" Daniel called from the table.

"His lord Professor Nathaniel Cormorant," said Gorov with stiff dignity.

Another rival for the office of High Grand Osteomancer.

Daniel wasn't up to facing such an encounter on an empty stomach.

"Put out a breakfast spread," he instructed. "I trust you'll see it meets San Simeon's customary standards."

Gorov dared a "hmmph" before retreating to do as his master commanded.

Y ou smell odd, boy."

Cormorant buried his nose, roughly the size of an eggplant, in Daniel's hair and held him in a captive embrace.

"I've been some odd places recently," Daniel said, his voice muffled in Cormorant's chest.

Cormorant exploded with guffawing laughter, which distracted him long enough for Daniel to push off and away and taste the sweet air of freedom.

A man of Falstaffian proportions, with ruddy cheeks and a white skunk stripe running down the center of a wilderness of brown hair, Cormorant wore a monk's robe of luxuriant purple wool.

He cocked his head to one side and fixed Daniel with an analytical frown. "You look wan, my lad. Have your cooks not supplied you with my revivifying soup? You, man!" he thundered at a startled Gorov. "Look at the state your lord is in. He's the color of a mushroom. Well, I can take care of that. All I need is seven pots and a stove." He began rolling up his sleeves and was ready to march off to the kitchen.

"No, no, that's not necessary my . . . I'm fine, I'm fine. Please, join me in breakfast." Daniel wasn't sure if Paul addressed Cormorant as "Lord" or "Professor" or "Lord Professor" or Nathaniel or Nate or Old Bean. "Oh, I should warn you, my dinner and wine were poisoned last night."

Gorov squirmed, and Cormorant launched a cannon salvo of laughter. "You've always had such a way with people."

He landed on a chair and took to sniffing the spread of scones and clotted cream and jams and juice and coffee, sucking in so much air through cavernous nostrils that Daniel was shocked his ears didn't pop.

Apparently, Cormorant considered the food safe. First one scone went into his mouth, and then another, washed down with a whole glass of orange juice. "Delicious," he declared, struggling to get all the syllables out while simultaneously destroying a third scone.

Daniel assembled a plate of pastry and fruit and, with less flamboyance than Cormorant, submitted his breakfast to his own olfactory inspection before tucking in.

After a few minutes of tasty chewing and sipping, Cormorant asked if they could speak in private. Moth glowered at the request.

"I like your new man," Cormorant said. "He's delightfully large. You can trust me, large, new man. I would never harm a hair on my favorite student's head. What a waste of my tutelage that would be, eh?"

Moth did not trust Cormorant. Nor did Daniel. But the more relevant question was if Paul did.

Daniel ordered Gorov and Moth and the serving footmen to clear the room.

Alone with Cormorant, he again found himself having to explain his year's absence, his injuries, and his long seclusion and recovery. Cormorant took it in as if Daniel were spinning a riveting adventure, responding with worried flinches and gasps and culminating in applause when Daniel got to his return to the shores of San Simeon.

"Splendid, my boy, just splendid. That was a proper odyssey you had. A rite of passage. An ordeal. When I was coming up, you weren't a true osteomancer without an ordeal. I wasn't even half your age when they sent me up Mount Rainier after the mountain dragon's tooth. But I've bored you with that story enough times."

"No, no, I can't hear it enough."

Cormorant gave Daniel a rueful smile, but Daniel meant it sincerely. The more he knew about Cormorant and how osteomancy was practiced in the North, the better his chances of pulling off a successful scam.

But Cormorant waved him off. "I didn't come here to regale you with tales of glories long past. You're back. And I am relieved and delighted. But it does raise issues."

"Yes, there's the matter of who's going to be the realm's next High Grand Osteomancer."

Cormorant smeared a great blob of jam on another scone.

"Our Hierarch hates an empty office. She's been eyeing me for it."

Would Paul be happy about this? Threatened? Angry? Daniel decided to test the waters. "You should consider it. You'd make a fine High Grand Osteomancer."

Cormorant reacted as if he'd smelled something foul. "What offense have I ever given you that you would wish such a drab future for me? I'm a scholar."

"But you think I'd be happy in the seat?"

"Happy? No, you'll be miserable. But when have I ever successfully talked you out of misery? What I know is the realm would be a kinder place with you in that office rather than Cynara or Allaster Doring. I'm a man of libraries and museums. With one of the siblings in office, he or she will likely take away my access to them, just to spite me. You, my lad, will be quite content to let an old man read into the night. But you must tell me now, with no prevarication: Are you strong enough?"

"My body is strong. My osteomancy is strong. I have some memory lapses, but being at home among my things is helping with that."

"That's welcome news. But that's not the kind of strength I'm talking about. You need strength of desire. And strength of stomach. Have you thought what to do about the Dorings?"

"I've had conversations with both of them," Daniel said, trying not to commit to anything.

Cormorant harrumphed. "No doubt Allaster tried to appeal to your old friendship."

Daniel allowed that he did.

"I hope you weren't fooled. He sincerely loves you, and he sincerely would love to return to the old days. Who wouldn't? Two young princes, shoulder to shoulder, trying to outmatch each other with fire? Those jousts were the highlight of many a great gathering. Those were fine, blazing days. But the one thing greater than his love for you is his hate for you. He still fights that battle in his heart, but the war was lost a long time ago."

Daniel decided to take a risk. "Is there anything I can do to change the outcome?"

"Can you bring back his father?"

Oh, god, thought Daniel. What had Paul done to the Dorings' father? What kind of man had Paul been?

"No, I can't," Daniel said, because he assumed that was the truth.

"Then don't stir those coals. You were exonerated by the Hierarch. Nothing else matters. Except that Allaster is your enemy, and he won't settle for being a mere spectator to your elevation."

Daniel rubbed his temples, betraying a sign of stress. But if Paul wouldn't be stressed about facing major opposition just after returning home from an ordeal, then he was even stranger than Daniel thought.

"And what about Cynara?"

Cormorant tsked. "You've created your own problem there, my boy. Toying with her, promising to support her for an office you crave . . . bad idea. She forgave you for her father, but she'll be the death of you if . . . when . . . you betray her. And giving her a daughter was a gamble you lost. I warned you it wouldn't make her beholden to you, but rather the other way around."

So that's what Ethelinda was to Paul? A tactic. A game chip. An emotional bribe. In the South, osteomancers ate children. Things weren't so different in the North. Just more subtle.

Daniel refilled Cormorant's empty coffee cup. "You know how much I value your counsel. How should I proceed?"

"Just as we agreed before your departure. My blades are still ready. They only await my word." Cormorant added sugar and cream and stirred with concentration, as if he were mixing an osteomantic formula.

Daniel found himself hating Paul more with every new thing he learned about him. Paul would have made a fine successor to the Hierarch.

But maybe Daniel's hate was misplaced.

What the Hierarch was to Daniel, Daniel had become to Ethelinda: a killer of fathers.

"Paul? My blades. Shall I employ them?"

"Hold off. Just a few more days. There will be repercussions, and I must prepare myself. Until then, I'll keep the Dorings at arm's length."

"That will be impossible, assuming you keep them alive. Oh, I volunteered to deliver something to you." Cormorant reached into the folds of his robes and produced an envelope. He placed it on the table as if it weighed tons and slid it toward Daniel. It was sealed in wax, and the stamp was of a human skull with a dragon's frill. This was the seal of the Northern Hierarch. The letter came from the palace.

Opening it, Daniel felt as though he were unsealing his own death sentence.

He read it.

The Lord Chamberlain is commanded by the Hierarch to invite Baron Osteomancer Paul Sigilo to court reception, dinner, royal audience, and investiture, commencing Monday, 21st April, 6:00 P.M., and to conclude Friday, 25th April, noon.

Oh, god. Not a death sentence. Even worse. A party invitation.

"A whole week of formal rum-mummery," Cormorant said, wiping his lips with a napkin and throwing it down, his breakfast good and well conquered. "By Friday, either you or one of the Dorings will be High Grand Osteomancer. And I do like my library privileges, Paul, so try to curb your resolute disregard for etiquette. Don't pull a book out of your pocket and read at the Hierarch's supper table."

"Disregard for etiquette. Yes."

Cormorant let out a long breath of existential weariness. "Well, at least try not to be murdered before your investiture. Can you do that, at least?"

Daniel promised he would try.

With dread and solemnity, he took a silent oath, to which he was the only witness.

He wouldn't just save Sam.

He'd save Ethelinda, too.

THIRTEEN

Sam could see nothing out the dragon's eyes. No stars, no moon, no furtive movement of prey below. Nor could he hear anything outside the cockpit. And most disconcerting of all, no smells reached him. He could only assume the dragon was still dangling from the airships and being hauled away to some unknown destination.

"We're blind," he said, trying to tamp down a burgeoning panic. "What's capable of blinding a Pacific firedrake?"

Annabel lay on her back with her legs sticking out from beneath the control panel, like a mechanic under a car. "No osteomancy that I know of."

Sam fiddled with the steering yoke, just to see if by some near-miracle the controls worked now. They didn't.

"So, let's proceed from there," she said, crawling out from under the panel. "Who's got enough big magic in quantity to do something like this, and access to airships? Sounds like the North to me."

Sam got up from his chair. "Well, we can't have that. If they can neutralize—or tranquilize, or paralyze, or whatever-ize—us then they probably have the know-how to gain control of the dragon. Which means they'll have their weapon. Trying to stop that from happening is how I ended up in here in the first place. So we keep trying to pilot this machine." Sam gestured at his worthless control panel. "Any ideas?"

Annabel's smile made Sam nervous. "Have you ever been to the brain?"

And so, Sam and Annabel set out to find the firedrake's brain.

It turned out Annabel did not actually know the way to the brain.

The obvious direction was up and back, deep into the skull. But the meaty passageway from the cockpit didn't lead that way.

As they moved along, Annabel tapped a bone against the wet walls and put her ear close to listen.

"Looking for hollow spaces," she explained. "Rooms, chambers, some place big enough to house a brain."

That sounded reasonable to Sam. "And if we find it?"

She waggled the piece of bone in her hand. "We don't have a manual, so if we do get to the brain, we'll just have to monkey with it."

"Monkey with a dragon's brain. What could possibly go wrong?"

They kept on, Annabel tapping away, and Sam searching the air in vain for a telling odor. There were still no obvious noises from outside the dragon, but inside, a low bass hum and subterranean rumbles persisted.

Annabel tapped another tunnel wall, pressed her ear against it, and came away disappointed. They'd been at it for hours. Sam's hamstrings burned from steep climbs.

"So, what's your life like?" Annabel asked him. "Or what was it like?"

"Why? You think there might be some clue in my past that'll help us figure out the dragon's layout?"

"No, but you're the only human contact I've had in a long time. Make conversation with me, please?"

"Talking. Oh. Okay." Talking was not something Sam ever did much on the outside, much less talking with girls near his age. Practically every time he did, he fell in love with them. If he was asked the time of day, or road directions, or asked if he could stop blocking the soda fountain at a gas station, he would often find himself smitten for days.

Sam discovered he wanted to tell Annabel everything.

But Daniel's voice in his head told him not to tell her anything.

"My uncle raised me," he began. "We moved around a lot. He was sort of a . . . what would you call it . . . a thief. So we were always on the run, trying to stay ahead of the law. I didn't go to regular schools or anything like that."

There. That was largely true. Just a lot of omission.

"So, your uncle. He was a great osteomancer." She said it as though it were incontrovertible fact.

"What makes you say that?"

"Because you're a powerful osteomancer yourself, with no formal schooling. Powerful enough to dive into a Pacific fire-drake's osteomantic essence and not lose your own magical co-herence. So your uncle must have taught you. And it takes a powerful osteomancer to train another one. Was he the guy who shot us down on Mount Whitney?"

"Yeah. But he was trying to help. Daniel wouldn't do anything to hurt me."

"Hm" was her only response. They continued down a nar-rowing passageway. "What about the other two on the moun-taintop? The big guy and the girl?"

Moth and Em.

He'd fallen hard for Em. They'd spent more than just a few

moments together. They'd spent days, and they'd shared danger and pain. Also, she was so . . . so *Em*.

"Friends," Sam said.

Maybe Daniel was right and Sam should have kept his mouth shut. He didn't want to go into Moth's and Em's biographies, much less Daniel's.

Annabel saved him with another question. "Okay, what's your earliest memory?"

"Earliest. Let me think."

He didn't have to think hard. His earliest memory was also one of his clearest. He remembered waking up fully submersed in a tank of fluid. Later, he would learn the fluid was osteomantic medium, a soup of magical essences designed to accelerate cellular growth and turn him from a scrap of flesh into a fully formed body. And what he remembered most was how delicious it was, a chimerical blend of creatures. He remembered opening his eyes and looking out on a kaleidoscopic world as the medium boiled around him. After a while, he became aware of a fleshy umbilical cord winding around his belly and chest and entering his body through the back of his head. And there was a small square of glass in the tank. A window. And through the window, the face of the Hierarch looked in on him.

He wanted to tell her what he was. How long was it okay to keep secrets from the only other person in the world?

"I remember a birthday," Sam said to Annabel. "My first."

"That sounds nice. Presents? Cake? Ice cream?"

"Nothing like that. I was born in a tank. I'm a golem. I'm a magically grown duplicate of the Hierarch. The guy who ate you. So, whatever magical essence the Hierarch absorbed by consuming you is also in me. Which is probably why you're here now, in the dragon. The Hierarch ate you, I'm grown from the Hierarch's substance. The firedrake consumed me, and so here we are, together."

There. It was out, all in a gush of honesty, and he wished he could scoop it back up with his hands and shovel it in his mouth and make it disappear.

She looked at him, stunned. Horrified. Maybe repulsed. She walked a few steps away from him, then turned.

"How was I?"

"What do you mean?"

"As a meal. How was I? Tasty? Nutritious?"

"That wasn't me. That was the Hierarch."

She tilted her head, like someone trying to understand a painting with no obvious appeal. "You *are* the Hierarch. I don't know how I missed it before. But it's right there in front of me. Your nose, your chin . . . He was a lot older than you when he ate me, but it's so clear now."

She resumed walking, now at a fast pace. Sam struggled to keep up, hunching beneath the low, fleshy, wet ceiling.

"So, is he still in charge of things?" Annabel said without turning her head.

Sam dreaded having to give her the next bit of bad news. "No. A lot of time's passed since he consumed you."

"I figured. You have a weird haircut. And you're dressed like Buck Rogers."

Sam was still in the black fatigues and tactical boots he'd worn for the Catalina mission.

"So what's it been, Sam? Ten years or a hundred?"

He didn't say anything right away. She stopped and turned.

"More than a hundred?"

"About seventy," Sam said. Enough for everyone she'd known and loved to have died, for the places she found familiar to have been razed and rebuilt upon a dozen times over. History and architecture weren't sacred in Los Angeles. Not much was.

Annabel continued down the passage. Sam didn't know if he should follow or let her be alone, until she spoke again.

"Seventy years wouldn't be much to the Hierarch. Did another osteomancer finally gather the bones to do him in?"

"My uncle, Daniel. He's not really my uncle—"

"So, you lied about that."

"Er. Yeah? I guess. Anyway. The Hierarch was going to put his consciousness in my body—"

"Just like you put your consciousness in the firedrake's body. Oh, but you're nothing like the Hierarch, are you?"

"Look, do you want to know how the Hierarch died or not?" Sam had a hard time accepting guilt just for having been born from the Hierarch's essence. Yet his power came from everything the Hierarch ate, and one of those things—those people—was Annabel. Could he deserve her anger even without having done anything wrong?

Annabel walked faster.

"Daniel killed the Hierarch," he said to Annabel's back. "He reached into his chest and pried his heart out. And then, like I said, I grew up on the run. Daniel kept me away from all the shitty people who would've eaten me."

"I wish I'd had a Daniel on my last day of work."

Ducking her head, she stepped through a gap in a pink wall, like a bulkhead partition.

"So do I," Sam said, following.

He knew he should let her be, at least for a while. If he'd found himself in an afterlife where the only other person was the closest thing remaining of the sorcerer who'd eaten him,

Sam wouldn't want to spend another second with that person. But what if he left her alone and never found her again?

He needed an ally.

He needed someone. Anyone.

And maybe he owed Annabel.

He opened his mouth to say something, not knowing what he was going to say, but remained silent when he took in their surroundings.

The space was a jungle of white trunks and branches and tendrils. Pulses of light traveled along them, a great, crackling forest. Sam's skin prickled. The hair on his arms stood erect.

"I think we've found the brain," Annabel said. Loose strands of her hair floated in a halo. "I'm going to go deeper in."

Sam restrained himself from reaching out for her hand. "Do you want me to leave you alone?"

"Hell, no," she said. "You got me into this mess. If I'm getting deeper in it, you're coming with me."

Not letting her see him smile, Sam followed Annabel into the firedrake's brain.

FOURTEEN

Things were going decently well until Max got shot.
Gabriel's sigils had gotten him and Cassandra and Max through black tunnels and cold shafts, down de-commissioned aqueducts and raging subterranean rivers. They had just inched past hydroelectric turbine blades whose barest touch would have removed a limb or a head or a bellyful of guts when Cassandra started getting uncomfortably inquisitive about his magic.

"That's quite a bag of tricks you've got there," she said chirpily.

"They're not tricks. They're tools."

"So, you packed the bomb nice and safe, right? You're not going to jiggle it and kill us all?" She remained chirpy. Maybe that was bothering Gabriel more than her nosiness.

"It's inert unless activated, and I activate it with a tuning fork. And, before you ask, the tuning fork is packed in a nice, padded case, if by chance I fall down again."

"That sounds real good," she said, and Gabriel hoped they were done.

Cassandra wasn't done.

"It's really a powerful bomb, right?"

"Very powerful. But safe. You're safe. We're all safe."

They trudged on in blissful silence. The bliss was brief.

"Is it powerful enough to destroy a Pacific firedrake? Because it'd have to be a really powerful bomb."

She was still being chirpy. Max walked faster and moved ahead. He didn't like chirpy any more than Gabriel did.

"It's a really, really powerful bomb, Cassandra. Look, see?"

He unzipped his backpack and got out a foam-padded case. He opened it, showing her the little globe of silvery water.

"Huh. It doesn't look like much."

"Do you want me to strike the tuning fork now and show you?"

She actually seemed to consider it.

"No, that's okay. You can put it back."

Gabriel did so.

"Are you prepared to use it?" Now, she was not chirpy. Now, her look was as hard as hammers.

"Yes. But that's not the plan, is it? The plan is we find the firedrake, and it's up to Daniel to extract Sam."

"That's Daniel's plan," Cassandra agreed.

The distinction was not lost on Gabriel. "But . . . that's not your plan? The bomb is only supposed to be a last resort."

"My plan is to do whatever's necessary," Cassandra said. "I hope that means no more than telling Daniel where the dragon is."

She quickened her pace, leaving Gabriel behind.

Gabriel truly did intend the bomb to be the last resort. But saving Sam was never part of his plan.

And, if he wasn't mistaken, Cassandra had just told him she was okay with however he used his bomb.

He imagined she'd be less okay if she knew what he was planning to do with the memory water in his flask. The dragon was too dangerous to be left to its own devices. They could agree on that. But the memory water wasn't for destroying the dragon. The memory water was for bending the dragon to Gabriel's will.

Max held his hand up and signaled the team to stop.

Gabriel peered into the darkness ahead. "What is it? You smell something?"

"No, but I heard something," Max said. "There it is again."

"Echo of our own footsteps," Gabriel suggested hopefully.

Cassandra unholstered her gun. "But we're not moving."

The last access hatch they'd passed was over a mile behind them. The next one was two miles ahead. That left them trapped inside a tube without a handy escape.

"How far away was that noise?" Gabriel asked.

"Close enough that I could hear it, far enough that you couldn't," Max replied.

"But you still don't smell it?" Cassandra was a little incredulous.

"My nose is keener than yours, but it's trained to detect magic. This could be a repair crew, or maybe a hobo camp."

"Well, we've got a distant early warning," Gabriel said. "What do we do with it?"

Cassandra moved forward, the barrel of her gun leading the way. "We keep moving."

"Wait," Gabriel said.

Max and Cassandra turned to look at him.

There was no need to risk walking into an ambush or getting attacked from behind. Gabriel could erect a sigil and flush out anyone waiting to do them harm. Whoever got in the way of tons of water thundering down the tunnel like a freight train would be crushed. He'd probably never even have to see the bloated corpses.

But he would always know what he'd done, without ever knowing whom he'd done it to: monsters, mercenaries, or Northern water department workers just trying to fix a leak.

The other option was to continue down the tunnel. He and his team might be killed, and then there'd be nobody to destroy the firedrake, and the dragon might rage free, or the Northern Hierarch might discover how to wield it, and in either case, thousands upon thousands of people would die.

Kill a few by water, or risk many dying by flame. It was at moments like this that Gabriel could let himself hate Daniel Blackland. Gabriel had to look after millions of people who considered him yet another tyrant, while all Daniel ever had to care about were his friends.

"Cassandra," he said. "I can take care of the threat."

She flicked a glance at him before returning her attention to the path ahead. "I know you can. I don't want you to."

"Because . . . ?"

"We don't know if they mean us harm."

"But what if they do?"

She stopped to face him. "When we signed on for this, we accepted risk. Anyone who tries to kill us accepts risk. Maybe they're guys with guns. But maybe they're guys with wrenches. I don't want to guess wrong and make someone pay for my mistake. You'd think someone with power over a whole kingdom would've worked out some of these ethical equations."

"I have a feeling, Cassandra, that you and I aren't plugging in the same figures. By the way. How's Otis Roth?"

Max drew his pistol. "Closer now."

They hugged the sides of the tunnel. Max and Cassandra took up firing positions; Gabriel hadn't even brought a gun. He barely knew how to use one and figured he was more likely to shoot himself in the crotch than hit an intended target. Instead, he reached into his pack to retrieve the components of a flash-flood-generating sigil.

Out from the flickering light emerged three women, all with black guns outfitted with lots of textured grips and add-ons and built-in flashlights and things that emitted red beams. Gabriel noticed red dots on Cassandra's and Max's chest. He looked down to see one on his own.

The women ranged in age from late-thirties to late teens. They resembled one another, their faces hauntingly familiar.

The oldest of them stepped forward. She was the one whose gun was trained on Gabriel. "Have we caught you in a bad moment?"

"Everyone holster," Cassandra said, pointing her gun at the ceiling. "You're Emmas."

Now Gabriel knew why they seemed familiar. They were golems of Emmaline Walker, the osteomancer who developed the technique of growing duplicates of living humans. Walker had worked for the Hierarch, and her progeny were scattered across the Southern realm. Daniel had left one of them—Em—guarding Sam's gestating golem body.

The Emmas redirected the muzzles of their rifles to less-threatening trajectories.

"Who's the one with the pipes?" the older Emma asked.

"He's a plumber," Cassandra said. "How are you getting through the system without one?"

The Emma didn't answer, only smiled, and Cassandra smiled back. They trusted each other enough to stop waving their guns around, but not to share operational information. Gabriel was just happy the gun-pointing situation had improved.

He let Cassandra handle the conversation, and she got from the Emmas that they were in the aqueducts to "do some recon."

Cassandra told them that she and Gabriel and Max were here "on business."

"Break bread?" Cassandra suggested. She passed around her ration of chocolate bars, and in exchange, the Emmas shared foil-wrapped lumpia.

Max sniffed his lumpia thoroughly before taking a bite, and only then did Gabriel dig in. The lumpia was hot, even though it was cold here in the tunnels. The Emmas' base must be close.

"So how do you know us?" asked another of the Emmas. Her face was pink except for a mask of lighter flesh around her eyes, giving her the look of a reverse raccoon.

"I know some of your sisters," Cassandra said.

The third of the Emmas, the youngest, had a pale, thin face and long, delicate fingers that made Gabriel think of harp strings, not guns. She spent most of the time looking down at her shoes and her food, taking only furtive glances at Gabriel and his companions.

Cassandra asked what they could expect farther down the tunnel.

"Way's clear all the way to San Francisco," the oldest Emma said. "Not counting running water and turbines and various other bits of engineering. But no human obstacles. Or anything odd. How about in the direction you came from?"

"Clear sailing all the way to Hetch Hetchy."

The oldest Emma stood and offered Cassandra her hand. "Well, we should be off. Wherever you're headed, good luck."

She and Cassandra shook. "Same to you."

Gabriel accepted an offered handshake with Reverse-Raccoon Emma. And the youngest Emma, the meek, reedy one, took out her gun and shot Max in the leg.

The muzzle flash and thunder stunned Gabriel. But he heard

Max cry out, and maybe he heard the tree-branch snap of his
femur breaking, and he heard himself scream out Max's name.

Or maybe he inferred all these sounds. He felt as if he'd been
clubbed in the ears by the gunfire, and everything was dim and
far away.

The only thing he knew for sure was that Max was writhing
on the ground, his face and neck coated with sweat, with blood
pouring out of him.

Gabriel begged the Emmas to save Max's life. Their answer was no.

The rain had finally stopped, but water still dripped and
streamed from the silhouetted pine boughs, and the way was
sloppy with mud. Moonlight came down between patchy clouds.
Gabriel struggled along, carrying Max by his armpits while
Cassandra carried his legs like the handles of a wheelbarrow.
The Emmas made them haul their backpacks, as well, after determining that the weapons, gear, and provisions they contained
were too valuable to leave behind. With their guns pointed at
him, Gabriel couldn't go into his pack to assemble a sigil. He
couldn't reach bottles of water, nor his tuning forks.

"He's going to bleed out," Gabriel said, breathing hard. "He
needs hydra regenerative, or eocorn horn, or surgery. Please—"

"I bandaged him myself," said the young, willowy Emma girl
who'd shot him. "He'll live. For a while yet."

Max was still breathing, but he hadn't uttered so much as a
grunt in a long time.

"What is it you want with us?" Cassandra asked.

"Not you. Him." The oldest Emma made eye contact with
Gabriel.

"Me? What do you want with me?"

"I used to live in Los Angeles," she said. "I know what the South's chief hydromancer looks like, Lord Argent."

Gabriel trudged through mud, his arms and shoulders and back screaming. Max wasn't a large man, but he was dead weight.

"I'm not a lord. And you didn't have to shoot Max to take me captive."

The Emmas had nothing to say to this. Of course they had to shoot Max. He was unmistakably Gabriel's protector.

"So, what's your plan for me? If you have some drains you need unclogged, you came to the right man."

"How much are you worth to your Department of Water and Power in Los Angeles? Or to your enemies in San Francisco?"

"You're going to ransom me."

"An underground network to free enslaved golems doesn't run on hope and miracles," said the oldest Emma. "We need funds for guns and ammunition, for food and safe houses, for bribing rangers and border guards."

Gabriel stepped into a knee-deep puddle. He managed not to drop Max, but just barely.

"You're doing this the hard way," he said. "You're murdering my friend, and it's not necessary. Treat his gunshot wound before he dies, and I'll submit to whatever you want to do with me. Let me talk to my people in L.A. I'll negotiate the best price for myself. Or sell me to whoever you want. Help Max and I'll be the best hostage anyone could want."

The oldest Emma stopped to check her compass. "You're already the best hostage we could want."

"Then heal Max because it's the decent thing to do."

"We can't afford to be decent. I don't know what it's like in the South. Maybe your cupboards are stuffed with things like hydra and eocorn. Maybe you pick your teeth with griffin bones. We're not so lucky. I'm sorry it was necessary to shoot him, but he would have fought to keep us from taking you. We didn't shoot him in the head. We didn't leave him for dead in the tunnel. It might not seem like much to be grateful for."

A twig snapped in the darkness of the woods. The Emma raised her fist and the group froze. Another snap. She motioned for everyone to get down. The two other Emmas crouched, peering through the narrow gaps in the trees. Cassandra and Gabriel carefully lowered Max to the ground, and Gabriel was ashamed at the relief he felt. Max had borne his weight enough times, and it seemed to Gabriel that he should be able to pay him back without complaint.

The oldest Emma issued directives with finger gestures, and the other two Emmas crept toward the nearest trees with guns drawn.

An antlered creature emerged from the woods to meet them, its fur silvered by the moon.

"I'm not an expert," Gabriel whispered, "but I think it's a deer."

The Emma gave Gabriel a warning look, but after a moment of regarding the intruders, the deer moved off peacefully, and there were no more noises from the forest except the constant drip of water.

"Pick him up," the oldest Emma commanded, and the exhausting slog through the mud continued.

Apparently the Emmas hadn't noticed that when they were huddled on the ground, Cassandra had slipped her hand into his backpack, palmed something, and tucked it into her pocket.

The Emmas' shack lurked among trees at the top of a slippery path. The windows were shuttered. The roof sagged under a pile of pine needles and pinecones. Milk crates and rusty spools of barbwire littered the yard like flotsam and jetsam in a muddy sea.

When the oldest Emma unlocked and pushed open the front door, Gabriel realized the house's slovenly appearance was costuming. The door was a solid slab of wood. The interior walls were concrete block.

"Through here." Reverse-Raccoon Emma ushered them into a bedroom and let them lay Max down. With the other two Emmas standing guard, she retrieved a pair of shears from a black leather bag on a bureau and split open his pant leg.

The bandage over Max's wound was filthy with blood and water and mud. If Gabriel hadn't seen it applied with his own eyes, he would never have believed it had started out white. The Emma removed the bandage and revealed worse. There was no bullet hole. Instead, it looked as if someone had rammed a fist into a bag of blood, pounded it with a sledgehammer, and set fire to it. The rest of his leg was shades of black and pallid blue.

Reverse-Raccoon Emma unzipped her med kit all the way open, revealing an array of gleaming surgical instruments. Gabriel's eye fell on the long knife and bone saw.

Gabriel caught his breath. "Hydra. If you have any, give it to him. If you don't, get some. Quickly."

"Drop your packs and go with my sister," the oldest Emma said. The youngest Emma's gun was still drawn.

"I am one of the great powers," Gabriel said. "I am the darkest hydromancer of the Southern realm. You did this to my friend. Undo it, or you'll die with water in your lungs."

"Come with me, or I'll shoot her next." The youngest Emma's gun was pointed at Cassandra's leg.

"Gabriel, please." Cassandra's voice betrayed a thin shudder.

Max wouldn't have been scared, even if he'd been conscious. When Gabriel first met him he'd been under a death sentence, and he'd never shed the certainty that every day he lived was just a short reprieve.

Gabriel found himself resenting Cassandra and her fear. It complicated his emotions and limited his options.

But what were his options, exactly? What could he really do here? Expect the Emmas to simply watch him construct a sigil? Grant him access to a faucet?

"Gabriel," Cassandra said again, with unconcealed desperation.

He dragged his eyes away from Max and from the Emma's amputation kit, and only then did he remember that Cassandra had snuck something out of his backpack.

"Please don't cut off his leg," he said before the Emmas took him away.

A few outbuildings stuck out of the sodden ground like mushrooms. The youngest Emma put Gabriel in a shed of concrete block where they stored bags of flour, road salt, and plant fertilizer. Rain clattered on the aluminum roof, but the shed remained dry. Never a bad plan to keep a water mage away from water.

He kept his mouth shut as she handcuffed his wrists behind his back. He didn't resist as she patted his back and chest, probed his armpits, felt her way up his legs, stripped his belt off, unfastened his pants, searched under his scrotum. He met this humiliation with silence until the Emma took her lantern with her and left him alone in the dark.

He paced the shed, hoping to find a forgotten bottle of water, a spray bottle of window cleaner, a puddle from a leak in the roof. He wasn't sure what he'd do if he found any such thing—not handcuffed with his bag of sigil pipes and puzzle valves locked up in the house—but a water mage must seek water.

Max won't die, he told himself. Max was strong, and smart, and fierce. He couldn't die.

But there was no rational reason to believe any of this. Max wouldn't make it through the night simply because Gabriel wanted him to. Max was a man of flesh, blood, and bone. A bullet had plowed into his leg, possibly fracturing his femur and severing his femoral artery.

Possibly? No, probably.

Gabriel sat on the cold, dry concrete floor.

Say the Reverse-Raccoon Emma managed to save Max's life, he thought. Let's just go all the way and say she even managed to save his leg. Max still wouldn't be able to walk. Not for a long time. Not through woods and mud, not through the aqueducts.

And what about himself? Would Gabriel's underlings pay his ransom, or would they welcome his absence, pop some champagne, and throw a usurpation party?

So far, this had turned out to be a really bad day.

Gabriel shouldn't have surrendered so easily. He should have stayed with Max, convinced the Emmas to administer whatever magic they had in their stores to save him. He was a coward.

And, no, that wasn't true, either. He let himself be trundled off because if he'd stayed to argue and fight, they would have shot Cassandra as well.

So, not a coward.

But weak?

Yes, absolutely weak. Confronted by three guns, the great and mighty hydromancer, master of the mandala, bringer of life and destruction, was weak.

The metallic sounds of lock and key and the rattle of a chain brought Gabriel off the floor. The door slid open, revealing Cassandra, standing in the moonlight like a goddess of the hunt with gleaming black blood spattered on her face and a gun tucked in her waistband.

"What happened?" Gabriel said, astonished.

"Idiot tried to search me."

She uncuffed him with one of the Emmas' keys and led him outside.

"There're still two in the house," she said.

"How do we deal with them?"

"I'm good at locks and I can kick down a door, but the second they hear us coming, they'll shoot Max."

"Right. You still have the thing you took from my backpack?"

She dug into her pocket and handed him a brass nozzle. "Can you do anything with this?"

Outwardly, it was just a nozzle, not that different from the kind of thing you screwed onto the end of a garden hose, with a simple-looking valve. But inside was a sigil over a hundred miles long. Gabriel felt its satisfying weight in his palm.

"I can do a lot with this," he said. "But it might kill Max."

"'Might.' He's in there, dying right now. I'm sorry, Gabriel. 'Might' is the best we can do for Max right now."

They crept up to the house, Cassandra leading the way, but Gabriel stopped her when they were still a few dozen yards away.

He bent down and dipped the nozzle in a puddle. The nozzle

drank up the water, not just of the puddle at his feet, but from surrounding puddles, from deep underground. The mud around them grew dry and cracked as the nozzle drew up hundreds of gallons of water.

The nozzle should have weighed tons. In fact, if you hung it from a scale, that's what the needle would show. But the pattern inside the nozzle extended to the pattern of Gabriel's own circulatory system, and the pattern of his own circulatory system drew strength from the water in the earth, in the trees, in the air.

He aimed the nozzle at the front door. "Get ready," he said, and he turned a valve.

The water didn't come out right away. It had miles of capillaries to travel first, hundreds of sigil patterns to run through and repeat inside the nozzle. Then, with an unnatural gleam, the water shot out in a laser-thin stream. The door collapsed into splinters. An instant later, the windows and half the roof blew out, and tiny fragments of wood and plaster rained down amid a diffuse mist of water.

Gabriel trailed behind Cassandra as she raced up to the house. Inside, it was dry. The walls were cracked, with ragged holes where the windows had been. Gabriel saw stars through the remains of the roof.

They found the oldest Emma facedown on the living room floor. Blood ran from her ears.

They left her there and charged to the bedroom. The damage was less extensive here, the door hanging on one hinge but still intact. Max lay on the bed. A tourniquet of surgical rubber was tied around his upper thigh. Scattered over the floor lay the contents of Reverse-Raccoon Emma's surgeon's kit: hooks and probes and scissors and scalpels and saws for separating bones.

Gabriel's water cannon hadn't taken out the last remaining Emma. She held a foot-long knife to Max's ruined flesh. With her other hand, she raised a gun.

Cassandra raised her own gun. There was a harsh *pop*. A small, red hole appeared in the Emma's forehead. A trail of blood fell from the hole, like a fat, wet raindrop, and she pitched forward over Max's body.

Gabriel pulled the Emma off Max. He let her drop to the floor.

Max's skin was white wax. His gray tongue sat dry in his open mouth.

Cassandra felt for his pulse and closed her eyes. "I just don't know, Gabriel."

Gabriel sorted through the surgical supplies but found nothing of use. He pulled the drawers out of the small bureau and dumped their contents on the floor. Just towels and ammo clips.

"I'll look around," Cassandra said. She left the room to search the house, and Gabriel despaired. Hydra was a treasure. Even if the Emmas had any, it would be well hidden, or buried under debris. Or maybe he'd destroyed it with the nozzle.

He sat on the bed and gripped Max's cold, white hand.

"I need you to wake up now, Max. I know it's a shitty thing to do, to need you when you've got your hands full just staying alive." He pried loose some hair stuck by dried sweat to Max's brow. "I know I ask a lot of you, all the time. You'd think after a bullet and all the blood and muck, I could take care of things myself, mighty sorcerer and all that. But I need you. And the only thing that's going to help you now is hydra, or eocorn. We'll probably need both, actually. So, I need your nose. You don't even have to get out of bed. Just open your eyes, drink up some air through that magnificent beak of yours, and point.

You can do that for me, right? It's not like I don't pay you well. It's not my fault if you don't know how to enjoy money." He squeezed Max's hand tighter. "I need you, Max, and you have to wake up."

How absurd it would be if Max actually did open his eyes. If his nostrils twitched and he raised himself up, leaned on one elbow, and said, "Under the kitchen sink." What a strange world it would be, where good things could happen simply because you wished for them.

Gabriel gently set Max's hand down and released it. Max's hand slid off the mattress, palm up.

His index finger was slightly extended. Pointing.

"Oh, come on," Gabriel said, not allowing himself to hope.

He followed the trajectory of Max's finger to a floorboard and got down on his hands and knees. The floorboard didn't look different from any of the others. He dug his fingernails in and tried to lift it, but the fit was too snug, and the floorboard wasn't going anywhere.

Cassandra found Gabriel on his knees.

"There was a substantial safe in the basement," she said. "I got it open, but it was empty." She watched him for a moment. "What are you doing?"

"I let myself believe Max pointed at this floorboard, and I find I can't give up." Blood welled beneath his fingernails. He scrabbled over to the surgeon's tools and grabbed a scalpel. Jamming the blade in the seam, he tried to lever the floorboard out. It would not budge. No matter what, it remained stuck.

"There's osteomancy under here."

She gave him a pitying look.

"Why else is this floorboard so tight? There's *something* under there."

Cassandra moved him aside and crouched. She ran her fingers

around the board. Taking the scalpel, she dug deep into the wood and gouged a long line.

"You hear that?"

Gabriel heard nothing.

"Listen for it. It's air moving around, like a whisper."

Gabriel closed his eyes. He heard his own breathing, and Cassandra's. The softest of thumps: drops of the shot Emma's blood hitting the floor.

"I don't hear it."

"That's because you haven't been doing this all your adult life. It's sphinx oil. You don't expend sphinx oil just to keep a squeaky floorboard in place. Go get my pack. They stashed it in the bathroom down the hall."

Gabriel ran, returning seconds later with Cassandra's backpack.

She found her pouch of lock picks and skeleton keys and osteomantic devices and took out a cube of bone. It was the size of a child's alphabet block, etched with cartouches containing symbols and vaguely Egyptian animal figures. She placed it on the floorboard.

Also from her pack came a folding knife with a serrated blade, much meaner-looking than the scalpel. She attacked the floorboard, stabbing, digging, carving wounds in the wood.

And now Gabriel heard it: whispers floating on moving air, scratching like the claws of rats against the sandstone walls of a dark, dry tomb. The sounds resolved into voices, unintelligible at first, and then merely foreign, and then, not English, but somehow understandable.

"The black eye watches but never sees," Gabriel said, repeating words forming in his head.

It was a riddle encoded into the sphinx oil. The Emmas

would have known the answer, and speaking it would unlock the floorboard.

"Do you know this one?"

Cassandra shook her head. "The cube will. It was carved from the sagittal crest of an Akkadian cave sphinx. That's the oldest of the sphinxes. All the riddles originate from it. It knows the answers."

With Max's face the blue-white color of glacial ice, Gabriel couldn't allow himself to hope. "There must be thousands of sphinx riddles."

"Tens of thousands," Cassandra said.

Another voice emerged, thin and weak, and the whispers grew stronger. The air became thick with the sense of an invisible battle waged with words, challenges and responses, a swirling, violent rush.

Then, all at once, the voices fell silent.

Cassandra inserted her blade in the seam. With only a little rocking, she lifted the floorboard free. In a hollowed-out space rested a blue velvet bag with "Wolfskill Whiskey" embroidered on it in gold thread. Gabriel loosened the drawstrings. Inside was a tiny glass vial of particles, like pepper flakes, pearly black. He could feel the warmth through the glass. There was also a small foil packet. He unpeeled it and found a wad of dark green paste, no bigger than a piece of bubble gum.

He brought the items over to the bed.

"Pretty good work for a sick day, Max."

He sprinkled the ground eocorn horn directly into Max's wound. The hydra regenerative, he placed under Max's tongue. Max breathed deeply, and Gabriel closed his eyes and swallowed to keep from weeping.

FIFTEEN

T he highway up to San Francisco teetered high above coasts of jade and turquoise waters. Cypress trees clung to weathered crags, their trunks and limbs distorted into tortuous shapes by centuries of wind.

"You call the Hierarch 'Her Majesty' or 'Her Highness' the first time you address her. After that, it's okay to call her 'ma'am.' Remember, it's just like I said it. Rhymes with 'damn,' not 'mom.' "

Daniel might have enjoyed the scenery more if Moth hadn't decided to use the time in the back of the limousine to drill him on royal etiquette and protocol.

" 'Damn,' " he said.

"Right. She's first in the line of royal precedence. That's like the pecking order. Next comes her husband. His full name is Reginald Creighton, and following tradition, he'd be 'Your Majesty' or 'Your Highness,' never 'Lord Consort,' even though that's what he is. As a matter of preference, though, he likes 'Lord General.' Okay, next in precedence are those of the Grand Ducal ranks. But none of them go by 'Grand Duke,' because that would be too easy. For instance, the High Grand Osteo-mancer, who carries the rank of Grand Duke, goes by 'High

Grand Osteomancer.' You won't have to worry about that, of course, because the seat is empty. Now, as for Master of Bones, Master of Keys, Master of the Fire Eternal, you can call them 'my lord.' "

"And if it's a lady?"

"Also 'my lord.' "

"Moth, how do you *know* all this stuff?"

"Books, my lord. There are books about this stuff. Right in your very own library. Along with family genealogies, royal histories, etiquette manuals . . . I've been staying up late with a flashlight under the covers."

"Do you know which fork I'm supposed to use?"

"That's in *Beernan's Etiquette of Court Dining*. It's a little musty, but I don't think those things change much." Moth paused, waiting until Daniel turned away from the scenery. "This stuff is important, D. I'll be shunted off to wait in some antechamber with the other domestics. I won't be there to help you."

"I'll be fine. I'll bet my bones against any of theirs."

"I'm not worried about you in a fight. I mean a wizardly fight, not a proper fight with fists and biting. But that sort of thing at dinner would scupper our operation. And so would acting like you don't belong at court. Minding your p's and q's is important."

Daniel gave Moth's barrel-sized leg an affectionate pat. "I know. You're right. You are the rock upon which I am building this scam. So, I call the Master of the Fire Eternal 'sir,' except, actually, in this case, she's a ma'am, rhymes-with-'damn.' But I still call her 'my lord.' See? I'm paying attention."

The highway turned inland, winding through magisterial redwoods with tunnels built right through the trunks. Moth led lessons for another three hours, until Daniel's head was stuffed full of curtsies and forms of address and gravy spoons. When they arrived in San Francisco, Daniel had time only to catch a glimpse of mansion-infested hills before being transferred to an elephant-driven coach that took him and Moth the rest of the way to the palace.

By now, Cassandra and her team ought to be less than a day's journey from here, and he shouldn't worry that he hadn't received any message from her yet. He didn't expect to for another two days.

He worried anyway.

Moth tapped him on the shoulder. "We're here."

Heavy chains clanked as guards in red livery drove elephants around a pair of massive windlasses to draw back the palace gates. The elephants trumpeted, straining. Even riding in back of a plush coach over the drawbridge, Daniel couldn't shake the feeling he was being let into an overbuilt prison.

At least it was a nice prison, set in botanical gardens with acres of tropical ferns, a stand of redwoods, cacti and other weird, spiky things. Rising above even the tallest of the trees soared a spire of glass, paned in emerald, sapphire, and ruby: the Jewel Palace.

Moth looked out with his nose pressed to the window as they drew up before a welcoming committee. On the flagstone courtyard, ceremonial guards and dignitaries stood in formation, while musicians blared a fanfare on long trumpets. It looked like a lot of inconvenience, and it drove home the idea that Paul had been a very important man in this kingdom.

Daniel was relieved that neither Cynara nor Allaster Doring were in view.

Porters unloaded Paul's trunks, packed by Gorov with clothes and household items that apparently Paul couldn't travel without. This was supposed to be only a few-night's stay, but he'd brought enough for a months-long grand tour.

Getting Daniel out of the coach required a crew of six footmen plus the coach driver to open the door and bring over stairs for the one-foot drop to a spotless red carpet.

"Do you get out first, or am I supposed to?" Daniel whispered.

"Did you sleep through finishing school?" Moth clambered out and took his place at the end of the line of footmen, respectful of the occasion in a black formal coat. Daniel stepped down onto the carpet. What Paul would make of all this pomp. Was he openly disdainful of it? Resigned to it? Or maybe he enjoyed it and considered it his due.

Daniel decided to play it as though he were weary of everything. He was, after all, supposed to be convalescing.

Some guy—Daniel had no idea who he was, Minister of Groveling or something—greeted Daniel with a lot of curlicue words and escorted him and Moth into the palace. Daniel's eyes instinctively probed the entry hall for things to steal and places to conceal himself: ceiling vents, broom closets. But from what he could see, the palace was a glass box. The gleaming floors, the high walls, the stratospheric ceiling were all facets of bright emerald. This was not so much a building as it was the interior of the world's most colossal gemstone. It was kind of beautiful. And unnerving. It made Daniel feel like a flaw.

The Minister of Groveling took them deeper into the palace. Through a doorway, Daniel caught a glimpse into a vast chamber. At the far wall, a hundred yards away, a gargantuan reptilian skull curved over the back of an empty throne. He kept moving, but the scents of osteomancy stayed with him. He smelled flight in high, thin air, and rich undersea powers, and more than anything else, magma and pressure and gases rushing from shattered earth. He hoped the scents had been left lurking in the room as a deliberate display of power and weren't just what the Hierarch left effortlessly in her wake. In any case, if the throne room was so rich in osteomantic tells when empty, he could only imagine what it might smell like when she sat upon her throne.

They finally arrived at Daniel's suite of rooms. The dominant theme of the main sitting room was the color red, with red-glassed windows and walls covered in red silk and furniture of red mahogany and redwood upholstered in red. The Hierarch had put him up in a slab of rare prime rib.

Moth chased off their escort and shut the doors with a sigh of relief. He took a stroll around the room, presumably checking the paintings on the walls and the statues on plinths for any dangers. The place smelled clean to Daniel.

Daniel turned his attention to the exotic cut orchids, the quality liquor and wine and cheese on a sideboard. A sealed envelope of creamy, thick paper stock sat on a writing desk.

"Dude, can you just imagine?" Moth enthused. "Back in the day I'd be cramming everything in this room in a pillowcase."

"I take it this stuff is valuable?"

Moth jabbed his finger toward a painting of red boxes the size of a garage door. "That's a Rothko. It's worth millions."

"How do you know?"

"What's that thing when the little inky bugs go into your eyes and make brain knowledge? Reading."

"Art books are mostly pictures, aren't they?"

"Don't insult me when I'm busy insulting you. Your thief-craft is flabby. You've always got to be on the lookout for the score. You've got to be sharp enough to devise a plan to get it, and smooth enough to execute it. My job is to be the muscle, but you're supposed to be the criminal mastermind. I can't do everything myself."

"I've been working. I've already discovered that the Hierarch's treasury is in the palace, which means the crown jewels are also likely in the palace."

"Which means the *axis mundi* bone is probably somewhere in the palace. Okay, that *is* a nice bit of work. When did that happen?"

Daniel showed him the piece of paper he'd found in the envelope.

"It's a schedule," Daniel said. "Cocktails at six. Dinner at seven. Brandy and cigars at nine. Guided tour of the treasury at ten."

"Cheater."

A discreet knock on the door, and Moth went to answer. A servant stood in the hall bearing a small wooden chest.

"My apologies, sir. The porters missed this one."

"What's in it?"

"Sir. His lordship's handkerchiefs."

"Let's see them."

The servant grew pale as Moth used his size and growl to threaten him.

Daniel silently formulated a joke: How many guys did it take to deliver Paul's hankies? Two. One to bring them, and Moth to make him pee his pants.

The joke still needed some work.

With a shaky hand, the servant opened the chest.

"Yes, those indeed are his lordship's" was Moth's haughty verdict. "I'll take them."

As soon as the chest was in Moth's hands, the servant punched Moth in the jaw, hard enough that Daniel heard the crack of facial bones. Moth stumbled and fell back. Before he could recover and counter, the servant flicked his hand, and three flechettes penetrated Moth's chest. Daniel smelled basilisk venom. Moth sagged to one knee, tried to rise back up but collapsed. Coal-black blotches formed on his face, and he stared lifelessly at the ceiling, foam spilling from his slightly parted lips and mingling with blood from his mouth.

The man leaped nimbly over Moth's body and turned his full attention to Daniel.

"What do you want?" Daniel said, though the answer was obvious. He stepped back and away.

The assassin was a professional. He'd been hired to kill, not to chat. Three flechettes identical to those he'd subdued Moth with were tucked between his fingers.

Daniel kept backing away, and the assassin watched him warily. Paul was no easy target. Surely the assassin knew that, as did whoever sent him.

"Who hired you? Did you try to poison me at San Simeon?" Daniel backed into an armchair. The assassin allowed himself a hint of a smile, satisfied that he'd cornered his prey, but that's what Daniel wanted. He'd drawn the assassin away from Moth, and now he could strike with kraken lightning or vomit fire without catching Moth accidentally.

He drew upon the Colombian dragon in his bones. Essences of dragon scales hardened his chest. The assassin flung the flechettes. They struck Daniel over his heart, only to fall on the carpet like dead birds.

The assassin jerked his arms, and knives popped from the cuffs of his jacket and into his hands.

Daniel let him have kraken electricity, enough to stun even Moth unconscious. He pushed out the sizzling forks of energy, but the assassin only faltered, then shook it off. His knives whizzed past Daniel's head, and Daniel smelled seps. The blades thunked into the Rothko painting, and the canvas disintegrated like dry paper in a fire.

Daniel had had enough. He wanted the assassin alive, but

not at the expense of his own life. He unleashed another bolt of kraken, this time enough to kill a monoceros. The assassin went down, smoke rising from his back. The air smelled of basilisk, seps, kraken, and smoldering fabric.

Moth groaned.

"You okay, buddy?"

"I'm fine." His voice was weak, his breathing labored. But a new scent joined the others: the green, fungal aromas of hydra, which told Daniel that Moth was healing. Daniel swallowed with relief.

"You better not have killed that guy," Moth croaked. "Because I'm going to hit him so hard his grandchildren will need occupational therapy."

"You just sit and rest a spell, Moth."

Daniel turned the assassin over. He was still breathing.

"Golly, you're a tough one," Daniel said. "You can take a hit, and you can certainly give it. I don't think I've ever seen my friend smacked that hard."

"It wasn't that hard," Moth protested, spitting blood on the carpet.

"But I don't smell enough osteomancy to make you such a strong fellow. And I didn't smell your basilisk and seps blades until it was too late. Concealing aromas like that is high-level magic."

"I'm not telling you who hired me," the assassin rasped. It sounded as if Daniel had cooked his throat.

"I think you are going to tell me."

Daniel exhaled. Blue flame flared from his lungs. In an instant, the assassin's singed eyebrows turned to flaking carbon.

"Tell him what he wants to know," Moth said, "or else I'm going to fetch graham crackers and chocolate. That makes you the marshmallow, in case you're not following."

The assassin glared at Daniel with contempt, but his expression was mixed with fear, and horror, and a profound sadness. Daniel recognized the combination.

"I don't want to die."

Moth huffed, impatient. "S'mores, is what I'm saying."

"I don't want to die, I don't want to die." He said it again and again, breaking into sobs, and despite the fact that the assassin had meant to murder him, Daniel felt pity. He'd never been good at interrogation. Instilling fear just made him feel vaguely sick.

"This is the second attempt on my life in as many days. And before that someone tried to murder my daughter. Tell me who hired you, and I won't kill you. I won't even hurt you worse."

The man worked his lips but couldn't form words. His tears dried to salt on his face. His skin paled, turned gray and began to splinter. Daniel smelled gorgon. He moved away from him and told Moth to get back. The man's fingers curled. He drew his knees in and bent himself into a fetal position, his skin crackling, his limbs growing rigid, his hair crusting over as he turned to stone. Gray dust and flakes sifted off his body with the sound of wind over sand. A powder like dry cement sifted from his servant's costume.

Moth gaped. "What the hell?"

"An assassin with an expiration date. This took expensive magic. What's Gorov's salary?"

"Not enough to buy gorgon. Which means whoever wants you dead is high up. But I guess that's nothing new for you."

"They don't want *me* dead. They want the guy I'm pretending to be dead."

"Okay, that is new."

"Sounds strange, but I have bigger priorities than not getting assassinated. I'm not sure what I should be doing about this."

"I have some ideas."

Moth's ideas turned out to be simple and practical. First, he poured each of them a glass of expensive brandy. Then he went to the phone and dialed zero.

"Send up a maid to Lord Paul's chambers," he ordered, looking at the assassin's remains. "There's a spill to clean up."

All through cocktails Daniel felt as if he were walking the edge of a sandstone cliff. It wasn't enough to step carefully when accepting the good wishes of the realm's lords and ladies, government figures, business titans, and osteomancers. He felt he could get everything right, convince everyone he was Paul, and still falter, because Paul walked a more perilous road than Daniel had imagined.

At least he didn't have to pretend to know people's names. They were announced upon each guest's entrance, and then a flurry of gossip would fill him in on the basics of their biographies, scandals included.

"The Countess Helena, High Osteomancer of Sausalito, and Count Lourdes," honked a crier at the door, and anyone with ears would soon learn of the count's infidelities and the countess's misguided attempt to grow wings, which would explain the voluminous sleeves of her gown.

Paul's own announcement had been followed by at least ten minutes of delicious mutterings, and Daniel overheard seven different reasons for Paul's long absence, including time spent living on the bottom of the sea, as well as in a volcano, as well as a yearlong cleansing that involved fasting and enemas. Nobody mentioned anything about Catalina Island and dragons.

There were murmurs about the afternoon's assassination

attempt and the poisoned food at San Simeon. He heard the name Doring dropped more than once.

He also learned that people were careful around him. Those who approached to give their respects did so with stiff caution. This suited Daniel fine.

When Allaster Doring was announced, he entered the room as though he were penetrating it. Snagging a champagne glass from a waiter, he strode toward Daniel, and the party-goers cleared a space around them. They watched with salacious interest, as if they were expecting a bare-knuckle brawl to break out.

The murmurers and titterers fell silent. The string quartet decided to play everything pianissimo before their bows stopped entirely. Ice cubes clinked inside glasses.

Allaster came to a stop before Daniel.

"For crying out loud," he roared. "We're not going to fight in the middle of cocktail hour. Go back to your prattling." He made shooing motions with his hand, and the murmuring started up again, and the music resumed, and the clusters of conversation re-formed.

Allaster brushed an invisible speck of lint from his sleeve and sipped champagne. "Bread and circuses are a fine idea, but damned if I'm going to be the circus."

"Better than being the bread," Daniel said.

"Good point." Allaster flashed a winning smile and raised his glass to Daniel. "Just so you know, that assassin wasn't mine."

"That's lovely to hear, Allaster. Why should I believe you?"

"Have you ever known me to be subtle? About anything?"

Daniel took a drink.

"The whole point of killing you would be to prove I'm the stronger osteomancer. Paying someone else to do it, behind closed doors, out of view . . . ? That would prove nothing."

"So if it wasn't you, who, then? Your sister, maybe."

Allaster's face became thoughtful. "We did have one governess who punished Cynara for melting a rather expensive statue in her cauldron. I think it was a Rodin? I don't know, I was only six."

"And the governess?"

There was some commotion at the door, and Allaster's smile became resplendent. "Here's your chance to ask her yourself."

The crier announced Cynara's name, and Allaster's sister entered in a black gown that flowed over her like liquid, carrying with her a cloud of potent magical scents. As she approached, Daniel found himself unable to stop staring at her exposed shoulders. He had to force himself to look up from them and acknowledge her eyes. Unfortunately, they were beguiling as well. Her clavicles were beguiling. Even her nostrils were beguiling.

He drank.

"I was just telling Paul about the . . . conflict . . . you had with our governess," Allaster said. "The thing with the Rodin. What happened to that governess, anyway?"

"Same thing as happened to the Rodin. I don't suppose my brother told you the part about him being the one to melt the sculpture and blaming me for it."

Allaster gazed off in the distance, as if looking into the past. "Is that what happened? It was a long time ago."

Cynara smiled at him, not without some affection. Then she turned to Daniel. "Who's trying to kill you, Paul?"

She gave him a significant look. The attempts on Ethelinda's life weren't public knowledge, but maybe Cynara wasn't wrong to suspect a connection with the attempts on Paul's.

Daniel made a dismissive gesture. "I have larger concerns." An absurdly true statement. Or it ought to be. Playing Paul made this the most complicated heist Daniel had ever tried to pull, and though assassination attempts were troubling, every job came with problems: extra guards and alarms you didn't anticipate, or the getaway vehicle springing an inopportune oil leak. It was just stuff to be dealt with. But the fact that Ethelinda had been targeted as well somehow made it more than just stuff.

"Is Ethelinda still at San Simeon?"

"She's here, with her governess," Cynara said, as if it were something Paul would have known.

"Formidable woman," Allaster said approvingly. "Unmeltable."

"Ah, my three musketeers," came a booming voice. Lord Professor Nathaniel Cormorant shouldered through the crowd, a glass of white wine in each hand. He sipped first from one glass, then the other, and swished the mixture in his mouth before swallowing.

He didn't seem to like what he tasted.

"Problem?" Allaster asked.

"The butler said these were from the same bottle, but he's lying." He held up the glass in his left hand. "This one was stored higher to the ceiling. I hope you youngsters have been exercising your tongues."

"I assure you, Professor," Allaster said, "I give my tongue a regular workout."

Cynara sighed, and Cormorant shook his head like an indulgent uncle.

"I imagine the party's favorite topic has been the latest attempt on your life, Paul?"

Daniel took a noncommittal sip of champagne.

"You know, it's really not something to take so lightly," Cormorant said, reproving. "You're the favored candidate for

High Grand Osteomancer. Has it occurred to you that whoever's got it in for you is less interested in killing you than in showing you're not able to protect yourself from threats? Nobody wants a weak High Grand Osteomancer."

"I suppose you could ask the assassin if he finds me weak."

"Paul turned him to dust," Allaster said, with an air of confidentiality.

"Little more than a freshman exercise," Cormorant said, sipping and swishing.

The string quartet ended their piece on an abrupt note and launched into a march. An elderly man made his way through the room, bent under the weight of his outfit: a military dress uniform of pristine white, pinned with medals and ribbons. A circlet of bone crowned the old man's head.

Lord Creighton, the Hierarch's consort, was known in Southern California as the Butcher of Bakersfield. Daniel did not fail to take notice of the scabbarded sword buckled to his belt. It was almost as long as his leg and was said to have separated thousands of soldiers' heads from their necks.

Guests of all ranks bowed deeply as he passed.

When his slow progress finally brought him near, Cormorant and the Dorings bowed almost to the floor, and Daniel joined them.

Creighton took Daniel's forearms and raised him out of his bow, either gently or weakly. "My lord Paul, you look like a wreck."

"His Lord General is not the first to notice. But I'm sure some time in the Jewel Palace will restore me to my full vigor."

"I shall see to it," declared Creighton with the force of conviction one might bring to sealing a military alliance. "We are so pleased to have you home. It feels like the realm has been on hold, ever hopeful for your return. And now that you're back, the wheels of progress spin once more."

"No one could be more pleased than I, my lord."

Creighton smiled and nodded heartily. "Indeed. And Her Majesty and I would like to express our regret for the . . . incident . . . earlier this afternoon. I have been assured that any reminders of the unpleasantness have been scrubbed from your chambers. But if you should like to be lodged elsewhere, it shall be done."

"Thank you, Lord General, but I am comfortable where I am."

"I have looked into the identity of your attacker."

Daniel wondered what "looked into" meant. He imagined maids and gardeners and houseboys in dark places with apparatus involving ropes and pincers and hot coals.

"From what I have gathered," Creighton went on, "the assassin was not of our household, but rather of yours. I understand this isn't the first time something of this nature has happened. Will you accept a word of advice from an old hand?"

"I would be grateful, Lord General."

His advice was unsurprising. "Kill your household. The whole bloody lot of them. Every butler and scullery maid and your head chef and the boy who peels the carrots. Kill the gardeners and your groomsmen and falconer. Kill your chamberlain and your new man, the big one. Build a bonfire in front of your castle and a tank of water and boil them all alive."

"But if I'm killing them all, who will I get to do the boiling?" Daniel just couldn't resist.

Creighton didn't smile, but there was a gleam in his eye. "I keep experts at this sort of thing on my staff. I'll lend them to you."

"You're very kind, Lord General. Thank you."

Dinner was announced soon thereafter, and the meal was mercifully easy to get through. Lord Creighton wasn't present, nor the Hierarch herself, and the chairs were placed around an oversized banquet table so far apart that conversation was physically awkward and easy to avoid. Someone must have decided that the elite of the realm didn't need another opportunity to talk among themselves without their liege present.

After dessert and coffee, Lord Creighton reappeared to personally lead the tour of the Hierarch's treasury.

It was a high, round chamber, paneled in battleship-gray glass. Daniel supposed it was hard as steel, possibly made from the tooth enamel of some monstrous Northern beast. He suppressed the urge to rap his knuckles against the walls.

Massive columns supported a gallery, where archers stood ready at close intervals. The scent of basilisk venom wafted down. A basilisk-laced arrow in the heart would certainly dissuade a thief.

The floor was staffed by a cadre of guards tricked out in helmets, body armor, and machine guns. A little rude for such a classy gathering, maybe, but Daniel couldn't blame the Hierarch. Some thieves needed a lot of dissuasion.

There were other smells—sphinx riddle and nhang locks and Hyakume eyes, and probably more sophisticated things that kept their aromas to themselves.

Glass cases rose in the center of the room like monuments, and they contained marvels: broaches, necklaces, bracelets, rings, tiaras of osteomantic bone.

Creighton dutifully recited the names and histories of these priceless objects, but his interest lay in arms. A breastplate of red and brown dragon scales shimmered on a mannequin at least eight feet tall. There was an entire suit of armor made from serrated megalodon teeth, hippogriff ribs, mammoth tusks, and dragon fangs, rising like horns from the helmet.

"I captured this one myself when I took Oregon," Creighton confided to Daniel.

But nothing made him prouder than a sword of glossy red, yellow, and orange enamel, like sculpted flame. "Of course, you all know this blade. The Hierarch claimed this as her personal prize in the Battle of Yosemite, right from the hand of the Southern Hierarch."

"El Serpiente," Daniel whispered, almost in spite of himself. His father had been the Southern Hierarch's sword smith, and in this beautiful, simple, powerful blade, he saw his father's hand.

"It seems rather a shame, doesn't it?" Lord Creighton said to Daniel. "To keep it locked away in a case. A weapon like this is meant to be wielded."

"Perhaps, someday, it will be again, Lord General."

"Indeed, my young lord, indeed."

Daniel followed along as the tour continued, paying more attention to the treasury itself than the treasure. The flooring alone was worth a king's ransom, with plates of Colombian dragon fused with basilisk hide and hardened steel, with no seams to wedge them apart. Even Daniel's favorite recipe of grootslang and seps venom would take hours to burn through it. And the guard presence was too large and well placed for Daniel to take them out with soporific magic or gorgon blood.

". . . but I know none of this is what you were hoping to see," Creighton was saying. "So, here it is."

The tour gathered around a case containing a six-foot-long scepter. The rod was crowned by a blue emerald braced in gold and jewels. From the top of the orb thrust a silver dagger, and set in the dagger's base was a black stone, about the size and shape of a guitar pick.

Reverence shined in Nathaniel Cormorant's eyes. Allaster moved closer, to get a better look. Cynara was right by his side, as if magic radiated from the bone and she wanted to make sure to get her share.

Creighton drew his own gaze away from the scepter. He cleared his throat. "Tomorrow, Her Highness the Hierarch will declare her choice for High Grand Osteomancer. And one of you will enjoy the privilege of being touched by the *axis mundi*."

SIXTEEN

Cassandra didn't want to have a conversation with Gabriel about leaving Max behind. But despite the hydra and eocorn treatment, Max remained laid up in the Emmas' cabin. His gunshot wound was bad, and the magic from the Emmas' stash had turned out to be heavily diluted.

Gabriel hadn't left his side in eight hours. Cassandra watched him doze in a chair beside Max's bed, even after it started to feel like she was intruding on an intimate moment.

Gabriel was not a monster.

She hadn't thought he looked like one, or acted like one. But deep down, she'd still believed he was. She'd met monsters. Anyone who'd climbed to the heights of influence Gabriel had achieved must be a monster.

But here he was, slumped in a chair beside a person he clearly cared a great deal about, dirty and beaten and tired and scared. A powerful man, but also a guy who'd gotten in over his head.

He mumbled something, lifted his chin, and looked anxiously over at Max. Then, wincing, he stretched and sniffed.

"What's that I smell?"

"I threw a soup together," Cassandra said. "Your water gun destroyed the kitchen, but I found a camp stove out back."

A bit of spark reignited in his eyes. He looked hopeful. "Soup. Soup is great. What's in it?"

"Turnips, some chicken, stuff from the herb garden. It's basically Frankensoup. Go have some. I can watch Max for a bit."

Gabriel still hesitated.

"Listen, if he gets well enough to walk, he won't be able to carry you to San Francisco. Get some nutrition in you, find somewhere to lie down for a couple of hours, preserve your strength. For the good of the job."

Gabriel creaked to his feet. "Get me in an hour."

Cassandra promised she would, and she listened to his receding footsteps.

She turned to his bag, lying on the floor next to the chair, and unzipped it.

"I hear you offed Otis Roth."

Max's eyes were open.

"Yeah, I did."

"How does that sit with you?"

"It sits fine. I feel lighter."

"You liked killing him?"

"No. But I like not having Otis Roth in my world anymore. If you knew him as well as I did, you'd feel the same way."

"Maybe I already do," Max said.

She began rooting around Gabriel's bag.

Max tried to rise on one elbow, but then winced and eased himself back down.

"What are you doing?"

"I'm searching Gabriel's bag," Cassandra said. "Back on the trail when I nicked his nozzle gadget, my hand ran into a lot of things that got me curious. There's all the plumbing he's using to get us through the aqueducts. There's the water bomb. But this . . ." She removed a stainless-steel flask. Whatever was inside sloshed with an odd gravity, like a spinning gyroscope. "What's in here? It seems . . . complicated."

"You shouldn't be tampering with his things."

"So stop me. Call for Gabriel."

Max just gave her a baleful stare.

"You have some concerns of your own about your boss, don't you?"

Max still said nothing.

Cassandra took a seat in the chair by the bed. "Okay, I'll go first. I don't think Gabriel's on this job to help Daniel get Sam back. I don't think he's even going to destroy the dragon."

"No? What, then?"

"I think he wants the dragon for himself."

Max sank deeper into his pillows. "You don't know Gabriel like I do. He's not power-hungry."

"Maybe not. But he is a control freak."

Max made a noise that might have been a tiny crumb of laughter. "I'll give you that. But he has to be. He's accountable for a lot."

"I know. He's accountable for an entire kingdom. He controls a lot of magic. Does he think he can control a Pacific firedrake?

"Does Daniel?"

"Hell, no. And he doesn't want to. He really just wants his kid back. That's the truth. Daniel's got the magic to be a great power, but he's seen close-up what that costs people. But Gabriel . . . Gabriel already is a great power. You know there's a price for that. And it's a price paid by more than the person with the power. You know that, Max."

Again, Max gave her no response, but she could tell he agreed with her.

"I'm going to ask you again: What's in the flask?"

He closed his eyes, in pain and stress. She reached over with a towel and daubed sweat off his forehead.

"I don't know what's in the flask," he said.

She believed him.

"Max, I'm on this job to keep Gabriel in check. If I don't like what he's doing, I've got a bullet for him. Him, and anyone else who threatens my friends."

"They go the way of Otis Roth?"

"And I'll lose sleep. But I'll do what's got to be done."

Max peeled off his blankets. Slowly, he swung his feet over the side of the bed, and after several seconds of concentration, he stood. He kept his face rigid, the muscles in his neck and jaw bulging.

Cassandra stood to face him.

"I've got some bullets, too," he said.

Cassandra nodded. "Warning noted. I'll go tell Gabriel you're up."

SEVENTEEN

D aniel re-created the Hierarch's treasury on a table in his sitting room. Upturned tumblers and water goblets stood in for the display cases. Toothpicks were the archers, and matchsticks were the guards. It took a little bit of searching through the suite to find enough matches.

He set one of Paul's cuff links in the middle of the diorama and placed a champagne flute over it. This was the score: the *axis mundi* scepter.

Moth leaned over the table, working on a roast beef sandwich the size of a fire hydrant. "I don't see what you're whining about. We've tackled tougher jobs."

"That is a blatant lie. And you are dripping horseradish on the *axis mundi* scepter."

Moth wiped the spilled horseradish with his finger and licked it. "Well, we'll do this job and then we'll be better thieves. You don't get better without practicing. It's like piano. Can't play 'Chopsticks' forever if you want to be good."

"We played a whole concerto when we broke into the Southern Hierarch's Ossuary. That didn't go so well." Daniel displayed the stump of his right pinky. "Anyway, this room is tougher."

"Why?"

Daniel took the remainder of the matches and scattered them around the diorama. He added tongs from the ice bucket, a box of face tissues, a pouch of tobacco, several books.

"Now you're just making art, Daniel."

"More guards, unknown palace layout, some of the most powerful osteomancers in the two Californias. And this." He planted a candlestick on the table. "By which I mean her. The Hierarch, in her seat of power."

Moth waved his sandwich. "Okay, stop it. You're depressing me. We're not going to burglarize the *axis mundi* from the treasury. Then what's plan B?"

"Here's plan B," Daniel said, with a bit of a flourish. "I'm going to steal the bone at the investiture. Right in the open, in front of everyone. Right under the Hierarch's nose."

Moth stared at him, holding a big clump of unchewed sandwich in his mouth. He picked up a match and struck it on the back of an antique chair. The flame danced. "Can't we go back to 'Chopsticks'?"

There was a knock at the door. Moth bit off the head off the burning match and spat it out. "Get down and stand back," he told Daniel, taking cautious steps toward the door as if he were approaching a vicious dog.

Daniel cut him off. "My turn to get the door."

"Could be another assassin."

"Yeah. That's why it's my turn."

Moth shrugged and scattered the pieces of the diorama. Now it was just a random assortment of stuff. He pulled a white cloth from his pocket like a matador flapping his cape and commenced polishing a glass.

Daniel reached back for sense memories of massive bodies slipping ghostlike through sunless depths, trailing sixty-foot tentacles that crackled with electricity. His fingertips tingled with kraken energy, and he opened the door. A towering woman filled the doorway, her sleeveless blouse revealing muscles clad in glyptodont-armored plates. Small, deep-set black eyes in a broad face stared holes through Daniel, and then over his head, into the room behind him.

"Yes?" Daniel said, somehow making his apprehension sound like impatience. "Who are you and what do you want?"

Her eyes didn't blink. Daniel wondered if she even had eyelids.

She dipped her boulder-sized head in a slight bow.

"I am commanded by Her Majesty the Hierarch to bring His Lord Baron into Her Majesty's presence for the purpose of audience."

"Oh," said Daniel. "Of course. And . . . when?"

Her eyes seemed to grow smaller without the assistance of a squint. "At once, my lord."

"Very good. I'll just need to change, then." He lifted the tails of his untucked shirt and wiggled the toes of his stocking feet to emphasize his slovenly and unfit-for-royal-audience appearance.

Her eyes shrank to pencil dots.

"I am commanded to bring His Lordship to Her Majesty *now,* my lord."

Moth came over with a dressing gown of gold silk and a pair of black loafers polished to an obsidian gloss. He helped Daniel step into his new costume, picked a speck of lint from Daniel's shoulder, appraised him, and graced him with an approving nod.

"Lead the way," Moth commanded the woman, stepping into the hall to follow.

The woman put a massive paw on Moth's chest.

"You're touching me," Moth said.

"I am not commanded to bring anyone save His Lord Baron."

"You're still touching me."

"I can assure His Lord Baron's manservant that His Lord Baron shall be delivered to Her Majesty the Hierarch's presence safely."

"I notice you didn't say delivered and returned. And you're still touching me."

Her eyes grew yet smaller and her voice dipped deeper. "His Lord Baron's manservant should know that His Lord Baron is in the care of Her Majesty the Hierarch's captain of the guard. To insult Her Majesty the Hierarch's captain of the guard is tantamount to insulting Her Majesty the Hierarch."

Daniel buried his hands in his face. "I'm losing track of all these possessives. I am perfectly confident in my ability to keep myself safe." That was an assertion so patently untrue Daniel almost choked on his own words.

"My lord," Moth began.

"You are commanded to remain here and await my return." Even as Paul, Daniel couldn't subject Moth to such high snottiness. More gently, he said, "Take some time off. Enjoy your sandwich."

He could tell Moth was exerting extraordinary muscle control to keep from reaching out and smacking Daniel.

"Yes, my lord."

The guard captain took Daniel up a staircase that spiraled around the outer perimeter of the palace. Glowing braziers lit the way, the light changing color with the hues of the glass walls. It struck Daniel that, despite being made of glass, the palace provided no views to the outer world.

He wondered if he was imagining scrutiny or increased interest from the guards posted at various stations. He was a candidate for the office reserved for the second most powerful osteomancer in the realm, and he was being escorted to a private audience with the first most powerful. On such occasions, word must spread through the palace. There were probably bets placed on whether or not Paul would return from the audience with all his bones still inside his skin. Daniel would have hedged and wagered both ways.

Higher and higher they climbed, and when his hamstrings burned and he was certain they must have reached the top of the tower, the staircase continued. Finally, they reached a door. Not a grand thing, just another pane of blue glass, hiding whatever it hid. The guard captain stood away and clear of it.

"You are to enter, my lord."

"What, you're not coming with me, stalwart captain?"

"Your presence is commanded, my lord, not mine."

Daniel put his hand on the door handle. It was all of one piece with the door, either crafted by an expert glass master or formed through some esoteric geological process, and touching it, Daniel found he did not wish to go any farther.

He had faced a Hierarch before. On the last occasion, he'd walked away with his opponent's still-beating heart clutched in his hands. If he desired a throne, he could be the Southern realm's Hierarch now, and this would be a meeting of two kings.

He did not fear her power. He feared making a mistake.

He couldn't remember if he was supposed to bow to her on the left knee or the right knee. What had Moth told him? The left knee. Yes, that was it. He was pretty sure.

He pushed open the door.

The chamber was high and claustrophobically narrow. Not a place for large assemblies. More for private audiences. The walls leaned inward, soaring to a point some fifty feet above. A single horn anchored to the floor rose with graceful undulations. Daniel had never seen such a thing, had no idea what gigantic creature it might come from, and under ordinary circumstances, it might have drawn all his fascination. But at its pinnacle, more felt than seen, sat the Hierarch on a throne. There were familiar magics in her smell, dragons and griffins and mammoths and monsters of sea and mountain and underground, but even stronger smells of osteomantic creatures unknown.

Daniel dropped to his left knee. "Your Majesty."

There was no answer, just a rush of air. Whether it was wind from outside or the breathing of a colossal animal, Daniel couldn't tell. At last, a voice commanded him to rise, and he obeyed.

He craned his neck, peering up at the figure on the throne. He saw black skirts draped over the top of the horn. White hands rested on the bone-white arms of a throne.

"I see a great deal from here," the Hierarch said. A black hood concealed her face. "I see out across my realm, the waves battering my shores, and all the pinpoints of light, and all the blackness between."

Somewhere, out in all the lights and the blackness, Cassandra and her team were working to find Sam. Daniel looked at the opaque glass walls and grew afraid for them once more.

"Who are you?" the voice demanded, like bats shrieking from a cave.

"Your Majesty. I am your servant Paul."

"I knew Paul. He is the man I sent afar, to build me a firedrake, and to sit at my right side. To wield my weapons, and to be my weapon. And, one day, to climb my throne, to take my crown, and leave me to my rest. That was Paul. But who is this man at my feet? You are not the man I sent. You are not Paul, the Hierarch's flame. You are not Paul, my finder of secrets."

Daniel readied himself for the fight. He called up sense memories of kraken, of bear, of mastodon and monoceros, of dragons and spiders, every magic he'd ever eaten, all the magic he'd breathed, all the magic he'd consumed from the Southern Hierarch's heart. He let it remain in his bones.

"You are a different Paul. You are a Paul who hides in his library rather than banging on the doors of my throne room until I let him in. You are a Paul who cannot rule his own house. A Paul who lets scavenger beetles attempt to assassinate him. You were to be my dragon-crafter, and my dragon is lost."

Daniel let out a breath he hadn't been aware he'd been holding.

He was still okay. She still thought he was Paul. Just not Paul as she remembered him.

"I remain your servant, Majesty."

The silence was long, and air moved around him. He could almost feel molecules being tugged from his body and drawn to the presence high above him. She was smelling him.

"You are not the High Grand Osteomancer I wished for. Not yet. If you wish to be, you will have to fight for it."

He bowed. "Your Majesty."

A full minute passed before Daniel realized the Hierarch was gone. A vanishing magic, or a hidden portal. It didn't matter. He'd been dismissed.

The guard captain opened the door for him and remained some paces behind as he returned to his suite.

He would be named High Grand Osteomancer, and he would take the *axis mundi* and run away with it, and no one would stop him. And if he had to fight both Dorings or even the Hierarch herself, he would.

His hands shook, but not with fear, and he wondered what their hearts tasted like.

EIGHTEEN

To climb out of a sewer grate on a bright, blue day felt more like an announcement than an infiltration. Gabriel couldn't help but feel conspicuous as he and Max and Cassandra emerged from an alley near the corner of Clay and Stockton after days of creeping through dark tunnels and navigating underground rivers. The sun warmed his face, and his spine and shoulders were happy to have traded his heavy pack for a lighter tool bag.

They melted into the lunchtime crowd. The men filling the sidewalks and getting on and off the elephant-drawn coaches wore a lot of tweed—coats, trousers, vests, and hats. Their socks were argyle. The women wore hats festooned with netting and cherries and little apples and feathers.

In a white, collarless, button-down shirt, gray cap, short jacket, and trousers tucked into boots, Gabriel felt ridiculous, a feeling made worse by Cassandra and Max wearing identical outfits. But Cassandra had picked their wardrobes, and he had to trust her. They were costumed as "fixits," registered roving repairmen and -women who were paid a government salary to take care of whatever small jobs needed doing, whether on public lands or private.

Marking the condition of the well-paved streets and sidewalks, the colorful bursts of fresh flowers in baskets hanging from the lampposts, the lack of broken glass and graffiti, Gabriel wondered if he should implement such a system back home.

Cassandra kept them moving. Escalators with lacy wrought-iron rails took them up to the sky-cable platform, where they boarded a car. Gabriel tried to imitate Cassandra's nonchalance, holding on to a strap near the back and gazing vacantly out a glassless window as the city passed below. Keeping his gaze vacant was the biggest challenge. This was Gabriel's first time outside the Southern realm, and he'd dreamed of visiting San Francisco since he was a child.

He drank in the views, the terraced buildings of Chinatown with their half-authentic Oriental filigree, rebuilt after the 1904 Earthquake War; the solid white-stone edifices and domes of government buildings and museums and skycar stations; the narrow Queen Anne houses lining the steep streets, painted in canary and flamingo and robin's-egg colors.

The Golden Gate Chain stretched across the strait between the San Francisco Peninsula and the Marin Headlands, its gigantic links blazing orange against the blue Pacific. Outside the chain, crane barges lifted cargo containers off a Siberian-flagged ship. Formations of tugs waited to tow the barges through the gaps in the chain guarded by sea patrol gunships.

Gabriel sighted the lush, green belt of Golden Gate Park, the Hierarch's seat of power. Her Jewel Palace soared like a stained-glass candle above her transplanted sequoias.

Max leaned toward the window, taking quiet, controlled inhalations. Gabriel wished he could smell all the new aromas Max did—a stew of new foods, new magics, distinct strains of sourdough yeast from the bakeries.

Los Angeles could be a disheartening sprawl with no semblance of rational layout. But Gabriel had spent countless hours poring over canal maps to understand and maintain and expand the mandala, and he'd learned to appreciate L.A.'s beauty, like dragon fire, perilous and apocalyptic. San Francisco was different, neatly contained by its hills, its bays, the Pacific Ocean. This was a place he could get his arms around.

They disembarked and walked a few blocks to arrive at Kapp & Street's Tamale Grotto and Refined Concert Hall. Above the door hung a bronze plaque emblazoned with the city's motto: GOLDEN IN PEACE, IRON IN WAR. A thin veneer of patriotism on the outside of a building probably didn't do much to deflect suspicion of illegal activity inside, but it couldn't hurt.

Before entering, Cassandra gave the team a last bit of coaching. "I know this isn't anyone's first piñata party, but I've been to this particular party before, and as dangerous as these people look, it's just show. They're actually far more dangerous than that. They smell something they don't like, they'll beat us to jelly before we can say, 'Please don't beat us to jelly.' Max, you'll be smelling all kinds of bone, a lot of it probably unfamiliar. So, keep it to yourself. I don't need reports."

"Are you sure you don't want to go in alone?" Max said. "I actually wouldn't mind a lunch break."

Max did his best to hide residual pain from the gunshot wound, but the steep streets presented him with a cruel challenge.

"My contact has her own hounds," Cassandra went on. "They'll smell you and everyone else on me, and before they'll deal with me, they'll want to know who I'm working with."

"No lunch, Max," Gabriel said.

"And you," Cassandra concluded, fixing on Gabriel, "just try not to do anything stupid."

Gabriel waved at her. "Chief Water Mage of the Southern Kingdom, Master of the Mandala, Bringer of Waves, Quencher of Thirst, Giver of Life. I'll try not to trip over a chair."

Cassandra knocked. The door was answered by a man Gabriel took for a cook by his apron and meat cleaver. He wore a necklace made up of dark lumps—dried fruit, or nuts, or roots, or desiccated animals, or fingers.

"Auntie know you're coming?"

"Auntie never knows I'm coming," Cassandra said. "That's not how Auntie and I work."

The man considered this, if raising and lowering his cleaver could be interpreted as consideration.

"Auntie's not here" was his verdict. "Make an appointment."

"Auntie is here. Auntie is always here. Let us up."

"Let you up? Let you past Emerson the Knife? Show the world you can get past him without paying Emerson's price? Southern girl's got thin brains, she thinks Emerson the Knife will allow this." Emerson smiled. His teeth were sharpened to points. He drew a finger along the edge of his cleaver—his none-too-spotless cleaver—and blood streamed down the blade like melting candle wax.

Cassandra was a model of patience. "I'll pay your price."

Gabriel watched with surprise and then dread as Cassandra extended her hand, as if offering it for a kiss. She let an object fall from her palm. The man, Emerson, turned his cleaver flat and caught it in the slick of his own blood. It was a withered, purple-black thing, and whatever it was, Emerson grinned sharp teeth, pleased.

He stepped aside.

"Every time, Emerson. We go through this every time." Cassandra climbed the stairs.

Gabriel followed. "What was that?"

"It's a mummified osteomancer who died in the form of a sparrow. They don't come cheap."

"Oh, come on, I know my bone magic, and that's not possible."

"More than is dreamed of in your philosophy, water mage."

Upstairs was a wide and cluttered space of worn furniture and ceiling fans that did little to freshen the stale air. A brood of monsters lived there.

Gabriel, who took comfort in numbers and neat columns and rows, tried to count them all—the ones with fur-covered faces, the ones with more than two eyes, the ones with claws and the ones with tusks and the ones with horns, the ones with blue veins visible beneath butter-yellow skin, the ones with scales, the ones in a rubber tub of water flapping wing-arms like stingrays, all contributing to an anarchy of chirps and clicks and whistles. They were the size of children.

Gabriel had never seen so many humans bodily transformed by magic in one place, and now the idea of dying in the form of a sparrow didn't seem so implausible.

And there was Auntie, an ordinary-looking woman of fifty or so, with black hair and strong hands and dark circles under her eyes. She seemed harried.

Max stood ramrod straight. All the new smells stressed him.

Cassandra had briefed the team on what to expect here. Auntie was a purveyor of osteomantic materials, with supply lines to Russia, Africa, the Far East, even to explorers of esoteric Antarctic magic. No one was quite certain about the origins of her children. Orphans, some said. Experiments, said others. Quite possibly both were true.

"I'm not doing business today." She struck Gabriel as brusque but not unfriendly. He sympathized, knowing what it was like to find his days more full of things needing done than hours in which to do them.

Cassandra patted the head of a girl who came up to her on four legs, sniffing her thigh. "I'm not here on usual business."

Auntie lifted an infant from a crib, and Gabriel caught a glimpse of golden, faceted eyes before Auntie wrapped it up in a swaddling blanket. "Very well," she said with an exasperated sigh. "I can give you five minutes. Beatrice, watch your brothers and sisters."

"Okay," the four-legged girl said.

Auntie took them into her kitchen. The baby mewled, but Auntie quickly put a stop to it with a bottle from one of her apron pockets. "You've always come to me alone, Cassandra, and now you're working with people. A hound. And a clerk of some kind. You're not here on trade. What kind of information are you looking for?"

"I'm looking for unusual movement of osteomancy, especially to large places. Big factories or warehouses. Shipyards hidden from public view. Airship hangars."

"What kind of osteomancy?"

Cassandra handed her a list that made Auntie raise her eyebrows.

"This has the look of a major project. Are you trying to be the customer or the dealer?"

Cassandra sidestepped the question. "The activity may be opaque to most, but you have children all over, eyes and ears in every corner of the city. Have they mentioned anything like this?"

"You exaggerate my reach."

"I saw three of your children just on the ride over here. They were on the same skycar as us."

Gabriel didn't know if she was bluffing.

Cassandra reached into her bag. "I can pay."

But Auntie handed Cassandra back her list.

"I don't sell my children's services, and I'm busy enough with my own affairs."

Gabriel thought Cassandra might start pushing, but instead, she seemed to accept Auntie's decision as final.

"Things do seem a little more chaotic around here than usual," she said.

Auntie burped the baby. "I've never had so many all at once, and we're moving house."

"Moving? But you've been here for almost a century."

"That's the problem. Old house. The walls are solid, and they're clean of bugs and rats, but the plumbing is shot. The toilets are backed up and the water pressure is but a drizzle. It's not a fit place for children."

"Where will you go?"

"That's a very good question, my newt."

Gabriel saw an opportunity.

"I might be able to help you with the plumbing."

"I've had fixits and plumbers in here enough, and it's all the same verdict: They have to tear the walls out and replace all the pipes. They say it'll take months."

"Just the same, I'd like to see what you're dealing with."

Auntie gave him a what-have-I-got-to-lose shrug and pointed him to a bathroom. After a quick inspection of the horror show he came back out. He dug into his pack and found a small brass cube. Pipe threads were drilled into two of its faces. On the inside was a precision-cut mandala.

"What if I fixed your plumbing problems?"

"With that little doohickey?"

"It's a puzzlebox valve. With this, I can get your water running strong and clean. And I can do it right now, in minutes.

No ripping out walls. No need to move house. Would you reconsider our request?"

Gabriel watched hope and skepticism fight a battle on Auntie's face.

"Fix my pipes for me, and I'll put my children to work."

Gabriel tossed the cube in the air and caught it. "I'll need a bucket and some rags."

"He's serious?" Auntie said to Cassandra. "He can really do this?"

"He can. He's pretty good with water."

The graceful winged pyramid of the Transamerica building glowed like an ember in the sunrise. To the west, the Golden Chain and the Marin Headlands remained in shadow. Yet, the Hierarch's palace blazed in jewel tones, as if whatever the sun and sky did wasn't relevant.

While Gabriel marveled at the skyline, Max walked ahead of him, sniffing the air all around. Cassandra had brought the team to the waterfront to give Max a chance to scent the warehouses and piers and docked ships. The marina bristled with the masts of yachts and fishing charters, and out on the harbor, a container ship eased past the sea-battered and guano-splattered rock of Alcatraz Island.

"Looks like his leg's improving," Cassandra said to Gabriel.

"Does it?"

"He's moving better than you are."

They'd spent the night sleeping in a vacant apartment on a cold, hardwood floor, and Gabriel's back hadn't yet rebounded. Crouching through tunnels and mud had killed his feet and knees and carrying his backpack left his neck and shoulders feeling like sharp rocks.

He observed Max's gait. "He's in pain, actually. He just isn't showing it. He never does."

"Is there something wrong with showing it?"

"He grew up in the kennels. A hound that can't hunt gets put down."

"You saved him from the kennels, didn't you?"

Saved him? Gabriel supposed he did. But he hadn't meant to. He'd simply needed Max for a job. Now, he needed Max for many things.

A group of homeless kids clustered in front of a pier warehouse. Most of them huddled on the ground, sleeping, but a few passed around a loaf of bread. A small figure in a hoodie weaved around his friends on a skateboard until deliberately swerving into Cassandra.

She barely nudged him away and kept on walking. The skater continued in the opposite direction, leaving his friends behind.

"What was that?" Gabriel asked her. "Pickpocket?"

"Just the opposite. He was one of Auntie's orphans. And he gave me something." She handed him a slip of paper, a fortune cookie fortune.

> *Treasures are found inside walls, but truth is found without.*

And on the opposite side, an address.

"I suppose this means something to someone who knows what things mean," he said.

"It's a puzzle. On one side, a place, on the other side, an admonition that you can't find truth in places."

"That last thing I said about things that mean something to someone: I'm saying it again."

"Auntie's given us a source with information. But not necessarily a source we can trust."

"I like toilets better than people," Gabriel said, following along. Cassandra picked up the pace as if she knew where she was going.

A narrow alley connected a pair of Barbary Coast back streets. Signs and banners in Mandarin blocked the bit of sky between the centuries-old brick buildings. Laundry hung from fire escapes. The alley contained trading companies, the headquarters of a few benevolent societies, and a printer's shop. Also, tucked between some buildings with no signs, was an attorney's office matching the address the boy had given Cassandra.

Cassandra told Max to stay outside in case she and Gabriel required a cavalry. A good idea, but as Gabriel climbed a staircase barely the width of his shoulders, he wished he could have stayed behind with the cavalry as well.

Stenciled on a frosted-glass door was LI & SAUL, ATTORNEYS-AT-LAW.

Cassandra tucked a throwing dart against her palm and knocked.

"Come in," said a woman's voice.

Cassandra entered first and fluttered her hand behind her back to signal Gabriel to follow her into the tiny office. A single window afforded a view of trousers and linens hanging from a line strung across the alley.

Behind a desk sat a Latina woman in her fifties with iron-streaked black hair. She had a handsome face that didn't look like it spent much time arranged in a smile.

Something about the woman was familiar.

"I didn't call a fixit," she said.

"We got a message to come see you," Cassandra replied.

"Is it about a legal matter?"

Gabriel knew where he'd seen her before. It was long ago, and she was much younger then, and he'd seen her only in a photo. "You're not an attorney," he said.

"And you're not a fixit."

"Cassandra, meet Messalina Sigilo. Daniel's mother."

Cassandra managed not to betray her surprise, and Gabriel wondered if she'd fling a dart into Messalina's eye. He wouldn't try to stop her.

Messalina offered a handshake that Cassandra did not return. "Cassandra Morales. I've wanted to meet you for a long time. And Gabriel Argent, the great administrator. Where's your hound, Mr. Argent?"

"You're Messalina Sigilo," Cassandra repeated. "Mom of the year."

"Yes, girl, I am. I hope we're not going to display any unseemly competition between a man's mother and his girl-friend. There are so many more interesting things we could talk about. I understand you killed Otis Roth."

"Who I did or didn't kill is none of your business."

"It must be very freeing to act with no regard to ethics, morality, or consequence."

"I didn't say I'm free from consequence. I just said it's none of your business."

"Between you and your god, then?"

"Between me and none of your business."

"Well, my dear, I wish you a long life before your consequences catch up to you."

Cassandra shrugged. "Objects in the mirror are usually closer
than they appear."

At first, Gabriel thought Cassandra was just using hostility
as a tactic, but he was mistaken. Cassandra's animosity for Sigilo was palpable. And this was too small an office for kicking
and punching and throwing darts and probably gunplay to
erupt without him catching a stray fist or bullet.

"Do you work for Auntie, or does Auntie work for you?"
he asked, eager to change the subject.

"What would be your guess, Mr. Argent?"

"I don't have to guess. You came down from the North
to Los Angeles all those years ago as a spy. You insinuated
yourself into the Ministry of Osteomancy, met Sebastian
Blackland, one of the South's most powerful and innovative
osteomancers, got him to marry you, and used Otis's smuggling network to send samples of his work back to your masters. Auntie is a black market magic trader with a network of
Dickensian orphans all through the city. Of course she works
for you."

Gabriel stopped himself. He was on the verge of feeling
smug. One should never feel smug in the presence of Messalina Sigilo. She hadn't liked his narrative, and he wondered if
he'd suffer because of it. Sniper bullet through his temple,
maybe. Anvil falling on his head. Poisoned anvil, probably.

"Mr. Argent has it in crude outline," she said, addressing
Cassandra. "But the details are important. I didn't make Sebastian marry me. We fell in love. We got married. As people do.
We had Daniel together. We loved him and raised him. And when
the marriage stopped working, we separated. And we continued to love and raise Daniel."

"And you continued to spy on Sebastian Blackland and report on his work," Gabriel said. "As spies do."

"Yes, I understand your outrage over that, Mr. Argent, because the Southern Hierarch's rule was fair and just, and your loyalty to him was so strong that you helped Daniel assassinate him."

"I didn't help much."

"Another thing Mr. Argent left out: I had two sons. Paul was my son, every bit as much as Daniel. I loved both my boys."

"One of them you loved enough to take with you to the North," Cassandra said. "Daniel, you abandoned."

Messalina glanced down at her desk. Cassandra had touched a raw spot. When Messalina spoke again, she seemed a little less sure of herself.

"After the Hierarch's purge, the families of the high-ranking osteomancers were targeted. I was Sebastian's wife. Daniel was his son. We both would have shared Sebastian's fate. So what choice did I have? I went North."

"You took Paul. You left Daniel. With Otis." Cassandra said Otis's name as if it was a foul piece of meat to be spit out.

"Daniel was hunted by a kingdom, while hardly anyone even knew Paul existed. The golem-creation process wasn't perfect. Paul was brain-damaged. He wouldn't be of any use to Otis, so Otis wouldn't shelter him. But if Paul and I were seen crossing the border, the Hierarch would assume it was Daniel. He would stop looking for him. Daniel would be safer. And as for Paul, I could keep him close by and protected."

"Pretty simple math," Cassandra said.

"When you have poor options, you choose the least poor."

"When your options are that poor," Cassandra said, "you ask yourself why you made choices that led to such a bad menu of options.

Gabriel observed the corners of Messalina's mouth tighten in frustration. It was important to her that she make Cassandra understand, probably because she knew she couldn't make Daniel understand. But she was trying to convince someone whose own parents had sold her to Otis to settle a debt. Messalina wouldn't find much sympathy here.

"She's still left one thing out," Gabriel said. "Why did Paul exist at all? Why did she make a golem from her own son?" Messalina didn't answer, so Gabriel did. "Because they don't make golems in the North. That's Southern magic, and it was something the Northern Hierarch wanted. What better intel could she bring her masters than a living golem?"

Cassandra didn't have a cutting remark. She just shook her head.

Messalina claimed back the tiny bit of composure she'd lost. "Well, you seem to have all the answers about my time in Los Angeles. And what are you two doing in San Francisco?"

"I'm a smuggler," Cassandra said.

"And . . . ?"

"And nothing. I'm a smuggler."

Gabriel knew Messalina wouldn't be satisfied with that.

"Two days ago, I got word that my son Paul has returned to the realm," she said. "That he is, right now, at the Jewel Palace. Which should be happy news." She closed her eyes. "Oh, such happy news if he weren't dead. But he is. I saw Daniel kill his brother with my own eyes. So it is strange to hear that he's home. And, now, at the same time, here are Daniel's friends, looking for large movements of magic, osteomancers, and support personnel. At the very same time Daniel has infiltrated the Hierarch's palace." Her eyes grew hard. "You're looking for Paul's firedrake. Why?"

Well, at least there was something she didn't know.

"I don't feel like telling you," Gabriel said.

"I could make you."

Gabriel pointed at the fire sprinkler above Messalina's desk. "It would get very wet in here."

Messalina placed her hands flat on the desk. Her knuckles were calloused, her fingers marked with old scars.

"We want different things, Mr. Argent, but that doesn't mean we can't all get what we want. You want to secure the firedrake for the safety of your realm. I want to secure Daniel's safety. And Daniel wants to save the Southern Hierarch's golem."

"Sam," Cassandra said. "His name is Sam."

Gabriel caught movement through the window behind Messalina's back. Max stood on the fire escape across the alley. He had no rifle, just his pistol, but he was a good shot, and the distance between the bore of his gun and the back of Messalina's head was less than twenty feet.

"What are you proposing?" Cassandra asked.

Messalina clasped her fingers. "I'm not proposing anything. You'll hear from me."

"When?"

"Not before tomorrow morning. I have a dinner engagement tonight."

The conversation was over.

"We'll look for you," Gabriel said.

Messalina swiveled in her chair to face Max across the alley. Max kept his aim.

"I mean to help you," Messalina said. "I mean to help Daniel."

Cassandra shook her head, and Max lowered his gun.

"Like Gabriel said. We'll look for you."

NINETEEN

D o you have a girlfriend?"

Sam and Annabel had been hiking through the fire-drake's brain in uncomfortable silence for a long time when Annabel posed the question.

"No. Not really."

"What about the girl on the mountaintop. Your friend. Em? It just seemed like you like her a lot."

"I do," Sam said, squeezing carefully past an electrically charged tendril. "Actually, I'm totally in love with her."

"But . . . ?"

"But we were too busy trying not to get killed to do anything else. We've never got to date. Not even once. I think that's what I'm saddest about. We've never taken a walk together just for the sake of taking a walk."

"That is sad," Annabel agreed. "But sad is good. It means you can still feel. It means you're still alive."

They maneuvered around a nest of pulsing brain junk.

"So, who have you eaten?"

"Me, personally?" Sam said, feeling a bit like he'd been ambushed. "Because if you mean who the Hierarch ate, it's a long menu."

"I mean you, personally."

"Oh. I ate the bones of a woman named Dolores. That's the only one." When Annabel didn't respond, Sam added, almost desperately, "She died in a car wreck, so I don't think that should count too much against me."

"Okay, that's fair," she said, much to Sam's relief. "I don't have anything against eating the dead. Any magic you gain from a dead osteomancer is magic they gained from something that preceded them in death. And good magic is rare enough not to waste." She stopped and looked at him, her face serious. "You're telling me the truth?"

He ducked under a low, pink, meaty branch. Was it a synapse or a neuron or something else? He knew even less about brain anatomy than he did about aeronautics. His scalp tingled as a pulse of light sizzled through the branch.

"I'm telling you the truth, Annabel. I've never killed someone to take their magic. Daniel hated that sort of thing. He raised me to hate it, too."

"I suppose a selfish person wouldn't have sacrificed his life to prevent people from being hurt by a weapon like a Pacific firedrake."

"That's right," Sam said. "I'm pretty much a hero. It should be obvious from my heroic physique."

She laughed. It'd been a long time since he'd heard a laugh.

"What about you? You said you learned your craft by finding an osteomancer's library. Were his remains part of the collection?"

"Oh, I wish. Somebody probably got there before me. But I've eaten plenty of other things."

"Such as?"

"I gorged myself in that library, Sam. Half-cooked bone, raw magic, I didn't care. I wanted to taste every kind of osteomancy there was. I couldn't get enough. And that was before I started working in the Ossuary."

"And what did you eat there?" Sam was afraid to ask, but he had to know.

"I told you, my work in the Ossuary involved hydra. You know how an osteomancer works. To perfect hydra magic, you have to eat a lot of hydra. I figure that's why the Hierarch ate me. Instead of giving that magic to the troops fighting his war, he gave it to himself." She stopped to assess him. "Do you see where I'm going with this?"

"Yes. I think so. Actually, no, probably not."

"I'm hydra essence, Sam. Regeneration. The Hierarch ate me. You were generated from the Hierarch. Along with the other osteomancy you inherited from the Hierarch, you got my hydra magic. You got me. When you jumped into the firedrake's magic soup and dissolved, you must have reached for your hydra magic to save yourself. You reached deeper than you probably thought was possible. Your body was gone, but your magical essence survived, in here." She tapped one of the brain tendrils with her stick of bone. "And by reaching for me, you brought me here, too."

They walked on awhile, Sam trying not to let on that he was watching her face.

"You seem remarkably okay with this," he said at last.

"We're magical constructs traipsing about the insides of a Pacific firedrake configured like a bomber made of meat. You've just got to roll with this stuff, Sam."

Sam found himself not quite able to roll.

"We're not really alive, are we?"

Annabel came to a stop and faced him. "Of course we are. I don't feel like I'm something you made. I feel autonomous.

I feel like I'm inside my own body. Like my thoughts are inside my own head. Don't you feel that way?"

"I guess. Yeah."

"But you're not. You're magical trace elements. You're the vapors of what's left of you."

"This is making me feel fairly awful. Can we talk about something else?"

She resumed her brisk pace.

"What I'm saying is: You still have consciousness. And a conscience. You have intentions and morals. That's more alive than many people I met before the Hierarch ate me."

Sam liked when people said nice things about him. And he liked that he could still like things. He didn't think much about morals and ethics, except he knew he had some decent ones, and the man who created him did not.

He realized he should say something nice and encouraging to Annabel, preferably something that would help her feel a little more alive, and he was about to do exactly that when she gasped.

"Oh my god."

Like a fly caught in a spider's web, an emaciated giant hung in a tangle of trunks and branches. Ribs as thick as baseball bats pushed against mushroom-white flesh. Limp white hair hung in his face. From the top of its head to its clam-shell toenails, it was twelve of fifteen feet tall.

Sam and Annabel crept closer.

"Is it alive?" Sam hoped the answer would be no.

But then the giant shuddered. Pulses of light flowed through the webbing, traveled along the giant's limbs, up his neck, crackling around his head like a crown of electricity.

Sam reached for Annabel's wrist. "I'm all for running away."

"Wait."

The giant raised his head. He blinked, staring out with eyes like fish bellies.

"Please don't go." Its groaning voice echoed through the chamber. It seemed to echo through Sam.

And Sam saw it then: The giant *was* Sam.

The planes of its face, the set of its brow, even the voice, all a version of Sam.

When the giant smiled and began climbing down from its web of brain tendrils, Sam grabbed Annabel's arm, and they raced through the white forest of the dragon's brain.

"Please don't go," the giant wailed. "I need your help."

"Don't listen to him," Sam said.

"Wasn't going to."

He didn't turn to look back, but Sam could hear the giant crashing behind them. When the nest of white limbs grew too dense to keep running, Sam and Annabel climbed.

"Please stop running. I just need your help."

"What for?" Sam didn't much care what for, but Daniel taught him that when people talked, they usually stopped paying as much attention to what was going on around them and started paying more attention to themselves. Getting someone talking could be a useful diversion if you wanted to palm a small item or make a getaway by chucking yourself out a window.

"Really, if you would just stop a moment."

The giant was directly below them now, reaching up with white fingers the length of Sam's forearms. Its teeth looked like shovel blades.

Sam stopped climbing. He motioned for Annabel to scrabble up above him, and once she was clear, he brought heat to his fingers and poured flames on the giant below.

Its shriek of pain was very satisfying.

Sam resumed the climb, the brain tendrils thinning to carrot-width vines. The traveling light pulses sent painful shocks through his hands.

"Please," the giant cried, pulling itself up on the web. "Please stop. I need you. I'm begging you."

There was a moment, just a second, when Sam pitied the sorrow in the giant's voice. How long had it been alone inside the brain, tortured by light pulses of thought and sensation? What kind of help did it need? What kind of help could Sam give it?

Of course he shouldn't help it at all. He knew what the giant was.

Just as Annabel Stokes was part of him, so was the giant.

It was the part of him that had melted out when he threw himself into the firedrake's gestational tank. It was the oldest part of him. The part of him that preceded himself. It was the part of him that created himself. The magic that Sam was born from.

It was the Hierarch, and it was the part of him that was awful.

Sam rained down more fire on it.

The giant's flesh reddened and blistered and charred. Bleeding, smoke curling from its body, the giant stretched and reached up with its long, scrawny arm, past Sam. White fingers closed on Annabel's ankle.

"Sam!"

"You smell so green," the giant said. "Is that hydra? Oh, yes, I think it must be. Just what I need."

"Let her go!" Sam screamed. He loosed more fire, but the giant didn't release Annabel. Like plucking a suction cup from a wall, he pulled Annabel away from the tendrils. He upended her and stretched his jaws wide, and he put Annabel's head in his mouth and bit.

She didn't scream, because she no longer could.

But Sam screamed as the giant chewed.

TWENTY

Daniel spent the day in his suite, contemplating his reassembled diorama of the treasury while practicing palming skills. He'd warmed up with coins, moved up to shot glasses, and was now working on making candles disappear.

Moth watched him. "You'll never be as good at that as Cassandra."

"The student does not always overtake the master."

Moth stopped watching Daniel's hands and now watched him. "You okay?"

Daniel moved some of the archer-stand-in toothpicks, using the movement to snatch up a six-inch candle and conceal it along his right wrist.

"Of course I'm okay."

"I said Cassandra's better at thiefcraft than you, and you didn't even get mad."

"Why would I get mad? She's better than you, too."

"I have the dexterity of a spider and the cunning of a rat. Also, thieving isn't hard if you just bang someone on the head and take their things. What I'm saying is, this is high-stakes stuff.

Sleight of hand isn't your game. I like it better when there's lightning shooting from your eyes."

Daniel reached up to scratch his head with his right hand and dropped the candle down the back of his shirt. "Hm."

"We haven't talked about your audience with the Hierarch."

"Yes, we did. Like I said, she's pretty scary, smells potent, and I didn't blow my cover."

"Yes, that is what you said," Moth agreed. "It's the stuff you're not saying that's bothering me."

Daniel stretched his back, retrieved the candle from his shirt, and hid it along his left wrist.

"She may have gotten to me a little," he admitted. "She made me feel . . . ambitious."

"Thinking of taking a crown as well as an *axis mundi* bone?"

"Maybe a little. But that's just magic talking, not my brain." Moving around some matchstick guards, he pushed the candle past his fingertips with his thumb and returned it to its original place. "Don't worry, I'm focused."

"Yeah. Okay." If Moth noticed the trick with the candle, he didn't say anything. "Better start getting dressed. You've got dinner in an hour."

Dinner was an intimate affair for thirty. Daniel was seated only two chairs down from the head of the table, where a pair of thrones of interwoven fangs remained empty, presumably awaiting the arrival of the royal couple. On his left, Professor Cormorant stuck his nose deep down his glass of white wine and was either closing his eyes in concentration or dozing. Across from him sat Cynara and Allaster Doring, both keeping their arms rigid at their sides as if struggling against the urge to drive their elbows into each other. They wore stiff, black military dress jackets plastered with ribbons and medals and family crests. Moth had quizzed Daniel on all their meanings and significance, but considering he was trying to plan a heist and worrying about Cassandra's team and fretting about Ethelinda and assassination attempts, he couldn't even keep track of the medals and ribbons affixed to his own jacket.

At Daniel's right was an empty chair. They didn't use place cards here, so the identity of his missing dining companion remained a mystery.

Other dukes and barons and generals filled out the table, waging a silent battle of scowls, suspicious squints, and ostentatious avoidance of eye contact. Butlers and footmen kept the wineglasses full and brought an appetizer of slivers that looked like light-colored oyster meat.

"Impressive work," Daniel said, indicating the stained-glass windows ringing the ceiling. They told a story in pictures, beginning at one end with a scene of devastation—a flaming city, buildings collapsed into piles of crumbled bricks and masonry, dead people and horses in the streets. In the next panel, a girl with skin rendered in golden glass emerged from a fissure in the earth. And damned if she wasn't wearing a halo. Other panels showed her quelling fires, healing the wounded, bringing back the dead. This was the benevolent Hierarch's rise to power.

Cormorant emerged from his wineglass. "I should think you'd find them impressive. They're by Nazaretti."

Allaster's smile was positively vulpine. "I'm sure my lord Paul recognizes her hand. I've always thought the domes of your bell towers were her finest work."

Daniel hadn't really taken notice of the stained-glass domes at San Simeon. Paul collected a lot of stuff in his big house.

"The reds in the flames are breathtaking," he said, only slightly changing the subject.

"Well, she made the pigment with her own blood. We'll never see her likes again."

Considering how many red panes of flame were in the windows, Daniel got a sense of why Allaster referred to her in the past tense.

Cormorant thoughtfully chewed a piece of his appetizer and closed his eyes in bliss. "Wherever did Her Majesty come by barnacle goose?"

"From the frozen Northern wastes." The voice belonged to a new arrival, and without turning around, Daniel knew who she was. He wasn't sure how he managed not to react.

No one stood as Messalina Sigilo took the vacant chair next to Daniel.

"My lords and ladies," she said. And then she turned to Daniel.

He'd known this moment would come. He couldn't expect to run around the Northern realm and not bump into his mother. Once he saw the empty chair next to him, he'd even suspected she'd end up sitting in it. He'd hoped otherwise.

And he knew this moment would hurt. Looking into her eyes was like looking into a mirror distorted by age. Her skin tone was his, only a little more freckled. Her nose was his, only never broken. People liked to remind him that he was Sebastian Blackland's son. But his mother had raised him till the age of twelve, and as painful as it was seeing his father murdered and eaten before his eyes, watching her take Paul by the hand and leave Daniel behind was worse.

But he expected this pain, and he was no longer a twelve-year-old boy. He'd made his own life. He'd taken on Sam and given him what his own parents couldn't.

What he didn't expect was the pain of seeing his mother's face staring back at him and not being able to read a single emotion, a single intention. Messalina Sigilo was very much alive, but for the first time, he felt her death.

"Mother," he said, with courtesy and feigned warmth.

If she blew his cover and called him Daniel he would flare with lightning and dragon fire. He would burn Allaster and Cynara and anyone else who moved to do him harm. He would fight the Hierarch's guards, and her consort, and even the Hierarch herself if he had to. He would go to war.

But if she called him Paul, he would just sit there and eat his shaved barnacle goose.

She nodded. "Son."

Two panels of the wall slid open where Daniel hadn't even noticed a seam. From a dark space—a closet, a vestibule, a passageway, or a yawning chasm—the Hierarch entered, with Lord General Creighton a pace behind.

Daniel had only glimpsed her during his audience, peering up at her high upon her throne. He assumed she'd be some kind of monster. But she wasn't so far removed from the girl depicted in the stained glass. Tall and regal, she was no beast or wraith. She wasn't constructed of exterior bone or armored skin plates. She wasn't covered in scales. She was a lovely, silver-haired woman apparently in her sixties, though, if history was to be believed, she was more than a century old. Her only badge of office was a simple diadem of silver set with a single griffin's claw.

The dinner party rose to their feet. Some, like the Dorings, stood gracefully. Others nearly fell over themselves, chair legs scraping on the glass floor.

Creighton pulled the chair out for his wife and liege, and the Hierarch took her place at the head of the table. Everyone took Creighton seating himself as the signal that they could stop standing at attention with backs so rigid that Daniel imagined them toppling like dominos.

Footmen in red livery flowed in and out of the room, bringing wines and plates of vivid purple mushrooms and gloppy soups and gelatinous swirls and the teeth of some herbivore prepared in a way that made them spongy and chewable. Every course was delicious, and Daniel would have given a lot to hang out in the Hierarch's kitchens.

The Hierarch set down her fork and dabbed her lips with a napkin. The footmen removed plates of crunchy black quills, whether or not people had finished eating them.

There was an interval of silence, and the air pressure seemed to decrease, like in the moments before a storm.

"My lords and ladies, we have a problem," the Hierarch began. "Arrayed before us we find our most respected osteomancers, four of whom we see fit to consider as our High Grand Osteomancer, an office that has sat vacant for too long. We would be displeased to see it continue as such. Fortunately, our realm is rich with talent. We have Lord Professor Cormorant, the most learned of our osteomancers, whose scholarship has advanced our art further than any other of our subjects we can name."

Rather than swell with pride, Cormorant seemed to shrink a little. He really seemed not to want a promotion.

"But the duties of the office are not only those of the scholar," the Hierarch continued. "We depend on our High Grand Osteomancer's counsel in matters of war, and internal security, as well. And is that where Lord Cormorant's passions lie?"

Cormorant issued a tiny grunt, as if to say, "Hell, no."

"As for Lord Allaster Doring, no one could question his passion for security and war. Nor his power. But, though we are not prejudiced against youth, we worry that Lord Allaster's wisdom lags behind even his modest age."

Daniel watched Allaster's Adam's apple bob as he swallowed.

"We are most delighted and relieved to welcome Lord Paul back to our bosom. Only the Lord Professor's knowledge of magic surpasses his, and his hunger for innovation is unmatched. A man who can build a living dragon from scraps is certainly fit to take a unique place beside our throne." She paused, and everyone seemed eager for the other shoe to drop. Daniel was, too. Her judgment determined who would be touched by the *axis mundi* scepter.

She went on: "But what are we to make of a man who both makes a dragon and loses it?"

That could have gone worse, Daniel thought as the Hierarch turned finally to Cynara.

"And we come to Lord Cynara, whom we have loved well since her birth. If she built a dragon—and we believe she could—we have confidence she would not then lose it. We do not, however, have full confidence that she would turn over such a wondrous creature to her Hierarch."

Her tone was that of a gentle scolding, but she'd just said that she suspected Cynara capable of treason. Cynara opened her mouth as if to protest, but apparently thought the better of it when the Hierarch stood abruptly. The dinner party scrambled to their feet again.

"The investiture is in two days," she said. "You shall know of our decision then."

When she returned to the black recess behind the glass panels, Daniel felt the air pressure rise again. His shoulders and neck ached.

More dishes were brought out, and the table hummed with conversation. Cormorant talked about wine and grapes, and Allaster made a joke, and Cynara asked Daniel's mother about espionage intelligence in the Southern realm and Daniel's mother countered by asking about Ethelinda.

When the dinner came to a merciful end, Daniel's mother touched his arm. "The moon bridge," she whispered in his ear. "Tonight at two."

Daniel went alone to meet her in the palace gardens. Japanese maples provided an illusion of concealment, but Daniel knew guards lurked among the croaking frogs in the dark. His mother was waiting for him on a decorative bridge arched over a pond sprinkled with cherry blossoms. Daniel drew close enough to touch her, but he didn't offer an embrace. He knew that made her sad.

"We can speak freely, Daniel. We're surrounded by meretsegar serpent dust. No one can overhear."

Daniel smelled dry bones and sand.

"You didn't fink on me at dinner."

"Of course not."

"No. Of course not. If you were going to tell the Hierarch I'm not Paul, you wouldn't do it in front of the court sorcerers. Secrets are your coin. You wouldn't splurge it on that bunch."

"I wouldn't do it because you're my son."

"I honestly don't know what that means."

"It means I love you."

Insects chirped. Water from the streams and fountains trickled in the night.

His mother looked into the pond, as if searching for something in the dark waters.

"Do you want to hear it now?" she said.

"Hear what?"

"The explanation. My story. The reason I abandoned you."

There was a time when Daniel did. All those years, being

raised by Otis Roth instead of a parent, always feeling there was a big, empty pit beneath him where the life he was supposed to have led had fallen away.

But he'd had help. He had Otis's other orphans. He had Moth and Cassandra and Jo and Punch. He had friends.

"You know," he said, "I look at your face, and I recognize it. I know your name. And I'm not going to say I don't have a mom, that my mom is dead. Because here you are. And I'm not even going to say that I don't care why you left me behind with Otis. Why you took Paul with you and not me. It's not that I don't care. Of course I care. You're my living mother, and you orphaned me. But right now, at this moment, I don't have time to care. You are not the most important thing to me. My pain is not the most important thing to me. I have a job to do, and all I care about is how your presence complicates it." Moonlight threw stark shadows across her face. "I'm sorry. I'm sure you had a whole speech worked out."

"Don't be petty. You must want an explanation."

"Not as much as you want to give it to me. But you don't get that. You don't get to explain. You don't get to let it off your chest. You don't get a chance to make me understand."

"This is the punishment you've chosen for me, Daniel?"

For a long time, neither of them spoke. Water flowed beneath their feet.

"If you're ever ready to hear my explanation, Daniel, ask Cassandra. She was willing to listen."

"When did you see Cassandra?"

"Today. She's in the city with Argent. And Argent's hound. They haven't found the dragon yet. I don't think they can without my help."

"Did you hurt them?" Heat came to his lungs.

"I'm a spy. That doesn't make me a monster. I want to help you, Daniel."

She reached out to touch him and he flinched away.

"How can you help?"

She closed her eyes, gathering herself, and he understood that it was costing her to stand here, so close to her son, not being able to get past the walls he'd erected to keep her out. He wouldn't even permit her to explain. He wouldn't even be angry at her. All he would talk to her about was business. All he would give her was coldness. It must be hurting her a lot. When she opened her eyes again, he saw how much.

"Your friends are on the right track," she said, "looking for large movements of osteomancy to a place big enough to house a dragon. And there is a lot of magic being moved around. The problem is, it's being moved to multiple locations, to the airship fields south of the city, to a flotilla of container ships docked off the coast, a few other places. Either someone's deliberately set up some decoys, or else there're multiple large-scale projects under way."

"Don't you know? You're the Hierarch's spymaster."

"That was a long time ago," she said. "And Paul's failure to deliver the dragon hasn't helped my position. I'm no longer privy to all the machinations of the Hierarch and her court. And there are a lot of machinations."

"Then what's your best guess?"

"I'd say the Presidio. It's got easy water access, large warehouse buildings, and they just got a delivery of two hundred feet of gleipnir chains."

"Gleipnir chains?"

"Not something you'd have seen in the South. It's an unbreakable compound."

"Just the kind of thing you'd need if you wanted to tie down a firedrake."

"Exactly." She smiled at him, proud.

Daniel made himself colder.

"My team needs better intel than that," he said. "I can't have them breaking into every possible facility in San Francisco."

"I just need a little more time," she said, encouraged. If Daniel wouldn't forgive her, then she'd have to settle for bonding with her son over a covert operation.

"How much time?"

"Two days. Maybe three."

"You have until the investiture the day after tomorrow."

She gave one brisk nod. Messalina Sigilo was a no-nonsense spy-mom.

He was ready to leave her here and go back to the palace, but hesitated.

"Just tell me one thing."

"Of course," she said, almost desperate. "Anything."

"Why are you helping me?"

"Because you're my son and I love you. Isn't that enough?"

"No. It's really not."

She drew a deep breath and exhaled it shakily.

"Well, accept it or not, that's my reason. But, no, it's not the only one. Paul was my son, too. I loved him. He gave his life trying to craft the firedrake. Call it foolish if you like. Call it inhuman. But he was my son, and this is what he would have wanted. I won't let the Hierarch keep his dragon as a toy."

He turned to go.

"Daniel, just one more thing. Ethelinda."

He stopped. "What about her?"

"When are you going to tell her that you're not her father?"

"Work in progress," he said, heading back to the palace.

TWENTY-ONE

W hat I would like to know, Paul, is precisely when you decided to make an enemy out of me."

Daniel and Cynara had been having a nice morning stroll through the palace gardens. Threads of fog softened the views and lent an authentic backdrop to the cloud forest. Daniel was admiring the pink polyps of fuchsia plants when Cynara made her accusation.

Taken aback, he fumbled for an adequate response. Lovers' quarrels were hard enough. Faking your way through one added an extra degree of difficulty.

"I'm not your enemy."

"Why haven't you taken yourself out of consideration? Why haven't you stepped aside for me? I don't understand your game. You can't really want the office for yourself." She looked at him with eyes like scalpels. "You were always about study. About pushing at the frontiers of magic. You wanted the power of osteomancy, but you never cared about power over people. You were the tweezers and the lens. I was the knife and hammer."

It disturbed Daniel how well Cynara had just described Daniel's father. Had there ever been a more powerful osteomancer who didn't want to be the Hierarch, or even hold a seat on the Council? All Sebastian wanted was a well-equipped laboratory and the freedom to work. Apparently, that's all Paul had wanted as well.

They came down the path into Sonoran desert. Saguaro cacti lurked behind the fog like sentries. A ship's horn wailed from nearby.

"You are not the man who left a year ago. I wish I had more time to let you become that man again, or to learn who this new version of you is. I mean that, Paul." She touched his hand, her fingers brushing across his palm and leaving a trail of warmth behind. "But the investiture is tomorrow. If the Hierarch names me, maybe there'll be some time for us yet. But if not, I will claim the Rite of Challenge."

The Rite of Challenge? There was a Rite of Challenge, for crying out loud?

"Isn't that a little extreme?" It sure sounded extreme to Daniel.

"You haven't left me much choice. Either I will be High Grand Osteomancer, or I will fight whomever the Hierarch names, be it my teacher, my brother, or the father of my child."

"And what if you lose?" If there was going to be a fight, then Daniel wanted to know what would happen to the loser.

"You think that's possible?"

"In a fight, anything's possible."

"Not if it comes down to tweezers against knife."

A figure came out of the fog, a man dressed in the green livery of Cynara's house.

"My lord," he said, out of breath. His face shone with sweat, even in this cold air. He graced Daniel with only the slightest head bob and turned his full attention back to Cynara. "It's Lady Ethelinda. Another attempt has been made upon her life."

There was a moment of paralyzed dread, surely just an instant in reality, but in that frozen moment, Daniel felt as if he'd fallen through the earth. He recognized the sensation, and the hollowness in his chest and gut. He'd felt the same way when he'd watched Sam plunge into a tank of raging firedrake amniotic fluid and thought he was dead. He looked at Cynara and saw the same horror and fear in her face.

They raced back to the tower.

Palace guards stood outside Cynara's guest apartments, but not within. A woman in a black housedress and white apron came up to Cynara. She was ordinary-looking, but magic curled off of her with powerful odors.

"Your daughter is unharmed, my lord." Her voice was rough with emotion. She must be Ethelinda's governess, the unmeltable one.

Cynara gathered herself, took a breath, and stood tall. She went in to see her daughter. Daniel followed.

Ethelinda was in the sitting room, working on a jigsaw puzzle. Controlled and graceful, Cynara lowered herself to her knees.

"Are you all right, my darling?"

Ethelinda nodded.

"Were you frightened?"

She shook her head. Cynara brushed hair off her forehead and planted a kiss, and they spoke in hushed tones.

Daniel went to the governess. "Where's palace security?"

"They were not informed, my lord. This is being handled by Lord Cynara's household."

"Good. Take me to Ethelinda's room."

The governess looked to her master, but Cynara was still fully occupied with Ethelinda. Reluctantly, she complied with Daniel's order.

Ethelinda's room was unfit for a child. The walls were opaque panels of dark green glass, almost black, and the furniture was all heavy slabs of wood. A few portraits of sinister old people glared from frames. Cynara never should have brought her here.

Daniel didn't spot the assassin's corpse immediately because it was strewn in parts across the room. One arm lay between the bed and the bedside table. Another had landed against the bathroom door, a trail of blood describing its trajectory. A leg lay near the wall across the end of the bed. The other lay on the black marble floor, bent at the knee into a bloody L.

Inside the tub, he found a woman's torso, with the head still attached.

He bent down and smelled the air around the assassin's open lips. There were essences of aranea, a creature whose closest living analogs were spiders.

The governess stood behind Daniel.

"Was she attacked in here or in bed?" he asked her.

"She was in bed. Still sleeping."

"And you?"

"Outside her door, in the vestibule."

Daniel didn't know this woman. Cynara trusted her enough to leave her alone with Ethelinda, but Daniel didn't really know Cynara, either. If it were up to him, Ethelinda would never be left alone. He'd load her in a car and haul her out to the remotest parts of the kingdom and beyond, never staying anywhere long, try his best to keep her a moving target. Just like he'd done with Sam.

Because, gosh, that had turned out so well.

Whether or not the governess was complicit in this, she'd done a good job of ripping the assassin to bits.

"Did she put up a good fight?"

"I wasn't there to see, my lord."

Now Daniel was confused. He gestured at the head and torso. "If this wasn't you . . ."

"Your daughter, my lord. She defended herself."

Daniel suppressed any reaction.

He returned to the bedroom and took another look at the dismembered limbs. Ethelinda was only four years old. One of the legs had struck the glass wall hard enough to leave a web of cracks.

A llaster laughed when Daniel demanded to know who was behind the assassination attempts. "Of course it was me."

Daniel had found him in the stables, about to set off on a chocolate-brown gelding for a morning ride around the palace grounds. Sunlight came through a patch in the fog to touch his hair with gold. In an open-collared white shirt tucked into tan riding pants, he was the picture of aristocracy.

"You're admitting this to me," Daniel said, unprepared for such an open confession.

"Well, who else would it be? Unless you're playing the game with someone else."

"The 'game.'" Daniel repeated the word with contempt, but he also meant it as a question.

Allaster's face grew serious. Maybe even sad. "I thought we could pick up where we left it before you went off to fool around with your patchwork dragon. And it was my turn, so I had your dinner poisoned. I'd tell you which one of your kitchen staff I paid, but if I developed a reputation for betraying the people who do my handiwork, then . . . well, you understand. Anyway, I waited. And waited. And waited. And you did nothing.

I found that vexing." He wagged a finger at Daniel. "So I sent the assassin to your room. And, yes, I know, I broke the rules. And I'm sorry for that. I guess. But what else could I do? You weren't playing your turn, so I took an extra. I thought I could smack you out of this boring lassitude you've been stuck in since you came back."

"All the assassination attempts. They were all you?"

Allaster frowned. He seemed confused.

"Just the two. Wait, have there been more?" The horse nickered, and Allaster ran a hand over its neck. "I suppose I owe you an apology."

"For trying to kill me? You think you should apologize for that?"

"I thought it would be a good way to welcome you back. It's schoolboy stuff, I know. But I suppose the closer one gets to the throne, the less time one has for games and old friends."

"The assassins. That was just a game."

"You've had a hard year, Paul, healing and recovering. I didn't anticipate it would injure your sense of humor so much."

Allaster put his foot in the stirrup and began lifting himself up to the saddle, but Daniel grabbed him by the shirt and threw him into the dust. The horse grunted and skittered away.

Allaster looked up at Daniel with a quizzical smile. "You're being violent."

"I'll—"

"Hit me with your little nubbin fist?"

"If you know me at all, then you know I can do much worse than that. I'll bury you, Allaster. Come at Ethelinda again, and even before Cynara gets to you, I'll bury you."

Allaster's face changed. He rose effortlessly back to his feet. "Ethelinda? Wait. You can't think I had anything to do with that."

Was Allaster playing Daniel? Was this part of his and Paul's game?

He looked sadly at Daniel and shook his head. "You really think I'd harm her? She's my niece, Paul. She's your daughter. Listen, I don't know what happened to you in the South, and you seem determined not to tell me. As you will. It's your business. But that doesn't mean we're strangers. We may have started off as rival apprentices. And we've had some bumps. And I'm not going to quite forgive you for everything you've done. But you brought us together. You, me, and Cynara. It was always us three, whether it was cheating on exams, or beating back other osteomancers. Cynara and I are family by blood, but you made the three of us family by choice. And you think I would hurt Ethelinda? You break my heart, Paul."

It had never occurred to Daniel that Paul might have friends. Close ones, as close as family, as close as Daniel was to Moth and Cassandra.

Allaster gathered his horse by the reins and mounted the saddle.

"Whatever happens at the investiture, Paul, just remember this: Whether we end up loving or hating each other by the time the sun goes down, there's always the chance we're both going to survive till the next morning. Let's make sure we can both live with whatever we've done."

TWENTY-TWO

Paul's field kit came in a briefcase of brushed aluminum. Precisely cut foam compartments kept all the little vials of powdered bone safe and snug, the tongs and thermometer and density calipers and balance and torch all fitting cleverly in place. This was luxury.

Daniel arrayed several items from the kit on the table. His hands craved work, because he knew it would help distract him from thinking about his mother. And as much as he didn't want to dwell on her, he wanted to ponder his inevitable conversation with Ethelinda even less. He was impatient for Moth to get back from his shopping trip.

He began by accumulating a little pile of bone, just pebbles and bits of grit, until he had a mass roughly equivalent to the *axis mundi* bone. He deposited it in his crucible and set the crucible on a tripod stand over Paul's torch.

The bones were all tiny fragments from various kinds of dragon—Colombian firedrake, western wyvern, Siberian yelbeghen. They didn't like to melt, so Daniel added a few drops of water spirit to give them encouragement. He set the torch for red-purple flame and left it to do its work.

"Ho, ho, ho, got your presents," Moth boomed, arriving

with shopping bags clutched in both hands. He set them on the table.

"Run into any troubles?"

"Only that I didn't want to come back to the palace. San Francisco's a really lovely town."

Moth unloaded the bags. There were mallets and hammers and pliers and tweezers, clamps and metal-bending tools, and an array of files and a soldering iron. There was a smaller bag containing four chunky, gold rings. Daniel weighed them in his palm.

"Where'd these come from?"

"Got them off a dead pirate. You want the fingers, too?"

"Pawnshop?"

"Yeah."

Most important, Moth had found him two books, both of them heavy slabs: *Slaker's Complete Manual of Lapidary* and a twin volume on making jewelry. Inside were pasted "City of San Francisco Library" stamps.

"You stole from a library?"

"Just what kind of man do you take me for?" Moth said. "I filled out a form and got a library card. You have these for nine days. And I better not get an overdue fine."

Daniel checked the dragon bones in the crucible. They were starting to soften.

"You still haven't told me what all this is for," Moth said.

"There's no way I'm going to be able to steal the *axis mundi* from the treasury. It's just too well guarded."

Moth frowned. "So you said. But we're good stealers, and I am always willing to employ my mastery of blunt force trauma."

"Well, sure, with a month of prep and a crew of dozens, we could maybe strongarm it."

"Instead, I'm a library patron. How do the books and junk fit in?"

"I'm making my own *axis mundi*. Or at least something that looks like it. That way, when I get invested as the High Grand Osteomancer—"

"You mean *if*."

"No, Moth. It's gotta be 'when.' There's no other way. The bone is in the scepter, and the scepter touches the new High Grand Osteomancer. So, that has to be me."

"And what if the Hierarch names someone else?"

"Then I'll be invoking the Rite of Challenge."

"The Rite of What the Hell?"

"It's a thing here. If you get passed up for a promotion you get a chance to prove yourself worthy."

"Like with a written exam?"

"No, it's an all-out fight."

"For crying out loud."

"You don't like my odds," Daniel said.

"That's between me and my bookie. Okay, then. What's next on our agenda?"

Daniel handed him a piece of paper on which he'd carefully drawn an exploded diagram of a device half the length of a pencil with a spring-loaded rod with a little hook on one end and a bladed tip on the other.

"It's a design for my new invention," Daniel said, proudly. "I call it the Blackland Popper."

"It looks like a dangerous penny whistle."

"You're holding it upside down."

Moth turned it. "Now it looks like a very horrible kind of catheter."

"I hope you contract ear cholera. It's a tool for doing heisty things. Do we have anyone handy on staff who can make things?"

Moth folded the paper and stuffed it in his pocket. "The

guy who winds your clocks has a knack. I'm sure he can handle it."

"Good." Daniel looked over the manuals and the tools Moth had brought him and felt some mix of panic and despair. "Okay, next job: We have to learn how to make first-class crown jewels. We begin with bezel mounting."

Moth went to pour himself a drink.

Morning light slanted through the windows of Daniel's suite like daggers in his eyes. He tried to calculate how many hours it had been since he'd last slept but gave up when he realized he was too tired to do the math. Moth snored in his chair at the table, his head pillowed on his crossed forearms.

Daniel stood, his spine cracking like thin ice. Today was a big day.

He took a hot shower. It wasn't just an indulgence: He couldn't afford to look like someone who'd been pulling all-nighters, scheming in the dark. He was supposed to be a prince of the realm on the verge of claiming his just reward. He shaved and dressed simply in a white dress shirt and black trousers. He was starting to get used to Paul's well-made clothes, the drapery and fit, the way they felt like more than just cloth wrappers. Daniel's wardrobe always came from charity thrift shops, but Paul was rich. He wondered if being High Grand Osteomancer came with a raise, and what Paul would have done with even more money.

Daniel bounced a grape off Moth's head.

"I will fucking kill you," Moth roared, his eyes bleary and enraged. Then he saw it was Daniel. He let his head drop back to the table. "Fucking kill you," he said again. "Where are you going?"

"Cynara's suite. I won't be gone long."

"Figured you'd give her one last chance to stab you in the back?"

"I think if she stabs me, it's going to be in the face. Don't worry, I'll be okay. I just need to have a conversation."

Moth yawned and rubbed his face. He slid his chair back and stood. "Not without me."

"Stay here, get some rest. Drink some juice. There's going to be a lot of running around tonight and I need you in top physical form."

"My physical form is the toppest, but it won't matter if you've got a knife poking out of your eye. I demand you see the wisdom in this."

"I do, but I need some more burnishing out of you."

Crafting the counterfeit *axis mundi* had taken Daniel all night, molding the melted dragon bones into something that looked authentic as long as one didn't really scrutinize it. Setting it in a border of gold from the melted pawnshop rings was actually the bigger challenge, but one at which Moth proved himself surprisingly talented.

Moth inspected the bone with a loupe and reached for a burnisher.

"Thanks," Daniel said.

"If you're not back in fifteen minutes I start breaking down walls."

"Twenty-five."

Moth grunted and burnished.

Daniel made his way to Cynara's suites. Her people were tense when he arrived, and they left him standing outside the entry for minutes, certain he was here to do their mistress harm.

He kept checking his pocket for the vial of lamassu bones he'd secreted there earlier. Here in the North, they called it the Sumerian sphinx. Paul had told him that.

The captain of Cynara's guard approached him. If looks could kill, Daniel would be a rotting corpse. There would be maggots and vultures.

"You may enter, my lord."

He found Cynara eating breakfast, slicing a honeydew melon with surgical precision.

"You're dressed early," she said. "Busy day?"

"I actually can't think of anything to do. The investiture's in, what, nine hours?" He checked Paul's watch.

"You kept it."

"Kept . . . oh, this?" She meant the watch. He hadn't given it much thought when putting it on. He'd found the watch in the same box with Paul's cuff links. Glancing at it now, it seemed familiar, the creamy white dial, the Roman numerals, the sharp points of the hands. Had his father worn a watch like this? Daniel hated the feeling of everything being at once so familiar and so alien.

"It's a good watch," he said.

"Do you remember what I told you when I gave it to you?"

Every time he talked to her, he felt they were fencing, only her blade was invisible and so sharp he never knew when he'd been cut. He wished she'd just throw her fork down and come for his head with a big, obvious swing.

"I don't, Cynara. I honestly don't remember what you said to me. I'm sorry. Remind me."

"I told you I loved you," she said. "And I did. I never told you a lie."

Daniel couldn't answer to that. Not to any lies Paul might

have told her, and not to the massive lies he, himself, had. He still didn't know if she was his enemy, but there was no escaping that he had made himself into hers.

"I came to see Ethelinda," he said.

Cynara took a bite of honeydew. "In her room."

"Will her governess let me pass?"

"Of course she will. Aren't you Ethelinda's father?"

He went to see Paul's daughter.

Four guards stood watch outside Ethelinda's door, as well as the governess.

"Still no progress finding out who's been trying to kill my daughter?" he said, making it an accusation.

The governess squared her shoulders. "This is not Lady Cynara's house, my lord, and her questions only go so far here. And if I may ask, my lord, have you made any progress determining who is trying to kill your daughter?" She made it sound like an accusation, too, and even more, a challenge.

And, no, Daniel hadn't come any closer to figuring it out. In fact, he'd barely tried. He couldn't save both Sam and Ethelinda. So, he'd chosen Sam.

But he still owed Ethelinda something.

"I'll see her now," he said, moving past the governess.

Ethelinda was in a tiny rocking chair by a gently crackling fire, gazing out the window. Daniel stood behind her. From here, he could see the bay, with just a bare hint of the headlands emerging from the fog.

"And what are we looking at with such rapt attention?"

"Things I can't see," Ethelinda said.

"How can you see things you can't see?"

He surprised himself at how much he sounded like his father, asking one of his koanlike questions for which he expected a single, concrete answer.

"You just look until you can see them," Ethelinda said, as if the answer were obvious.

"So? Anything yet?"

She turned to him, staring with unsettling intensity. "I haven't looked long enough."

Daniel paced the room, glancing at her toys and books and stuffed animals. Her mother must have brought trunks of her things, even her bed. He piled another log on the fire and worried it with the poker until he was satisfied with the strengthened flames.

"So, we haven't talked about what happened the other night. With the spider-person."

Ethelinda rocked in her chair, cradling a plush mallard in her lap. "I fought her."

"That must have been scary for you."

"I beat her. I killed her."

"I'm always scared when I fight," Daniel said. "It doesn't matter if I'm stronger, I'm always scared. Weren't you?"

The staff had done a good job of cleaning the blood and clearing out the body parts. Ethelinda's face was pink. Freshly scrubbed.

"I was scared. But Mommy says being scared doesn't mean you don't have to do the things you're scared to do."

Such good, bitter advice. Daniel picked up a stuffed rabbit. "Trade you for the duck?"

Ethelinda took her time considering this proposition.

"Okay," she said, and they made the swap.

He went to the window, his back to her. It was easy to transfer lamassu particles from the vial in his pocket to the fuzzy fabric of the rabbit. It didn't even require osteomancy. Just a thief's sleight of hand. He steeled himself and turned back to face her.

"Can you keep a secret?"

Ethelinda nodded. "I do all the time."

"But this is a big one. You can't tell anyone. Not even your mom. Can you keep a secret from her?"

"I do all the time," she said again.

"I'm leaving after tonight. After the investiture."

She didn't react to this. Paul was often not at home. This was only what she expected of him.

"You can come with me," he said.

She looked up at him, this little girl in a little chair with a plush rabbit, who'd ripped apart an assassin with her bare hands. What was it he was seeing in her eyes? Confusion? Hope in conflict with caution?

"Where are you going?"

"South," Daniel said. "The Southern realm."

"Is Mommy coming with us?"

"No."

"When will you be coming back?"

"I won't be coming back, Ethelinda. This time, I have to stay away. And if you come with me, Mommy won't be able to visit. And you won't be able to come back and see Mommy. Not for a very long time."

"Why do you want me to come with you?"

"Why do you think, Ethelinda?"

She should have been able to come up with an effortless answer. Why would a father want to be with his daughter? Because he loved her. Because he wanted to take care of her. And Daniel didn't love her, but he did want to protect her, because he'd killed her father, and he'd created a debt so deep he'd never pay it off. He could at least make some payments.

"You want me to come because it's dangerous here," Ethelinda said. "Because of all the people who want to kill me."

Life would be no safer for her in the Southern realm. It hadn't been for Sam.

"It might be a little safer," he said. "I'm stronger than your mom. And I have friends who will help me keep you safe. As safe as can be."

"Do I have to go with you?"

A funny question. He could have just abducted her. But Daniel was a thief and a murderer, not a kidnapper.

"No, Ethelinda. Of course not. You have a choice."

"Then I want to stay with my mommy."

Not "Mommy." *Her* mommy. There was something about the way she emphasized that, as if marking a clear line around herself and Cynara that left Paul on the outside. And if Paul was on the outside, then Daniel was even farther away.

"Well," Daniel said. "Then it's settled. Okay."

But things were not settled. He held the stuffed duck down near his waist where there was less danger of him accidentally inhaling the fumes coming off the lamassu particles.

"Want your duck back?"

She nodded. Daniel exchanged it for the rabbit, and osteomancy made contact with her chubby little hands.

"There's something else I need to tell you, Ethelinda. There's really no easy way to say it."

She looked at him, and for the first time since meeting her, he finally understood something about her: She wasn't stoic. Her flat, emotionless responses to attempted assassinations, to yanking limbs from sockets, weren't because there was something strange or wrong about her. She wasn't broken. She was just in a constant state of terror. And Daniel should have recognized it sooner. He'd been the same way after the Hierarch murdered his father. After he'd seen his father eaten, skin, flesh, muscle, and bone. The terror had never subsided.

"Ethelinda," he said, "I'm not your dad."

Her face registered no change, but she clutched the duck tighter. Holding on for dear life.

"I'm like his brother," Daniel went on. "But closer than that. We're made of the same flesh. The same osteomantic essence."

"You're a golem?"

"Something like that."

"Where's my daddy?"

And now Daniel wanted to run. To leap from the window. To escape this moment.

"I'm sorry, Ethelinda. He died. A year ago."

For a while, everything was silent except Ethelinda rocking in the chair. Each little thud of wood on wood like the bang of a gavel.

"How did he die?"

Lie to her, Daniel told himself. *Why does she need to know? Will it make her happier?*

Maybe not. It would make him happier if she didn't know.

"I killed him," Daniel said. "We were on an island, he was building a dragon, and he was . . . I don't know what he was going to use it for, but dragons are very dangerous and . . . I don't know if this helps. My father was killed by the Southern Hierarch. I don't think there's anything he could have said that . . . We fought, your dad and I."

He was babbling now, trying to explain without justifying, as if that would make things better.

Ethelinda was glassy-eyed now, partially from shock, but also from the lamassu.

"Look, here's the thing. It's not up to me to tell you what to think. To explain what your father did. Or how you should feel about it. In a minute, you'll forget this conversation. I gave you lamassu."

"Sumerian sphinx," she said, groggy.

"That's right."

Her eyes sharpened and she pegged him with a look of accusation. "You're stealing my memories."

"Yes."

Ethelinda tried to rise from her chair but fell back. Weeping in frustration, she flung the duck across the room.

"You won't remember what we talked about. Not for a while, anyway." Not until he was hundreds of miles away, his thefts accomplished. "But I'll make sure you always know where you can find me. If you need help. Or if you need justice. Or if you need revenge. I'll be there for you, to make sure you have whatever you need."

He stood watching her fight against sleep. Her chin dipped, and her legs fluttered with feeble kicks. It was nothing at all like watching a small child trying to stay awake past bedtime. It was exactly like watching her battling not to be a victim of his magic.

She couldn't win. She would sleep, and when she awoke, she wouldn't remember his crimes. Later, he would send her a message. He would make sure she knew.

He crossed the room to retrieve her stuffed duck. She had a lot of stuffed animals. Maybe she wouldn't miss this one. Or maybe she'd grieve for its loss.

He threw it in the fire and drew sense memories from his bones of lava, of diamond-hard claws and powerful muscles raking away earth and climbing to the surface. His lungs burned, and he breathed out a jet of blue flame, and now the toy was fully engulfed.

Before leaving the room, he gave once last glance at Paul's daughter. He couldn't predict what would become of her, but he knew he'd changed her, as surely as the Hierarch changed him when he ate his father.

Maybe the only difference between Daniel and the Hierarch was that the Hierarch had used a fork.

TWENTY-THREE

Gabriel's team followed Messalina Sigilo.

They rode the sky-trolley, one car behind her, to North Beach, where she browsed books at City Lights. Gabriel hoped to find her delivering or receiving a message at a dead-drop there, maybe in a hole carved into the pages of a thick volume on the history of Constantinople or something equally colorful, but Cassandra insisted no such thing had happened under her watchful gaze.

It wasn't until Messalina stopped at a fruit stand that they caught her making an exchange. She picked through a bin of Gala apples, and from Gabriel's vantage point at a newsstand across the street, it looked like she was just shopping for an attractive specimen. Then a small white woman came up to the opposite side of the bin. Messalina slipped an apple from her pocket and placed it on the mound with the other apples.

"It's happening," Cassandra said. "Keep your eye on the apple."

The stranger selected Messalina's apple and tucked it neatly into her own pocket. Messalina chose another apple from the top of the pile, paid for it, and took a bite as she and the other woman parted company.

Gabriel watched Messalina blend into the sidewalk crowd. "Do we follow her or her contact?"

"We stay on Messalina," Cassandra said. "If I'm reading this right, Messalina just passed an order. I want to be there when the apple-carrier reports back."

They rejoined the chase.

Messalina shopped.

She had lunch at a seafood restaurant.

She visited an art museum, and as far as Cassandra could tell, did nothing but enjoy a gallery of Japanese woodcuts.

She caught a movie.

It was edging on midnight when Messalina walked to a crowded late-night sushi restaurant in an alley near Union Square. She took a table on the patio beneath paper-lantern lights.

From across the street, they watched a waiter bring her a menu and a glass of water. Messalina sipped and ignored the menu.

Gabriel produced a small bottle of water from his bag. "Can you get this into her glass?"

Cassandra took it from him. "What is it?"

"It's tuned water," Gabriel said. "I just need you to get some on the table, and I'll be able to listen in."

Cassandra pocketed the jar. "I'll try." And she was off. She joined a group of pedestrians crossing the street, and by the time they got to the other side, Gabriel had lost sight of her.

"Is she lying about not being osteomantic? She just vanished right before my eyes."

"She pivoted when the big guy with the beard turned to talk to the guy on his right," Max said. "Then she slipped around the other side of the blue moped—don't bother looking for it, it's gone now—and ducked into the alley behind the restaurant. She's not magic. She's just sneaky."

What Gabriel wouldn't give to have her on his staff. There had to be something he could offer her. Everyone had a price, and Gabriel had gotten good at finding it.

"There," Max said. "Sigilo's contact." The woman from the fruit cart entered through the gate in the patio fence and sat opposite Messalina. The waiter brought a fresh glass of water, topped off Messalina's, and Messalina said a few words. The waiter nodded without writing anything down and headed off to the kitchen.

"It's going to be twice as hard for Cassandra with the two of them there," Gabriel said.

"Wasn't that hard."

Gabriel spun around. Cassandra stood behind him, a little out of breath.

"I didn't even see you get near her table. How did you . . . ?"

Never mind. She could explain all her methods and tricks to him later. And, yes, he would get her to work for him. If she was dead set against it, he would find a way to make her dead set in favor of it.

But he was getting ahead of himself. With an eyedropper, he let six drops from another bottle fall in his ear. The water was cold and heavy, and each drop felt like getting punched in the side of the head. He tried to breathe away pain and nausea.

Voices came at him, distorted echoes in a sluggish medium. It sounded like many people all talking at once, not just Messalina and her contact, but dozens.

I only go to church on Sundays unless Walter is there . . . got good ball-handling but his defense is shit . . . and she says she can cook but I get there and it reeks of burnt fish . . .

This wasn't very helpful. Usually transhydraulic listening was clearer than this.

"How many glasses did you dose the water with?" he asked Cassandra.

"All of them. I couldn't get farther than the service station so I spiked the whole pitcher. What, you thought I could just walk up to her table and say, 'Hey, look over there,' and dump shit right in her glass?"

Gabriel covered his ears with his hands and looked across the street at Messalina's table, trying to pick her voice out of a disorganized chorus.

. . . leverage 10.9 percent of the third-quarter sales and redistribute . . . if you'd just brush your hair over the trash bin instead of the sink then maybe I wouldn't have to start every morning digging out your clots . . . mauve or taupe or lilac or white or raindrop or parakeet . . . I'm not wasted . . . correlated ship passage through the Golden Chain with heavy fog activity . . . I don't know why you thought chimp noises were such a good idea . . . okay, first of all, that wasn't a chimp . . .

Gabriel couldn't read lips, but the voice talking about the Golden Chain and fog coincided with Messalina's companion moving her mouth. He concentrated on her.

. . . two miles offshore. It's registered as a garbage scow and licensed for dumping landfill farther out to sea, but it's been anchored for the last two weeks. My sources confirmed three airships heading for it eleven days ago.

There was some more talk about a PO box and a promise of delivery from Messalina, wrapping up the exchange with confirmation of payment. As the effects of the drops wore off and the voices began to fade, a waiter arrived with a sushi platter. Messalina's companion plucked up a morsel of something with her fingers, got up from the table, and walked away chewing.

"Garbage scow, anchored offshore, possibly took delivery from three airships," Gabriel said. "She also said something about shipping activity through the Gate coinciding with heavy fog."

"You can generate fog with osteomancy," Cassandra said. "Thick fog would be perfect cover for deliveries anywhere in the bay, especially at night. Even somewhere surrounded by heavy traffic. Seems credible to me."

Messalina tossed some bills on the table and got up.

"Do we question her?" Max asked.

"No," Cassandra said. "We question her source."

They tracked Messalina's contact to an amusement pier jutting out from the wharf. She had a bowl of clam chowder, then ducked into a video arcade. Beeps and bells and buzzes from the games played to a nearly empty arcade. The one attendant Gabriel spotted was preoccupied trying to drag a sleeping drunk woman out from under the air hockey table.

Max found their quarry at a pinball machine. She was well into a game and gave no signs of ever losing a ball when Max set down a coin on the game.

"I've got next," he said.

"You can have this one." Without even glancing at him, she hurried off, and the game beeped mournfully as her ball passed through the flippers.

She spotted Cassandra blocking the entrance and made a quick detour for the back of the arcade, but Gabriel beat her to the emergency exit.

"We just have some questions about your dinner conversation."

"I talked to a sea gull. It was all, 'I want your chowder,' and I was all, 'Fuck off.'"

"No, we mean at the sushi place."

"Oh, that. Yeah, well, same thing I said to the sea gull."

"How much did Messalina Sigilo pay you?"

"I don't discuss business with strangers." The woman took a step to leave but was stopped short by Max's hand on her shoulder.

She shook it off. Max reapplied it.

"I'm not kidding. I'm a professional. I'm not discussing it."

"My proposal is this," Gabriel said. "You tell me what you told her, and we'll all be really happy. Happiness is good, isn't it?"

"If you're going to beat it out of me, can you just get started? I've been beaten before. The worst part is the coy banter."

A great power who didn't ever resort to torture was a rare thing in Los Angeles, and Gabriel had ordered people tortured on behalf of his bosses when he worked at the Ministry of Osteomancy. But not since he took charge of his own operation.

Cassandra came over to join them.

"I was hoping I could just bribe you," he said.

"Are you rich? You'd have to be rich."

"I'm pretty rich."

The woman looked at Gabriel from head to foot.

"You don't look rich."

"Looks can be deceiving. And I have deceived you. Ha!"

She gave him a glare of weary contempt. "You can't scare the intel out of me. You can't hurt it out of me. And you can't bribe it out of me. So, what have you got?

"Well, for starters, I know what you told Messalina Sigilo."

"Bullshit."

"Deliveries of osteomancy to a garbage scow outside the Golden Chain, cloaked in heavy fog. Ha!"

"Why does he keep saying, 'Ha!'?" she asked Max.

Max looked embarrassed. "Because no one else is complimenting him on his cleverness, so he has to do it. It's a cry for help."

"I'll pay you ten thousand crowns," Gabriel said, hoping to avoid making this all about him.

"No."

"Fifteen thousand."

"If you already know what I told Sigilo, what is it you want to pay me for?"

"The truth."

"You can't afford the truth," she said.

"Try me. Name a price."

"It's not how much you can pay me now. It's how much Sigilo's paid me in the past. It's what she'll pay me for more work later."

"Thirty thousand."

That got her attention. But she still wouldn't come to terms. "It's also what she'll do to me if she knows I told you."

Cassandra stepped in closer. She hesitated, as if she was trying to decide something. "What if I assured you that Sigilo won't be around much longer."

Gabriel raised an eyebrow at her and Cassandra looked away.

She wasn't kidding. She was thinking about offing Messalina Sigilo.

"I'd say good luck with that," the woman said.

Cassandra was not discouraged. "With Sigilo out of the picture, you'll lose a lucrative client. You should reconsider my associate's offer."

Gabriel jumped on that. "Fifty-three thousand, and that's it, because that's all the cash I brought with me, and we won't be seeing each other again after this."

One of the arcade games rang a bell. It sounded a lot like a cash register.

"Okay," the woman said. "Where's your suitcase of cash?"

Gabriel reached into his fixit bag. "No suitcase. Just very large denominations."

He handed over a stack of bills. Once she counted them, the woman made them vanish into a pocket.

"Treasure Island," she said. "They've got the dragon on Treasure Island."

They stood in the parking lot of an import/export warehouse across the bay from Treasure Island. Gabriel pressed the binoculars to his eyes.

Treasure Island was the site of the Golden Gate International Exposition of 1939. It had served as a naval base during the United States War and was decommissioned and abandoned after the Northern Hierarch secured her state. Most of the military structures were gone, but a few remained, as well as some buildings from the fair.

The silhouette of a hill rose from the water next to the span of the Bay Bridge. A narrow roadway connected the hilly part to a flat apron of artificial island, crenellated with structures, some intact, some in ruins.

Cassandra reached out her hand. "Pass them back."

"You look worried," he said, while she peered through the binoculars across the water. "Is it really so bad?"

"I don't like islands. Landing is one thing. Getting off is another. But the dragon could be there. That big structure on the north side?" She gave Gabriel the binoculars back. He trained them on an Art Deco building composed of vertical concrete slabs. "That's the Cavalcade of the Golden West in the Court of Pacifica," she said. "It's big enough to house a dragon. Or it could be one of those other big buildings. Several candidates, anyway."

"Assuming the dragon's even on the island," Max said. "Assuming our intel is good."

Gabriel sighed. "It's as good as we're going to get. And we're on the clock now."

Cassandra packed her binoculars away and handed Gabriel a sheaf of papers in a leather pouch. She'd spent forty minutes prowling through the basement of the City Planning Office to steal the Treasure Island water and electrical diagrams.

Gabriel paged through the diagrams. "These are only current up to 1979."

"Maybe we can request current ones through inter-library loan. Those were the only ones they had."

Gabriel traced his finger along pipes and drains and sewers, not just getting a sense of the layout, but looking for patterns. When he found them, he traced over them again and again, looking for things hidden among the obvious, things that tickled the parts of his brain he'd trained to understand sigils and labyrinths. The routes his finger took began to describe a mandala, and he imagined hydraulic energy traveling its path, and when he could feel the blood in his body traveling a route that matched the mandala, he knew he was ready.

He handed Cassandra the papers back. "Okay. Follow me."

He found what he was looking for almost a mile away in North Beach, on a street corner near a liquor store and an Italian restaurant.

Moments later, they were below the street in a tunnel lined with jade-colored tile. Inlaid brass figures of mermaids and tridents and spouting whales gleamed in Gabriel's flashlight beam.

"Pretty fancy for a sewer," Cassandra said.

Gabriel spent a few seconds orienting himself, then led off down the tunnel. "It's not a sewer. The sewer runs parallel behind this wall." He patted the tile. "That's what caught my attention. Tunneling is expensive, so nobody builds this kind of redundancy. But we water mages like to have our own transportation systems. We don't like depending on surface conveyances."

Gabriel wasn't thrilled by having to walk beneath the bay. He didn't know how structurally sound this tunnel was, not having had anything to do with its construction and maintenance. It'd be just his luck for an earthquake to choose this exact moment to strike and crumble the walls like a saltine, and then, water mage or not, he'd die in a crush of seawater.

"Dawdling is death," he said, and he hurried the team along the two miles to Treasure Island.

The tunnel terminated at a marble staircase with an iron gate at the top. They hunkered on the top step and looked out through the bars. They'd surfaced about a hundred feet away from the Cavalcade of the Golden West building. Dominating a weed-cracked courtyard rose a monumental statue of a woman, at least eighty feet tall. She had a strong carved face reminiscent of an Easter Island moia mixed with classical features. A great span of dragon wings spread from her back. This had to be Pacifica, goddess of the Pacific. Gabriel's mother had told him of this monstrous creature who devoured one hundred osteomancers every day. She was said to be patterned on the Northern Hierarch.

A guard with a rifle slung over his shoulder paced around the base of the statue.

Cassandra screwed together a length of pipe and poked it between the bars. She put it to her lips, and blew a strong puff of air. The guard let out a small squeal and put a hand on his neck before sinking to his knees. He fell forward on his face.

Cassandra made quick work of the gate with bolt cutters, and they were on the island.

Sniffing the air, Max motioned for Gabriel and Cassandra to come away from the tunnel. They sprinted across the courtyard and gathered at the feet of the statue.

"It's this way," Max said, pointing across a field to a long building standing in a tangle of neglected brush. It might have been a factory or a massive barracks, but more likely, it was one of the fair exhibition pavilions.

Max's face shone with sweat, and his breathing was labored.

Gabriel put a steadying hand on his shoulder. "Max? Your face looks like cookie dough."

"Don't you smell that?"

"The dragon?"

"Yes, the dragon," he snapped. "How can you not smell it?"

"Plug your nose and keep quiet," Cassandra whispered. Then, she seemed to notice Max was suffering. She reached for her med kit. "What's wrong?"

"The magic's hitting him hard," Gabriel said. "It does that sometimes. He'll be okay. Max, drink some water." He offered Max his canteen, but Max pushed it away, splashing water on Gabriel's shirt.

"We shouldn't have come here," Max said, gasping. "Why did you ever think you could tame a dragon? It's not an animal. It's a god. It's *burning* me, Gabriel."

"We need to get him away from here," Cassandra said.

She was right, of course. Gabriel had seen Max stricken by the presence of strong magic, but never like this. His eyelids fluttered, and his breaths came in short, ragged gasps.

"All right," Gabriel said. "All right. Max, back into the tunnel, back under the bay."

"No," Max murmured.

"You're no good to me like this. And I can go the rest of the way on my own." He looked at Cassandra. "Take him."

Gabriel felt rather shitty right now. Of course he was worried about Max. But that wasn't why he was telling Cassandra to get Max away from the thick magic overtaking him. He wanted *her* out of the way. He *needed* her out of the way. He couldn't have her interfering when he tried to take control of the dragon.

TWENTY-FOUR

There were lots of buttons and buckles in places that couldn't be reached without assistance, and Daniel had to rely on Moth to help him get dressed. The jacket was black as nothing, with silver epaulets and braids and stiff collar tabs, padded and cut in a way that gave Daniel an actual physique.

"Where did all these clothes come from, anyway?" he said, as Moth puzzled out complicated cuff fasteners.

"Your closets. Your tailors. Your seamstresses."

"I have tailors and seamstresses?"

"You even have a valet. But I sent him on vacation to the wine country. I'm not letting anyone get close enough to you to insert pins."

Daniel examined himself in the full-length mirror. It was framed in bone, just because. "Look at us. We're so fancy."

Moth was similarly dressed in a simpler version of Daniel's black with silver doodads. "This hasn't been such a bad gig in some ways. I like the threads and the nice cheeses and booze. I'm going to miss this life when it's done."

"We've come a long way from scams and heists and doing

incredibly dangerous and ill-advised things to take something that doesn't belong to us."

Moth snorted.

Their first heist together had been a complicated operation to steal beer from the back of Kelly's Liquor on Centinela and Venice. They'd spent two days planning it: staggered entrance, a diversion involving Moth knocking over a jerky display, the snatch of one six-pack, and an exit that required running like hell with the beer tucked under Daniel's arm. As jobs had a tendency to do, this one went to shit. Daniel got caught and Otis had to bribe a cop to get him out of the back of the squad boat. If he'd ended up being taken to jail as Sebastian Blackland's fugitive son, he might have found himself dead and deboned in less than twenty-four hours.

Daniel reached up high to pluck lint off Moth's shoulder. "In case I haven't said it, thanks. Not just for this job. Or even for the last year of chasing after Sam. But for all of it. You know? From day one. I couldn't ask for a better friend."

"That's it? A friend? What about brother? Am I not more like a brother? I would have said brother, if I were the one getting all goopy."

"I killed my brother."

"Friend is okay, then. Friend is fine. Now stop being morbid and let's go get you your promotion."

"Wish we could delay this." Daniel hadn't gotten word yet from Cassandra or Gabriel. Either they still hadn't located the dragon, or else they had but couldn't get word to him for some reason. Which meant that Daniel would have to snatch the *axis mundi* and escape the palace, and then lay low for an undetermined period of time.

More risk.

"Nothing we can do about the schedule," Moth said, dour. He was just as worried about Cassandra as Daniel was.

Daniel checked his pockets for the last time. The counterfeit *axis mundi*. His old and reliable thief's tools. Altogether, fewer than five ounces of metal and bone, upon which Sam's life depended.

Not until he entered the main throne room did Daniel appreciate the Hierarch's genius. Walls of glass could be cold, but here, lit by fires in braziers, the grand hall was a symphony of color. The oranges and reds were primordial fire. The greens and golds, forests of spring and autumn. The blues were all the colors of water, from tropics to arctic seas, and the ceiling seemed to change with every flicker, from pristine blue sky to the blackness between the stars. The Hierarch's throne room had become the universe.

Atop her throne, the Hierarch presided over her world like a god. She sat perched on a pillar of skulls, with claws and vertebrae and armored plates hanging on the walls in her orbit, as if she were the sun. She was dressed in an emerald gown and a crown of black griffin teeth, elegant and simple, but undeniably rich. Across her lap lay her sword, and in her right hand, she gripped the slender golden *axis mundi* scepter. The bone set in its crest gleamed darkly in the flames.

"Thought she'd come in last to make an entrance," Daniel said to Moth.

"The throne room is her world. Here, she's eternal. You're supposed to believe she was present long before you arrived and will be here long after you're gone. Kitchen assistant told me that."

Daniel tried to make eye contact with her, to show that he had nothing to hide, but she seemed to look through and beyond him.

Lord General Creighton stood at attention at the foot of the Hierarch's throne, and despite all the medals festooning his coat, he looked more like her receptionist than her consort. To be fair, Daniel supposed anyone in proximity to her would suffer by comparison.

The competing candidates for the High Grand Osteomancer's office took to different corners of the chamber.

Allaster, in the red and black colors of the Doring family, was there with his retinue of courtiers, happily chatting, a confident star quarterback before the big game. He gave Daniel a quick smile and pointed at him in greeting, then turned his attention back to his pals.

"He's so cool," Moth muttered.

Daniel didn't fault Allaster for it. He could only envy his ability to stay relaxed at a time like this. Or his ability to fake it.

Even Professor Cormorant was dressed smart, in purple and gold academic garb. He mingled with his flock of gray-haired companions, fluttering in their voluminous sleeves. Daniel couldn't hear them from across the room, but it seemed like they were pestering him with free advice and getting rebuffed.

Cormorant winced a smile at Daniel across the room. Daniel gave him a wave.

Cynara was the last to enter, in a long coat of brilliant scarlet that rivaled the Hierarch's flame-and-magma glass effects. She had paired it with a simple black button-down shirt and narrow-cut pants tucked into boots. Daniel admired her outfit. She looked smashing in it, and the coat could be easily shed for freedom of movement. He suddenly felt encumbered.

Ethelinda's governess led a procession in red plate armor, followed by twelve of Cynara's household. None carried weapons—the only blade in sight belonged to the Hierarch—but Cynara's private guard didn't need weapons. Daniel smelled lethal magic on them. Coming to a precision halt behind Cynara, they separated just enough to give Daniel a view of Ethelinda. His heart sank. If Cynara challenged him, he would have to fight her. At least when he'd killed Ethelinda's father, she wasn't there to witness it.

The flames in the braziers lowered and the room changed, like theater house lights dimming to signal the show was starting. Only a single beam of red remained, projecting from the Hierarch. Murmuring ceased. Court observers took their places in seats around the room's perimeter.

"This is my cue," Moth whispered in Daniel's ear. "I gotta go stand with the other toadies. I'll make sure I'm right by the door. When you're done, get over to me as quick as you can. Don't get killed."

This was basically a summation of all their jobs: Do a thing, get out quick, don't die. Over the course of Daniel's career this plan had succeeded only to a limited degree.

Once everyone else had taken their places, the Hierarch's light expanded to bathe Daniel, Cynara, Allaster, and Cormorant in its blood-tinged glow.

"The candidates will approach," Lord Creighton called out.

Daniel joined the others to stand before the throne. The Hierarch's gaze felt like extra gravity.

He expected a speech. A lengthy pronouncement. Something more than a single, incontrovertible sentence: "Lord Baron Paul Sigilo shall be our High Grand Osteomancer."

There was a silence in the chamber, no actual echo, but surely her words bounced inside the heads of the assembly, just as they bounced inside Daniel's. He refrained from pumping his fist and emitting a hearty, "Yeah!"

Moth had coached him on what might happen next. This was one of the most crucial and dangerous moments of the job. Daniel took a breath to gather himself and stepped forward.

In the early days of the Northern realm, the High Grand Osteomancer was the victor of a battle. It was a contest of blood and magic, and the red light of the throne room was one relic of that tradition. Another relic was the Rite of Challenge. Any of the other candidates could invoke it. They could even take turns, one after the other, and make Daniel survive a contest against them all.

He could feel Cynara's eyes on his back as he climbed the steps to the Hierarch's throne. He was almost at the top step, mere feet away from the Hierarch's thrumming magic, his eyes on the scepter, when a voice thundered:

"I invoke the Rite of Challenge."

Gasps escaped from every corner of the room. Daniel suppressed a bark of profanity. He turned to face his challenger, Lord Professor Nathaniel Cormorant.

TWENTY-FIVE

There was a scream. It was the sound of the sky tearing in half, of such pain and fury that Gabriel clawed the earth with the instinct of a primitive little mammal trying to hide from a world filled with giant predators. He threw himself over Max, trying to protect him with his own body, just a flimsy strip of flesh. Max was right. They should never have come here.

The pavilion came apart in a tumble of masonry and cracking timbers, and a great, dark shape shifted behind swirling clouds of dust. The firedrake raised its head on the soaring tower of its neck, armored with blue and green iridescent plates. The arrow-shaped head was as long as a bus, fringed with javelin spikes. Its eyes were the color of molten steel, so bright they hurt to look at.

The neck swayed drunkenly, and it shuddered with the clang of massive slabs of metal. Cables embedded in its flesh snapped like thread, and chunks of the ruined building went flying. Spreading its wings, it flung away debris, broken blocks of concrete tumbling through the air and smashing craters when they landed. The broad sails of its wings stretched out, kaleidoscopic blues and greens and purples, undulating grace-fully like a liquid curtain.

Hot air wavered before the dragon's snout.

Anyone inside the pavilion was surely dead under tons of rubble. Everyone on this island would surely die.

Pointing its head skyward, the dragon unhinged its jaw, and from the gaping, saber-lined cavern, it roared fire into the air.

Hunkering at the base of a fountain with Max and Cassandra, Gabriel dug into his bag for a rack of bell-shaped glass bulbs. Daniel had an identical set and they'd agreed that Gabriel would contact him over the hydromantic organ once his team had found the dragon.

Gabriel never intended to tell him the truth. With tuning forks, he'd inform Daniel they'd found Sam outside the Golden Chain on a garbage scow hidden in the heavy fog. Cassandra and Max would never know he was lying.

"Treasure Island."

Two words that made Gabriel's heart sink.

Near her lips, Cassandra held a thin, hollow bone, half the length of a pencil.

"No need to call Daniel," she said. "I just did."

TWENTY-SIX

The Northern realm was such an absurd place, thought Daniel. Back home in the South, you got ahead by killing whoever was in your spot. There were no rites, no gilding of tradition and ritual to obscure the bloodstains. Naked aggression was easier to figure out. What the hell was Cormorant doing, challenging him?

There was a sharp stab in Daniel's ear, and then a voice: "Treasure Island."

That's all it said, but the two words were significant. The voice was Cassandra's, spoken into a small fenghuang bone, and picked up by Daniel through an even smaller bone he'd shoved deeply and painfully in his ear canal.

The official plan had been for Gabriel to contact him, but Cassandra hadn't liked the official plan and insisted on this backup.

Hearing her message meant a few things:

She was still alive.

And she'd found Sam.

He wanted to murder Cormorant for throwing a complication into his plan when he was so close to stealing the *axis mundi* bone.

Daniel spared a glance over to Moth in the back of the grand chamber. Moth maintained his glower, which helped Daniel affect his own.

He descended a single step down the Hierarch's dais.

"Is this a jest, Professor?"

"No, Paul. Not everything is."

Allaster looked back from Cormorant to Daniel, his mouth hanging open.

Cynara squinted at both of them as if trying to solve a puzzle.

"Her Majesty has made her choice clear," Daniel said, loud enough for all to hear. "Do you believe your judgment superior to hers?"

That sounded sufficiently starchy. What he really wanted to say was, "Damn it, I've almost got my hands on the *axis mundi*; why do you have to reveal yourself as an asshole *now*?"

Cormorant bowed toward the throne. "I ask Her Majesty's forgiveness. I hope she trusts my profound devotion to her crown, and all the tradition it protects."

The Hierarch acknowledged his words with a regal nod, and Allaster and Cynara moved away to one side of the room.

Daniel never expected a challenge from Paul's mentor, but he was actually relieved it came from him instead of Cynara. This would just be a brawl with no emotional complications. No need to drag around additional anguish over Ethelinda.

He thought there might be some ceremony, some ritual, at least a recitation of the rules, but mysterious smells of osteomancy already crackled in Cormorant's bones. There was no jolliness in him, just the dark nerves of someone prepared to do ugly things. He exuded threads of oily, indigo smoke, like squid ink. It came from his mouth and nostrils and pores, accumulating into an opaque cloud around him.

Before he lost sight of Cormorant in the miasma, Daniel

reached for sense memories of monoceros. The beast weighed three tons. It ran at speeds topping seventy miles an hour. He brought it to the surface, letting it flow into his muscles, and launched himself at Cormorant. His fist made contact with Cormorant's jaw. It was like striking mud. He found himself wrist-deep in icy flesh. He lost feeling in his hand, a numbness traveling up his arm, past his elbow, all the way to his shoulder.

Cormorant shook his head like a horse. He snorted and lashed out with his own fist, smashing Daniel's cheek. Daniel saw spots. Pain thundered in his face, sharp spikes digging into his neck and between his shoulders. Blood filled his mouth.

He staggered away, trying to get distance before the next blow came, and wrapped himself in odors of reflection and refraction and confusion, the essences of the sint holo serpent. He treaded a wide circle around Cormorant's ink cloud. There was no movement in response. Either Daniel's sint holo cloak succeeded in making him invisible, or Cormorant was just waiting for Daniel to commit to an offensive move.

Daniel drew griffin essence from the small bones in his hands. His fingers curled into claws, sharp enough to rip open the hides of the crocodilian monsters that griffins preyed upon. He lunged at Cormorant, and the ink cloud shifted, like a swatting arm. Daniel's stealth magic was torn away, newspaper in the wind. He was exposed.

Cormorant turned his bulk, and the tail of some creature slammed into Daniel like a steel beam. His torso seized up, as if gripped in a giant hand, and he struggled for air.

A panicked thought took him: He might lose. He would die here in a foreign land, in pain and fear. And Moth would be alone in the enemy's palace, without resources and Daniel's protection. And Sam would remain lost.

"Don't toy with him, Paul. He's cleverer than you. Burn him."

Daniel tried to blink his vision clear. The voice was Allaster's. Allaster was coaching him, in full hearing of the entire court. He was declaring his allegiance to Daniel.

Daniel reached for his oldest magic. It was the first magic his father ever fed him, from the spine of a creature feared by whales. One to rival dragons. A great weight settled on his shoulders, a column of ocean a mile deep. He did not buckle under it. He was at home in the sunless sea, the eye of unseen storms.

He sent bolts of kraken lightning into the ink cloud. A cry of pain and the smell of boiling blood rewarded him.

Cormorant wanted to be High Grand Osteomancer? Over Daniel?

Daniel had held a Hierarch's beating heart in his hands. His teeth had sunk into a Hierarch's aorta. He knew what the heart of sorcery tasted like. He wondered about the taste of its brain.

He exhaled a hot gust and dissipated the ink cloud.

Cormorant's skin blistered and bled. Blood trickled from his nose, from the corner of his mouth, dribbling from his chin.

"Kraken magic," he croaked. "This is not you."

Daniel struck again with a blinding white bolt. Then another. And another. He let Cormorant eat lightning.

Cormorant fell.

He was still breathing, still moaning, conscious. Even now, electrocuted and burnt, rich magic wafted from him as he tried to draw upon the osteomantic stores deep inside his bones. His power was old and deep. Sweet, viscous odors wormed through the air to Daniel's nose. Cormorant's magic crawled out of dark nests.

Cormorant pushed himself up to one knee but fell back

down, and Daniel felt pity. His strongest adversaries suffered the most painful deaths. He would have to skin Cormorant. He would have to rip his bones out through his flesh. This was what you did to an enemy. To someone who had wronged you deeply, to someone who had hurt you. Daniel had done this to the Southern Hierarch, because he'd killed Daniel's father and was trying to kill him. Daniel would have done this to Otis.

But Cormorant meant nothing to him. He was just some guy, and whatever grievances he was acting out of were not with Daniel, but with Paul. He was suffering for nothing.

Daniel turned to the throne.

"Your Majesty, he is defeated."

"He still lives." The Hierarch's voice was the chilled edge of a knife, tainted with mirth.

"Only because I have learned to be thankful to those who have served me."

"He was your teacher. Not your servant."

"His tutelage served me, Your Majesty. I ask your permission to spare him. Perhaps I will dine on him later." Those were cold words, and they sounded too natural coming from his lips.

"He is yours to do with as you desire, my High Grand Osteomancer."

Daniel bowed deeply, displaying gratitude for the Hierarch's gift of bone and meat.

"Take him away," he snapped to Cormorant's attendants. "But he doesn't leave the palace. His body is no longer his own."

Uncertainly at first, but then picking up the pace when Daniel showed his displeasure, they came forward.

"Stop," Cynara said. Her voice was soft, but its sound filled the entire chamber, pushing away any relief Daniel felt at not having to kill Cormorant. The fight had just been a bitter appetizer.

"Cynara, please. I don't want to do this. Not in front of our daughter."

How could such dishonest words be the truest thing he'd spoken since arriving to this realm?

Cynara dismissed this with an irritated wave of her hand.

"This is what I've been waiting for," she said. "This aroma. This magic. You've revealed yourself. Was it the duress of combat, or your arrogance?"

She knew he wasn't Paul.

Electricity sparked in Daniel's finger bones.

"Don't you recognize it?" she said to him. "He's redolent with it."

"Oh," Daniel said. "Oh."

She wasn't talking about Daniel's unfamiliar scents. She was talking about Cormorant's.

He sniffed the fumes curling up from Cormorant's bloody flesh. It was the same spider scent from Ethelinda's would-be assassins.

Cormorant had tried to kill Ethelinda, and Daniel thought of someone doing that to Sam, and his anger was strong enough to numb his lips.

He let the electricity in his bones come to the surface again. Painful sparks flared under his fingernails. Blue webs arced between his fingers.

He knelt before Cormorant. "You tried to kill my daughter."

Stepping closer, Allaster nodded, as if approving of some daring polo move.

"Ethelinda is the common bond between you two," Allaster said to Cynara and Daniel. "With her death, there'd be no reason to maintain an alliance. Or maybe in grief you wouldn't want to be High Grand Osteomancer at all. That would leave only me in Cormorant's way. And me, he could beat."

"Look at me, Professor."

Cormorant moaned and sagged.

Daniel moved his sizzling hand near the old man's face. "Why?"

Cormorant smiled. His gums were bleeding. "Why? Why else, dear boy? Because I wanted to be High Grand Osteomancer."

And that was enough reason for him to murder a child. This was the world, as it was. This was what people were. They were not good. They were not evil. They were less than either. People were merely consumers.

Cynara took a few steps toward the throne. "Your Majesty. This man tried to murder my daughter. I want his life."

The Hierarch looked down at her, serene and beneficent.

"Lady Cynara. He belongs to my High Grand Osteomancer."

Cynara turned to Daniel. She searched his eyes, and he felt she was looking for something that she used to find in them.

"Will you make me ask, Paul?"

Daniel shook his head no.

"Thank you," she said, as if Daniel had done something wonderful. "Ethelinda, come here."

Ethelinda's footfalls made tiny clicks across the floor. She took her mother's hand and reached the other out to Daniel. He took it. It was small and warm.

"This is the man who tried to hurt you," Cynara said, her voice ringing to the very top of the glass room, so powerful Daniel wondered if she'd bring down a rain of shards. "Show the kingdom what happens to such people."

Ethelinda drew herself away and approached Cormorant.

With him still on his hands and knees, their eyes were level. She placed a tiny, pink hand on each of his cheeks.

"Make it quick, girl," he said.

She turned his head to the side. His breath quickened, and she kept turning. There was a startling scream, but it soon choked off, and she kept turning.

In sorrow, with the sounds of snapping tendons and fracturing vertebrae, Daniel watched Ethelinda claim her place in this world.

Palace servants came with mops and buckets and sponges and a crate for Professor Cormorant's body. The court looked on hungrily as they packed Cormorant away and wheeled him off. He'd make a richly magical meal for someone. A cloth and bowl of water were brought to clean the blood from Ethelinda's hands.

Moth still stood down at the far end of the throne room, ready to proceed. The duel with Cormorant had been an interruption, but the job was still on. Moth touched a button on his jacket. Daniel looked down and saw a partially undone button on his own. He fastened it, straightened his jacket, and ran a hand through his hair. He wanted to look appropriate when he knelt before the Hierarch.

From the foot of the dais, Lord General Creighton gave Daniel an approving nod. "The High Grand Osteomancer will approach our liege," he said in his commanding-the-troops voice.

It was time to claim his prize.

With each step Daniel climbed up the dais, his body grew

heavier. The Hierarch let her magic be known to him now, wafting from her body in potent waves of griffin and fenghuang and fucanglong and mammoth and baku, and dozens of other creatures. When he reached the top of the dais, something happened with the light. The flames in the braziers flared and danced, throwing shadows on the Hierarch's face, and her crown of griffin teeth no longer seemed like a crown. The teeth grew from her head and cheeks.

The flames lowered, and the crown was once again just a crown. She allowed a hint of a smile, and Daniel got the message. *Don't get too puffed up, High Grand Osteomancer. I'm still your boss.*

That's fine, boss, thought Daniel. I'm going to pick your pocket anyway.

Some circumstances were better than others for theft. Daniel liked dark basements when nobody was home. He liked places where he could use magic, undetected. Stealing something when all eyes were on him and he was inches away from the most powerful osteomancer in the land was not a good set of circumstances.

Something on the far end of the room clattered, the sound echoing through the chamber. Eyes went in that direction, where they would find a serving dish on the floor and a mortified servant standing near it, courtesy of Moth and a well-timed shoulder bump. Daniel used the distraction to dip his fingers in his pockets.

Tucked with his thumb against the palm of his left hand, he held the counterfeit *axis mundi* bone, set in a bezel of melted gold rings. In his right palm, he had his spring-loaded pry bar.

He lowered himself to his knees before the Hierarch. She stood, sword in one hand, scepter in the other.

She touched the scepter to his head. "I claim your thoughts," she said.

She touched the scepter to his left shoulder, then his right. "I claim your body."

Finally, she touched the scepter to his chest. "I claim your heart."

Daniel took the end of the scepter in both hands, in a praying position. With a clear voice, louder than any sound he'd ever uttered that wasn't a scream of pain, he said, "I surrender all to you."

Simultaneously with his declaration, he pushed the pry bar against the stone, sliding the blade under its bezel. With a twisting action and a push, he popped the stone almost, but not quite, out of its setting.

"I am yours," he thundered, which was a risk, because this wasn't part of the declaration, and it surprised the court, including the Hierarch. Surprising a volatile sorcerer was, generally speaking, not a good idea. But the surprise provided a small diversion, and he used the moment to dislodge the genuine bone and replace it with the counterfeit. With the real bone now in his right hand and the counterfeit in its place, he released the scepter.

Success or death. In the next second, he'd know which he'd just accomplished.

"I name you my High Grand Osteomancer," the Hierarch called out. And then, with a shockingly warm smile, she said, "Stand, Paul, and face your lessers."

"Thank you, your most gracious majesty." He turned toward a cheering court. Allaster applauded and beamed. Cynara's applause appeared more dutiful and somber. Ethelinda clapped politely with the same small hands she'd used to twist Cormorant's head around.

Even from across the room, Daniel recognized the message in Moth's posture. It said, "Let's get out of here."

Daniel raised his left arm in salute. The *axis mundi* bone was palmed in his right hand.

"Paul."

A whisper. Light fingers on his shoulder. The smell of potent magics snaking into his sinuses. The Hierarch stood beside him.

"Your Majesty?"

"You earned this," she said.

"Thank you, Your Majesty."

Hand in hand, they walked down the dais together.

TWENTY-SEVEN

A celebratory feast was held for Daniel's investiture, with a rotisserie-roasted bull given the place of honor. It was one of those deals where they stuffed the bull with a boar, and inside the boar was a goat, and inside the goat was a lamb, and inside the lamb was a turkey, and then a pheasant and maybe a baby and so on, until you ate your way down to a teeny-tiny succulent frog.

Daniel did not plan to see forks reach the center. With the *axis mundi* bone weighing heavy in his pocket, the next phase of the job was a quick and unobtrusive escape from the palace.

Allaster grabbed Daniel by the shoulders. "What's that I smell?" He sniffed one side of his face, then the other. "Ah, yes, the smell of success. You are a big, important man. You are a mighty wizard. And I find you beautiful." He guffawed and clapped Daniel hard enough on the back to make him cough.

"How deep into the wine have you gotten, Allaster?"

"Not yet to the bottom, my friend. I have much diving yet to do."

"You know what, Allaster?"

"What, High Grand Osteomancer Paul?"

"I like you."

Allaster crushed him in a bear hug. "And I. Like. You."

Moth smiled and made not a single move to help him.

"Allaster?"

"Yes, Grand Sorcerous Mage Paul?"

"I have to go pee now."

"You go do that," he said, mercifully releasing Daniel. "You go pee. You deserve it. You deserve a good pee."

Allaster went off to pursue a passing serving girl, and Daniel watched him go with something like wonder. He'd completely misread him. Paul was lucky to have counted him as a friend.

Daniel eyed the exit. A clot of courtiers blocked the path to a clean getaway, and he knew once he began moving, they'd converge on him with congratulations and well-wishes and please-notice-me's and I-supported-you-this-whole-time's.

Daniel's advantage was the splattering of Cormorant's blood on his clothes and hands. Nobody would think much of it if he excused himself to freshen up before digging into a meal of beasts within beasts.

"My lord, if I might have a word." It was some grand dame osteomancer dripping in jewelry and smells of basilisk magic, with an almost desperate eagerness in her eyes.

"Certainly," Daniel said. "But if you would only pardon me a moment." He gestured to his gore-freckled pants and continued toward the exit.

Near a stage where pipers filled the air with toots and whistles, Cynara and Ethelinda stood surrounded by their household.

Once Daniel was gone, the High Grand Osteomancer's seat would be vacant. Cynara would have a chance to claim it, but she'd find herself the target of rivals and assassins and having to fight battles. But hopefully some of those dangers would be mitigated by Ethelinda's demonstration of power. If the daughter could rip apart a ranking osteomancer with her bare hands, then what was the mother capable of?

They'd withstand challengers. But Daniel didn't know how they'd deal with losing Paul again. From the Hierarch, he'd stolen a bone. From Cynara and Ethelinda, he'd stolen something more valuable.

He wanted to go to them, to give them a full explanation. A full confession. To remove from them a gnawing doubt of the sort he had always had about his mother. If they were to be abandoned, they at least deserved to know why, from his lips instead of a cowardly letter some day down the road.

Moth moved his body to subtly hem Daniel in.

"My lord," he said. "This is still a job."

Moth was right.

Making eye contact with Cynara across the room, he affected his escape with all he had taken.

Leaving the stronghold of the Southern Hierarch with a treasure in pocket was the easiest getaway Daniel had ever accomplished. He and Moth simply walked through palace gates guarded by two dozen pikemen and gunners.

"Bum a cigarette?" Daniel said to an obsequiously bowing guard who reeked of dire wolf.

The guard happily obliged, proud to perform a personal service for the realm's new High Grand Osteomancer.

In gratitude, Daniel removed his fine black military jacket, festooned with medals and ribbons he'd never learned the meaning of, and bestowed it upon the guard as a gift.

"My lord, I . . . I don't know what . . . ," the guard stammered.

"Say thank you," Moth instructed.

"Thank you, my lord."

Daniel gave Moth an impatient stare until with genuine re-
luctance, Moth unbuttoned his own coat and tossed it to the
guard. Moth was going to miss the high life.

In white tailored shirts and black trousers, they walked
through the gates and out onto the busy sidewalk, looking
like gentlemen, but not at all royal. Moth waved down a taxi,
and a few minutes later, they were on their way to the Bay
Bridge.

It would be easy to fool themselves into thinking the job was
done. The hard part hadn't even begun. Daniel still had to employ the *axis mundi*, recover Sam, and get him home. And
before that, they had to rendezvous with Gabriel Argent's
team on Treasure Island. There were many moments in which
everything might collapse into tears and cussing.

Traffic slowed to a sludge as the taxi approached the gray
steel double-decker gridwork of the bridge. A line of unmov-
ing taillights stretched into the distance, across the expanse of
water, to Oakland on the other side.

"Driver, what's the holdup?" Daniel's first thought was *road-
block*.

"The holdup? There's no holdup. Every day's like this. It's
life. Life is the holdup."

Leaning into his window, Daniel could see the dark hump
of Yerba Buena Island, connected by roadway to the bridge,
and an unlit, flat expanse on the hilly part's northern side:
Treasure Island.

"We'll get out here," he said.

The driver looked back at him in his rearview mirror, and
Daniel hoped he wouldn't say anything or look like he was
going to say anything that would make Daniel have to hurt

him. He was ready to burn people to ash, but not a random driver who'd had the bad fortune to respond to Moth's hail.

The driver tapped the meter and read out the fare.

Reaching into his trouser pockets, Daniel found only his torch, his walnut-shell-sized bone crucible, and the *axis mundi* bone.

He turned to Moth. "Uh, hey, can you get this?"

"For crying out loud," Moth said, passing the driver a fifty note.

Before getting out, Daniel leaned toward the driver. "You know, you might want to consider avoiding the bridge for the next few hours. I don't think traffic's going to get any better."

He and Moth went out to the bridge sidewalk. They'd only walked a few hundred feet when there was a shrieking noise as if the sky had been torn open and all the air rushed out into space. A geyser of blue flame erupted from the island, aiming for the stars.

Sam.

Cassandra cowered beneath the Art Deco pagan statue of the goddess Pacifica while the dragon stirred in the wreckage. Flames cast an infernal glow over the dark mound of its back. The dragon breathed, a sound like the whoosh of igniting gas. Burst water pipes generated clouds of steam but did nothing to quell the fires. Glass shattered and wood framing collapsed with the dragon's every movement. The dragon seemed to be resting, or gathering itself for something bigger.

People fled from the buildings—technicians, guards,

osteomancers—some of them engulfed in fire. Bodies fell and burned. A figure stumbled from the building, clothes aflame. Cassandra stripped off her jacket and ran into the field of ruins, and she didn't stop running until she'd reached the woman. She tackled her to the ground and threw her jacket over her back, patting her hard to suffocate the flames. The woman didn't thrash, didn't struggle. When the flames were out, Cassandra moved her head to make sure her airway was clear, and she put her fingers to the woman's throat in search of a pulse. She knew she wouldn't find one.

The dragon exhaled a gust of swirling blue flame, almost like a cough. Just clearing its throat. It stretched out a wing, and another wall came down in an avalanche of masonry.

From the corner of her eye, Cassandra caught a glimpse of someone darting into the wreckage.

Now, why would anybody do a thing like that? Why would they get closer to the dragon when the only sane thing to do now was find an evacuation boat off the island? Why risk getting crushed and incinerated or accidentally disemboweled if the dragon scratched an itch with a saber toenail?

Maybe someone trying to help victims. But Cassandra knew better. She'd spent hours tailing Messalina Sigilo. She may not know how she thought, but she knew how she moved.

Cassandra sighed.

She'd have to take care of it.

Gabriel watched Cassandra zigzag through the old wreckage of the fairgrounds and into the dragon's nest of smoke and rubble and flame. He let her go.

Bricks and chunks of crumbled masonry slid off the dragon's smoking back. It hunched, curling its tail and long neck around its body. Steam poured from its nostrils, and with every ragged breath, a wave of heat struck Gabriel's face. He was sure its orange eyes were fixed specifically on him.

"I need to get closer to it, Max."

"How close?"

"I don't have a mathematical formula. Just closer. And I need you to warn me about any osteomancy."

Max sniffed sharply. "There's some." He pointed at the dragon.

"You know what I'm talking about, Max."

"You're afraid of Daniel Blackland."

"I need him to stay out of my way. Just for a few minutes."

"What exactly are you planning to do, Gabriel?"

Any other time, Max would have done as Gabriel asked. He would have snapped into action, guarding Gabriel against danger. He might have had something to say about it, but this was different.

"Just tell me if Daniel is close. Do you smell him?"

Max closed his eyes and searched the air. It would be hard to separate out distinct osteomantic indications with the dragon's magic flooding the atmosphere.

"He's near," Max said.

"Then we don't have a lot of time."

"Gabriel, if Daniel's right, then Sam is still in there. He's Daniel's son. Let Daniel take care of it."

There was pleading in Max's voice, something Gabriel had never heard before, and it broke his heart a little. Max never did arithmetic with people's lives. You could show him the numbers on paper, the potential lives of the thousands who'd burn if the dragon was left to rampage, versus the single life of Sam, a boy who'd suffered from the Hierarch's cruelty just as much as Gabriel and Max had, but Max would always see the math for what it was: a formula that justified doing awful things. A proof of awfulness itself.

Max was decent.

Gabriel wished he could afford to be. Instead, he had to be accountable.

"This may not work," Gabriel said. "Go back to the tunnel. Steal a car and make it to the Pulgas Water Temple. There'll be a plane waiting to take you back to Los Angeles."

"I know the plan. It doesn't involve leaving you here." He looked at Gabriel with disgust. Then, "Come on," he said, and he stepped out ahead of Gabriel, moving toward the dragon.

Cassandra found things almost peaceful closer to the dragon. The fires had reduced their fuel to ash and carbon sludge, and the sounds of the outer buildings burning seemed distant. Curled in on itself, the dragon was more like a geological formation than a living creature. Reflected flames wavered in its glossy scales. Its wings spread out across the ground, sheets of swirling iridescence. The wreckage of machinery lay scattered around it—shattered glass dials and gauges, pipes and pump works tangled like string, ruptured tanks and control panels with severed wires exposed. The dragon was at the center of it all, the focus of the project.

Cassandra spotted the figure she'd seen picking its way through the wreckage, approaching the dragon. In an ideal world, Cassandra could just stand back and watch the dragon lash out with a tongue of flame and burn the idiot to a crisp, and then that'd be one little extra worry off her plate. But Cassandra recognized Messalina Sigilo.

Sigilo positioned herself mere feet from the end of the dragon's snout. Her hair blew back with its exhalations.

"It's time to wake up, Paul. They're coming for you." Sigilo's voice was soothing.

Paul? That was the name of Daniel's golem. Messalina's other son.

Daniel hoped to extract Sam's essence from the dragon, but the dragon was Paul's creation. How long had he labored over it? Months. Years. Maybe decades, knitting bones together, building armor plating, cell by cell. Cooking pyrogenic fuel. Investing his magic in the dragon. Investing himself. Maybe something of Sam's consciousness was still in there, but the dragon was also Paul.

Sigilo began moving rubble around, searching for something. She tossed aside segments of broken pipe, burnt-out bits of electronics. Then she flashed a satisfied smile. With a grunt of effort, she unearthed a scratched and dented cylindrical metal tank.

"This gas contains your magical essence, Paul. Your own breath. It'll strengthen you. It'll make your magic more coherent. Breathe it in, deep into your lungs, and let it warm in your fires. It will help you assert control of the dragon. It will help you *become* the dragon, just like you wanted."

Cassandra drew her gun. She loaded a round and lined up an easy, unobstructed shot. She didn't know what Sigilo was up to, and she didn't need to. All she needed to know was that Daniel's mother was a poisonous vein running through her life. If not for her, Daniel would have never become Otis's tool. Otis would have never had the opportunity to sell him to the Southern Hierarch. There would never have been a Pacific firedrake, and Sam would have never gone to Catalina Island to sabotage it. Without Sigilo, none of them would be here now.

Cassandra knew Sigilo wanted the dragon to inhale Paul's breath. She knew she could not let that happen.

She took a breath and let her finger touch the trigger.

"Messalina. Take your hand away from that valve."

Sigilo didn't turn around. "Cassandra. I know what this looks like. I can explain."

"It looks like if you don't get your hand in the air, I'm going to put a bullet in the back of your head."

"You don't understand. What I'm trying to do—"

"I am going to shoot you. Take your hand off the valve."

"I'm trying to help Daniel."

Cassandra squeezed the trigger, and a bullet whizzed inches to the left of Messalina Sigilo's head.

Sigilo flinched, but she kept her hand on the tank. She half-turned to face Cassandra.

"If you kill me, Daniel will never forgive you."

"I can live with that."

She wasn't sure that was true. But, then, what other choice did she have? She would *have* to live with it.

She watched Sigilo's hand. She watched her fingers grip the valve tighter. She watched her muscles tense as she began to turn it.

Cassandra squeezed the trigger again and ended the life of Daniel's mother.

Messalina's body fell. And her hand slipped away from the valve, resting in the dirt, fingers curled as if asking for someone to hold it.

Through tears, Cassandra saw Messalina's victory and the cost of her own hesitation.

Messalina had opened the valve. Rich blue gas billowed from the tank, and with a great, powerful inhalation, the dragon drew it in.

The giant pursued Sam through the dragon's brain, barreling through the jungle of electrified strands and vines. Sam struggled up thick struts and supports to the chamber's ceiling. He made it up to a wider beam and chanced a look down. Blooms of osteomancy flared beneath the giant's translucent skin.

Sam was high up now, the floor of the brain no longer in sight, nothing but thickets of brainworks below. He kept climbing, but he was exhausted and hurt. The world turned sideways and he lost his balance. Falling, he reached out a desperate hand and caught a strut. Long lines of pain bolted from his fingertips to his neck. He grasped the strut with his other hand, but too weak to pull himself up, he could only dangle there.

"Please stop fighting me, Sam. It hurts." The Hierarch's voice seemed to come from far away. "It's hurting both of us. It's hurting the firedrake. This doesn't have to be a zero-sum game, either you or me surviving. We're both part of the dragon. We can both exist."

Sam had an answer for him: fire.

He released a torrent of flame that fell on the giant like a blanket. The Hierarch screamed, and when the fire gutted out, Sam glimpsed exposed skull.

Weeping with effort, Sam pulled himself up and managed to swing a leg over the support strut. He shuffled along to the intersection of the strut and a vertical column, a little place where he could tuck himself and not fall.

His heart pumped watery blood, and he forced himself to keep his eyes open.

He heard a hissing sound, like air escaping a punctured hose. Maybe his life was leaking through his pores, and he'd deflate like a balloon. Such a dignified way to die. He coughed a weak laugh.

Sam made out blueish tendrils diffusing in the hazy air. They were most dense around the walls. Gas was coming in.

The Hierarch lifted his head and took in a long breath. "Oh, I recognize this taste. Is that . . . yes. Sebastian Blackland. Something of him, anyway. Or his son? That boy who took my heart. He breathes rich magic."

Sam smelled something very close to Daniel's essence, but not quite him. His golem-brother, maybe. Paul.

The gas flowed to the Hierarch, as if rushing to fill a vacuum, and he seemed to grow taller. His flesh thickened, grew opaque, his body becoming a more solid vessel for magic.

"I'm getting stronger, Sam. I shouldn't give you another chance. You're a parasite. An antigen. I'd be better off cleansing you from my system."

Sam dug into his bones, desperately seeking more essence of dragon fire to vomit down on him. But he'd mined his sources of power too deeply.

The Hierarch's fingers sparked and he casually raised a hand. Threads of electricity arced and struck Sam. White-hot nerves flared, and Sam screamed and clung to his perch. The pain would never end. Sam's flesh and eyes would burst and spray his last magic in a messy stain.

The Hierarch released him. It had probably been only a few seconds, but Sam felt himself diluting. He coughed himself thin.

The hissing sound of gas stopped, and after the Hierarch took a few more breaths, the air cleared.

The Hierarch seemed surprised. Maybe alarmed.

"Didn't get your fill?" Sam said, resting his cheek on one of the struts.

"I got enough." He patted his chest with a fist, the sound like a kick drum. "I'm solid now. More solid than you, which is all I need to be. The dragon is mine, Sam. Be a part of us, or I'll have to eat you. I'll keep you locked away, in the deepest, darkest part of myself. You'll never see daylight again. You'll never have another coherent thought."

"Thinking's overrated."

The Hierarch sighed. "I'm sad that's your choice."

His lightning came without mercy and ripped Sam's flesh to shreds.

Sam's bones splintered.

His body came apart as his creator, the Hierarch, unmade him.

The dragon tossed its head back and roared.

Gabriel stepped into the rubble field, Max right behind him. All that was left of the dragon's hangar was a low fence of broken wall with bent fingers of rebar poking from shattered concrete. Fires still raged all around, except for near the dragon, where the fuel was already expended. Gabriel had hoped to get to the dragon sooner, while it was still being tranquilized or whatever its keepers were doing to prevent it from rampaging. Though the dragon had been quiet for several moments, it was no less spectacular, no less threatening. It was like a capped volcano. He knew when the cork blew, it was going to be terrifying.

But why dwell on the negative? At least the dragon was still here. It hadn't flown off to raze a city and incinerate thousands more people. Wasn't that swell?

He reached into his bag and withdrew a shoe-box-sized casket. Kneeling in the dirt, he thumbed open the clasps and lifted the lid. The glass tubes were still unbroken, the tuning forks still seated properly in their sockets, the hammer mechanisms in place and unbent.

He heard Max's footsteps behind him.

"Is that the thing you're going to use to kill the dragon?"

"No," Gabriel said.

The flask of memory water was nestled in a recess in the casket's padded foam lining. Gabriel lifted it from the casket.

Max looked from the flask to Gabriel. "What are you doing?"

Gabriel didn't want to answer.

"Gabriel," Max said. "I've done a lot of things for you. You owe me. Tell me what you're doing."

"You're not going to like it."

Max looked so tired. "Tell me."

Gabriel did owe Max. He owed Max for saving his life countless times. For being the one person in the world he could tell his secrets to. For being his only friend.

"Okay," Gabriel said. "All the hundreds of tons of current coursing through the canals, all the aqueducts and mains and sewer flows, all the pipes to all the bathtubs and kitchen sinks, all forming a circuit of great power . . . The flask contains memory water from the deepest well at the very center of my mandala. And the memory it holds is the voice of the *axis mundi*, the dragon at the center of the earth. It's a beast even stronger than the Pacific firedrake."

"Simpler explanation, please," said Max.

"Our cells are water, Max. I'm water. You're water. The dragon is water. I drink the memory water, and I can dominate the dragon."

"Dominate it. You mean kill it."

"No. I mean control it."

Max closed his eyes. When he opened them again, he looked scared. "You want to control it, so you can send it into a volcano or fly it into a mountain. To kill it."

"No, Max. Just control it."

He unsealed the flask.

"Gabriel."

The dragon raised its wings. Piles of debris slid off its hide and crashed to the ground.

"Gabriel," Max said again, as Gabriel lifted the flask.

Max's gun was leveled at his head.

Anybody but Gabriel might have expected this. The previous chief water mage of the Southern Kingdom had died when Max shot him in the head. Assassins were people you used, not people you kept near. Not people you loved. But Gabriel had never thought of Max as an assassin.

"I thought you were my friend," Gabriel said. His voice sounded mournful and afraid and pathetic to his own ears. He couldn't know how it sounded to Max.

"I am your friend, Gabriel. If I wasn't, I'd have shot you from behind. But I am your friend, and I have been for a long time now. I'm trying to make sure you don't become a monster."

"I guess putting me down for my own sake could be an act of friendship if you tilt your head and squint the right way."

"I wouldn't really be doing it for your sake, Gabriel. In the end, I guess this isn't really about friendship after all."

"No? What then?"

"It's about accountability."

Gabriel had to laugh a little at that. He could see Max's point.

"Put the flask down, Gabriel."

The dragon lifted itself on its legs. It pawed the ground, excavating trenches through cement and earth. It moved its tail, slowly as a sleepy cat, and the great mass of armor and spikes knocked over a pile of rubble.

"And who's going to be accountable for that?" Gabriel said, pointing at the dragon.

"The dragon's not my concern, Gabriel. It's a monster, and it's magic I can never begin to understand. But I'm accountable for you, and I won't let you become something even worse." Max thumbed back the hammer. His grip was firm, the barrel of the gun steady, as if time had stopped. "Please, Gabriel, put down the flask. Please."

Max's voice cracked.

Gabriel considered returning the flask to its case, and shutting the lid, and closing the clasps. And if he did, it wouldn't be because Max held a gun to his head. It wouldn't be because he feared dying. It would be because Gabriel knew how broken he'd be if he was forced to kill Max, so he knew how broken Max would be by having to pull the trigger. How could he make Max suffer like that?

Scents billowed around him. Burning. Smoke. Power. Love. Awe.

Gabriel was chief water mage of the Southern realm. Becoming great at it was a mistake, but one he could no longer correct. There was no one else but him.

He touched the flask to his lips.

He heard the gunshot, and there was an explosion of pain in his head. His cheek was in the dirt, where he lay. His face was wet with his own blood.

Max turned him over. Gabriel saw his eyes. Water fell from them.

Daniel arrived with Moth on Treasure Island to a scene that filled him with despair. The dragon was awake and enormous, looming over a field of wreckage and flame. Daniel had seen, handled, and eaten countless bones, but he had never witnessed the majesty of such magic. Could anything of Sam be left in such a creature? And if there was, how could Daniel be strong enough to draw him out?

He spotted Max and Gabriel Argent in the distance. Argent was on his knees, and the hound had a gun trained on him.

He didn't see Cassandra anywhere, and this scared him almost as much as the sight of the dragon.

"Looks like things went sour with Argent and Max," Moth said. "Should we do anything about that?"

Of all the great powers Daniel had come across, Gabriel was far from the worst. He could have been a despot. He could have been a Hierarch. Whoever controlled the water could control California, but Gabriel seemed more genuinely interested in making sure the crops got irrigated, the traffic moved, and people didn't die of thirst. They weren't friends, but they weren't enemies, either, and sometimes, in a world of Otises and Cormorants, that was enough for Daniel.

He didn't want to see Gabriel die. But he wanted to see Sam die even less.

Hard choices. Gabriel would've been the first to understand.

"They're going to have to sort it out between themselves," he said. "Sam comes first."

They worked their way through the rubble toward the remains of a long rectangular building, an old remnant of the fairgrounds, where the dragon loomed.

A figure came away from the building. Daniel recognized her gait right away.

"Cassie." He and Moth rushed toward her.

"I'm fine," she said with impatience when they reached her. But from the pained look in her eyes, Daniel could tell she was not fine.

"What is it?" he asked her.

She closed her eyes and took a breath, gathering herself, and Daniel prepared himself to hear the worst news.

"Is it Sam?"

"No," she said.

"What, then?"

"It can wait. Do what you came to do and take care of your boy."

Cassandra took Moth by the arm. "There's a tunnel. It goes under the bay and comes out in North Beach. Let's go."

Moth pulled his arm away. "Bullshit, I'm staying with Daniel."

"Daniel's mom is coming up the tunnel. We're going to deal with her so Daniel can take care of Sam."

Daniel and Cassandra exchanged a quick conversation of silent expressions.

Daniel's mom was not coming up the tunnel. Cassandra was lying to Moth, and she was doing it to help Daniel. The next few moments were going to be a time of flame and magic, and Daniel had enough to do without worrying about immolating his friends. He needed space to work, and Cassandra was going to make sure he had it.

But there was something else she wasn't telling Daniel. When he was about to question her, she shook her head no.

"Not something you need to know now," she said. "It can wait."

Moth jabbed a giant finger in Daniel's chest. "If you get killed, I'm going to punch you so hard I'll actually feel it in my knuckles."

"You do and I'll kick you so hard I'll get a compound leg fracture. Go."

"We'll be on the other side of the bay," Cassandra said. "Promise us you'll be there, too."

"I'll try," Daniel said. "That's the best I can give you."

She kissed him on the cheek. "Do better."

With great relief, Daniel watched his friends scramble off to a direction most resembling safety.

From his pocket, he withdrew the *axis mundi* bone. He used his knife to cut a groove all the way around it, and in the groove he wound the strand of Sam's hair he'd saved.

This was the very last bit of Sam he had left. The other hair was in Los Angeles with Issac Slough, the golem maker. So much depended upon fragile strands.

Cupping the bone in his hands, he blew on it with care, as if trying to ignite a smoldering bundle of dry grass. It grew heavier and heavier, tons of weight compressed into an object the size of a coin, like it wanted to drop through the earth's crust and plunge through dark zones of rock, back home to the molten center of the world. It wanted to drag Daniel down with it. He was holding on to a bullet in flight thundering toward the ground, and it wanted to burst through the cage of his clasped fingers.

Daniel held on. The magic of a thousand creatures lived in his bones, and he used their strength to maintain his grip on the *axis mundi*. He used the strength of the osteomancy his father had given him, and the osteomancy he'd claimed for himself, from every morsel of griffin claw to the Southern Hierarch's heart. He used the early lessons his mother gave him about doing whatever he had to do to survive, even if those things were ugly. He used his love for Sam.

The *axis mundi* was the most powerful bone Daniel had ever

touched, and it wanted to return to its deep source of magic. Daniel overrode what it wanted. He held on.

The dragon raised its head on the towering column of its neck. It swept back its wings to their full breadth, blotting out the sky behind sheets of swirling color and generating a wind gust that fed the flames. Blue fire exploded from its yawning mouth, high enough to reach the moon.

Daniel staggered in the heat blast. He fell, chin hitting baked concrete. He didn't search his bones for defensive magic. No Colombian dragon to protect him from the heat. No hippogriff to run away. He needed all his strength to keep hold of the *axis mundi* bone, and he couldn't spare the magic.

Writhing on the ground, he held on.

TWENTY-EIGHT

D oes it hurt?"

Sam could barely breathe. "Yes. It hurts a lot."

He'd been shot through with kraken lightning. He'd been yanked from his perch high in the brainworks and dashed to the ground far below. He tried to summon fire from his bones, but his bones were all cracked, and all his magic was spilling out.

The Hierarch sat cross-legged and leaned over him, his massive body occupying everything in Sam's vision. There was color to his flesh now. More muscle. He was a vision of what Sam might have become had he eaten more magic and grown in power.

The Hierarch winced, not with his own pain, but in sympathy with Sam's. "I'd really prefer not to eat you."

Sam tried to speak and coughed till he had spots in his eyes. He swallowed, took a breath, and tried again. "That's a first. Too full from gorging yourself on my friend?"

"Your friend. Oh, the girl with the hydra."

"Annabel Stokes."

The Hierarch looked confused.

"That was her name. Annabel Stokes."

"Annabel," the Hierarch said, as if trying to commit her name to memory. "Yes, Annabel's healing magic was helpful. But I don't want that kind of help from you, Sam. Discovering myself alive in the firedrake was a surprise. And a nice one. As I once gave you life, you gave it back to me. Thank you for that. I mean that. Thank you very much. But now I want your mind. My own isn't quite fully formed yet. I suppose you may have noticed."

"It's noticeable," Sam agreed, spitting the words out in a sob of pain.

The giant smiled. He was a good sport. "May I have it? Your mind?"

"I need to think about it," Sam said. "Catch my breath."

"You'll have to think quickly, I'm afraid. Daniel Blackland is right outside us. I don't know what he's doing, but I'm sure he means the dragon harm."

Of course Daniel was outside. Where else would he be? Daniel always showed up eventually.

Sam reached deep for the last of his magic.

His remaining fire wasn't strong enough to roast a marshmallow.

But fire wasn't what he needed.

He needed healing. He needed the hydra he'd inherited from the Hierarch. The hydra the Hierarch had devoured.

What he needed was Annabel Stokes.

He searched through his bones and through all his cells, reconstructing the memory of Annabel's scent, just as Daniel had taught him. She'd been inside the dragon as long as Sam, so she smelled mostly of sour acid and bitter flame, of viscera and meat. That's what everything smelled like in the dragon.

He thought of the sound of her voice. A bit of a gruff alto. He thought of her eyes, not afraid to look at Sam, not afraid to see him.

"I think you'd better go ahead and eat me," Sam said.

The Hierarch blinked. "I don't understand."

"I mean I don't want to be your copilot. I mean I would literally rather you eat me than force me to spend another minute with your pizza-dough face. I mean screw you, you idiot. Down the hatch with me."

The Hierarch leaned forward and brought his face close to Sam's. His breath smelled of his last meal. It smelled of hydra and of Annabel.

He opened his mouth wide, and the last thing Sam saw before he closed his eyes and braced himself against the pain of ripped flesh and muscle were the Hierarch's teeth.

The Hierarch let out a small squeal of surprise. White bumps formed on his forehead and grew outward, elongating like wriggling fingers. A pair of fully formed hands followed, and then wrists, and forearms, and then elbows.

"What are you doing?" the Hierarch said, his voice strangled with pain.

"Looks like something you ate doesn't agree with you."

His forehead bulged out with the crackle of dry spaghetti. It was the sound of a splintering skull. Sam watched in horrified fascination as a human form continued to grow out of him—the crown of a head, shoulders, and a back.

The Hierarch shrieked. And the dragon shrieked. And Sam shrieked.

"This *hurts*. This *hurts*."

Sam didn't know which one of them had spoken. He clutched his head, and the Hierarch's eyes bulged in pain.

"Stop it. It *hurts*."

They writhed together, the Hierarch's giant form and Sam's tiny body, joined by magic and pain. And if this was how it ended, so be it. The end of Sam and the end of the Hierarch.

But Sam changed his mind. Even in his agony, he didn't want to die. Even in this form, a thought inside a dragon, a reflection of the Hierarch, he wanted to live. He wanted grass tickling his bare feet. He wanted cool fog on his skin. He wanted flavors on his tongue. He wanted to feel a warm hand in his. He wanted to talk to someone, to tell truths and not hide behind made-up identities. He wanted these things and he wanted Em, and he wanted to live.

He wanted to heal.

The Hierarch's head came apart with a gush of liquid magic, and a form fell to the ground like a birthed calf.

Annabel lay curled among the Hierarch's remains, naked and gasping.

Sam held her, and even though she came out of the healing magic in his body, he hoped he could somehow give healing magic back to her. In a just universe, things would work that way.

He couldn't say how long they stayed together like this. He felt the firedrake's heart like a big, deep drum in his chest, strong and slow.

He didn't know how often the dragon's heart beat. A dozen times a minute or once an hour or once a year. But when Annabel opened her eyes, he felt the thudding in his chest quicken, and the flow of blood through his body strengthened him.

She was still healing him. He released her.

"I have to go to the cockpit," he said.

"Why? What's so great about the cockpit?" Her voice was rough, as though she'd swallowed acid.

"The Hierarch said Daniel's on the outside. I have to go see."

He began unbuttoning his shirt.

Annabel blinked. "Sam? Why are you taking off your clothes?"

"Because you're not wearing any. You can have my shirt."

"Oh. Turn around."

She plucked the shirt from Sam's outstretched hand.

"Thanks," she rasped.

"Well, you saved my life. You're my hydra."

"So I can keep the shirt?"

"Yeah. Sorry if it stinks." He helped her to her feet.

"It's a stinky world, Sam. The whole thing. Inside and out."

Leaning on each other like drunk friends stumbling home, they made their way to the cockpit.

Sam took the pilot's seat and turned a knob, and the dragon raised its head. With the movement of a few levers, he spread the dragon's wings out to their full span and laughed a little with delight.

"Are you doing that?" Annabel said.

"Yeah. The Hierarch's dead. Or . . . you healed the part of me that was the Hierarch. The part of me that wanted the dragon to burn people. The part of me that just wanted to consume. Hell, I don't know. But I think I can operate this thing now."

"Let's see what's happening on the ground," she said.

"Okay, okay . . . I think it's this one." He turned another knob, and the dragon stretched open its jaws and shrieked flame into the orange sky. "Oh, crap."

"Maybe you should be a little more careful."

"Sorry, sorry . . . here. It's definitely this one." He touched a control, and the dragon's head angled down. The scene outside the dragon's eyes was one of burning structures, charred mechanical equipment, melting wires, billowing smoke, and spreading flames.

Daniel knelt in the middle of it, a small man confronting a colossus. He struggled to his feet, his chin smeared with dirt and blood. He looked like a mess. He always did. It was almost comforting to see him this way.

Daniel clasped his hands and spread his legs, as if trying to lift an enormous weight, something the earth was trying to claim for its own. Sam felt its gravitational pull as well. He braced his feet against the control panel, afraid he'd fly through the dragon's eyes and out into . . . what, exactly?

Daniel was working some kind of magic. In his grip was probably an osteomantic bone, and he'd no doubt gone through great pains to obtain it, and to bring it here to Sam.

Annabel held him in the seat by his shoulders. "What's wrong with you?"

"Don't you feel it? Daniel's pulling."

"No," Annabel said, somber. "It's just you."

Sam flew from her and smashed into the control panel. He gasped, pain in his ribs.

Annabel wrapped her arms around him.

"Maybe you should let go," she whispered in his ear. Her breath was warm, her lips brushing his jaw. "Maybe you should go home."

"Go home to what?"

"He's your friend, right? You trust him?"

Sam didn't want to live in a world where he couldn't.

"I trust him," he said.

"Then stop fighting it."

It was decided, and they both knew it. But Sam still didn't want to give in to Daniel's magic.

"What about you, Annabel?"

"I have to stay here."

"But how can you? You're part of me. If I leave, then you—"

"Don't be so full of yourself. You are not my entire universe. And if you are, well, I'm willing to risk death to prove I'm really alive." She ran a hand across the control panel. "It's good this way. Someone's got to fly this thing."

A dragon with healing magic at its core? It was too good to believe in.

"Now," she said. "Do you want to jump, or shall I push?"

Clutching him tight, she pressed her body against his, and they kissed. Just when he was sure he should change his mind and remain with her in the Pacific firedrake, she pulled her hands free.

Sam became untethered, and everything he was—body, mind, magic—flew free.

TWENTY-NINE

Gabriel arrived at his office with an empty bag. After twenty minutes of sorting through his desk and shelves and files, the bag remained empty. It turned out there was nothing he wanted to keep. He was tempted to douse the whole place in gasoline and toss in a book of lit matches, but that would be pointless. He'd long ago outfitted all his facilities with quality fire-suppression systems.

Instead, he'd just walk away. One of his lieutenants would inherit a nice corner office with a view. Or maybe they'd seal the doors and leave the place in static perpetuity, like a pharaoh's tomb. Maybe Gabriel's office would serve as a cautionary tale of what happens to good bureaucrats when they try to promote themselves to rulers.

"How long are you going to mope?" Max said from the sofa. He'd been sitting there when Gabriel showed up and remained, silently drinking coffee.

Gabriel wore a patch over his right eye, and he had to turn his head nearly all the way around to see Max. He didn't like moving his head. It brought him nausea and fresh hammers of pain.

"Not much longer. I'm almost done here."

"Does that mean you're going to stop moping, or you're just going to mope somewhere else?"

"Don't mock me, Max. You don't get to do that anymore."

Max arched his eyebrows. "Why not?"

Gabriel zipped his still-empty bag shut and stuffed it in the wastepaper basket. "Because you shot me in the head."

"With a rubber bullet," Max said, apparently dismayed that Gabriel was even bringing this up.

"In the head, Max. I might have died."

"But you didn't." Indeed, Max had managed to drag an unconscious Gabriel to the waiting airplane at the Pulgas Water Temple south of San Francisco, and they were halfway home before Gabriel woke up with a concussion and blind in one eye.

"So, you're packing it all in, just because you're angry with me?"

Gabriel sat on the surface of his desk. It was exhausting to remain upright for longer than a few minutes. "I'm packing it in because you were right to shoot me. The water mage controls a lot of power. The minute he starts to think his job is more than delivering water to the realm, the minute he starts to think he should have his very own firedrake—"

"That's when he becomes another Hierarch," Max said.

"Yes. And that's when it's time to pack it in."

"So, you're not going to thank me?"

"No, I'm not going to thank you," Gabriel said, careful not to raise his voice, because raising his voice made him dizzy. "You shot me."

"With a rubber bullet."

"In the head."

"There are worse places to be shot, Gabriel. Anyway, here, I have something for you." He got up and dropped a file folder on Gabriel's desk.

"What's this? Going-away present?"

"Status reports from when we were gone."

Gabriel moved his hand away from the folder as if it were a venomous spider. "This no longer concerns me."

"Okay," Max said, opening the folder. The top page was a bullet-point list of priorities, and without realizing he was doing so, Gabriel started reading it.

There'd been a major reduction of water flow on the Ten Flumeway east of La Brea.

Electrical output at the Long Beach wave-generation facility was down 3 percent.

Someone had sabotaged the new dam under construction at Lake Castaic. The intelligence report indicated it was Mother Cauldron's work.

"You shot me, Max."

"I'm sorry."

Max hit a button on the wall, and the doors to Gabriel's private elevator opened. Together, they descended to the subbasement, where Gabriel climbed the ladder to his throne, a chair of moderate comfort poised before a sprawling array of switches and wheels. He reached out and opened a valve, and then another, and before long he found himself watching over the realm's water.

Below, standing at the foot of his throne, Max watched over the realm's water mage.

Daniel headed for the storage facility in San Pedro as soon as his boots hit Los Angeles. He rolled up the door and discovered a scene of violence. Bullet casings and fragments of cracked ruhk egg littered the floor. Scorch marks marred the walls.

"Em?"

When there was no answer, he called her name louder: "Em!"

"Back here." Her voice sounded weak from behind her sandbag barrier.

Daniel squeezed through a gap in the sandbags. Em sat on the folding camp chair in front of the crate, her rifle resting across her lap. Lines of encrusted blood striped her face. One of her eyes was swollen shut. Her left arm was in a sling. She gripped a pistol in her right hand.

The crate containing Sam's golem-body looked as pristine as when Daniel left it in Em's care.

"Did you get the bone?" she said.

"You need a hospital."

"I need to know if you got the bone."

Daniel set down his heavy bag, reached in with both hands, and lifted the bone. "Right here."

Em closed her good eye. "Great," she said.

He knelt before her and got out a jar of eocorn paste. "Looks like you had company. Who came for him?"

"Who didn't?" she said. "But nobody stayed very long."

"Of course they didn't. Not with you here." Gently, he dabbed her swollen eyelid with the paste.

She let out a long breath and smiled lazily. "That's warm. I like it. How'd the job go?"

He thought of Gabriel Argent, shot by Max.

He thought of Ethelinda.

"We got it done," he said. "Everyone did what they had to do."

The rest fell to Daniel.

He set up a folding table, little more than a cot, and fussed with a blanket to pad the metal framing. Em handed him a crowbar, and Daniel went to work on the crate. The nails came out with small cracks and squeaks, like extracted teeth. Inside the crate stood a steel tank, about the size of a large water heater. It bothered Daniel that the steel was dull, with lumpy welds like scars. He wished for everything to be clean and precise and sterile. But when was life ever really like that?

He could barely make out the golem's face through a small square of cloudy glass.

"How does this work?" Em asked him.

"Messily. Is there a bucket?"

"Here," Em said, passing him a yellow plastic pail.

Daniel placed it under a spout at the bottom of the tank and turned the spigot, and whatever osteomantic medium the golem hadn't already soaked up drained out. He waited until the last of it plinked into the bucket.

After unfastening some bolts, Daniel swung the front of the tank open. The golem's body steamed in the cold air. It was Sam's size, but seemed somehow younger, perhaps because its white skin had never been touched by sun, had never been cut or bruised. The body would never be so unharmed as it was in this moment, before its life had begun.

Daniel undid the straps holding the golem upright and maneuvered one of its arms under his shoulders.

"Maybe we should get Moth," Em said. "I'm not going to be much help with my busted arm."

"No, I can carry him."

"You won't prove anything by breaking your back."

But Daniel ignored her and managed to hoist the golem into a fireman's carry. After only three steps toward the table, he regretted not listening to Em. Yet he got the golem to the table, and he set the body down on its back without dropping it.

The golem lay there, chest rising and falling, eyes open, seeing but not comprehending.

Daniel took a moment to rest before getting out his knife. The blade was copper, a soft metal, but hardened by osteomancy. The cut would need to be deep.

He placed the point of the knife against the golem's skin above its heart. With a breath, he drew an inch-long line down and in. The golem gasped but lay there while Daniel cut it. Blood welled up in the incision, gleaming in the fluorescent lights.

Daniel lifted the *axis mundi* bone and inserted it into the wound. One edge remained above the skin. Daniel pushed it in with the heel of his palm, drawing more blood that ran in strands down the golem's white chest. He held his hand there, over the golem's heart.

The golem breathed. Its heart beat. Its skin felt warm against Daniel's hand. It blinked and swallowed and was by all indications alive. But would it ever be Sam?

Daniel wondered if there was something else he could do. Maybe he should slit his wrists open and bleed his own magic into Sam. Maybe it would give Sam the strength he needed to crawl out of the bone and into the golem's body.

But it didn't work that way. Daniel had brought Sam to the doorstep, and it was up to Sam to walk through the door.

Outside, tugs blew their horns, towing barges down the big canals. He could hear Em's breathing, and his own. The fluorescents buzzed overhead.

It felt more like a death watch than waiting for a birth, and when Em came and held Daniel's other hand, Daniel wondered if that was what it had become.

"You okay?"

It was barely a whisper, but the sound of Sam's voice knocked the air out of Daniel as if he'd been punched.

Daniel leaned over him and brushed his damp hair away from his eyes.

"Yes, Sam. I'm fine."

Sam blinked as though everything were bright, as if the world was new and everything in his vision a novel, unfamiliar sight. He raised himself halfway up and looked at the blankets, at the walls, at Daniel's face.

"I'm naked," he said. "I'm naked, and Em's in the room."

"It's nothing I haven't seen before," Em said.

"That doesn't make it better. It just means you can make comparisons."

Daniel tucked the blankets around Sam and pulled them up to give him some cover.

Sam's body gave off heat, and to Daniel, standing near it with Em, each of them holding one of Sam's hands, it felt like nothing so much as warming himself by a campfire.

Dinner itself was just okay, overpriced salads of bitter artisanal lettuce at a Santa Monica bistro, but Sam finally got to do a thing he thought he'd never accomplish: get through a meal with Em without anyone trying to kill them. Afterward, they walked along the beach with their pants rolled up, letting white-foam surf chill their toes.

Sam was telling Em about Annabel Stokes.

"What I don't get is, I'm what the Hierarch ate. And the Hierarch ate her. So why couldn't she heal him? Or the part of him that was leftover in me? Why was he still such an evil bastard?"

"Is that what you're wondering? Or is it really why *you* aren't an evil bastard?"

"Can't anyone just answer a question with an answer? Is that not allowed?"

"I don't know, is it?"

A flock of shorebirds picked the sand with long beaks and fled from a breaker. Sam and Em fled with them, giggling. Sam had never heard Em giggle before. It was unsettling. And wonderful.

"Listen," he said, "you're a golem of the original Emma Walker. You and all the other Emmas must have thought this through. Haven't you worked it out?"

"You've met my sisters. Do I seem much like them?"

"Not much."

"And Cassandra ran into more Emmas when she was with Argent and Max up North. It didn't sound like they were much like me."

"No. They sounded like evil bastards. So, why? Why were they like that but you're not? Why was the Hierarch like that and I'm not?"

Em held his arm and leaned into him. "Because we're not what we eat. We're what we do, and what we sacrifice, and what we love. And if we choose right more often than we choose wrong, we become who we want to be."

"You mean if we choose right, and we have a lot of luck."

"Luck," Em said. "Yeah. We need shitloads of luck."

Sam covered her hand with his own. His hand, grown from one of his hairs, from a body created by the Hierarch, generated from his own flesh.

Sam had a hand. And a body. He was still alive, here in the cooling night air, here with Em.

No, Sam was not what he ate.

He was friends, and magic, and luck.

Daniel had no photographs of himself with his mother, but he had an empty picture frame that used to contain one. He still remembered the photo. He was about five, on the saddle of a red bike with silver tassels flying back from white handlebar grips. The picture was a little blurry because he was pedaling with a fury. His mother was jogging along, not touching him or the bike, but her hand hovering near the sissy bar to catch him in case he teetered over. They were both grinning like lunatics.

Otis made him get rid of the picture when he was fifteen. It was too dangerous to keep evidence of Daniel's connection to his mother and father. Daniel hated Otis for making him do it, but he understood the wisdom in it, so he burned it in the gas jet of his osteomancer's torch.

He kept the empty frame.

He held it before him now and looked through it at the last house he'd lived in with his parents before they separated. His dad's salary at the Hierarch's Ministry of Osteomancy netted a two-story white colonial in the hills of Westwood. For some reason, Daniel had expected to find it gone. Maybe just a charred foundation on a hard-baked lot. But it looked exactly as he remembered it, shaded by maple trees and nestled in a cozy blanket of ivy.

His mother was dead.

Cassandra told him what she'd done as soon as he joined her and Moth on the other side of San Francisco Bay. Maybe she figured if he killed her on the spot, then she wouldn't have to go through the trouble of hauling her ass all the way back home to Los Angeles.

Daniel didn't kill her. He didn't do anything to her. He didn't speak to her. The job wasn't finished yet.

But now Sam was alive, and all his crew were accounted for, and Jo Alverado had restored his face so he didn't have to see Paul in the mirror every time he shaved.

There was nothing left to be done.

"Can I help you?"

A man came out of the house and down the porch steps, glaring at Daniel from across the lawn. He had the build and the iron-gray buzz cut of a football coach, and if he decided he wanted to pummel Daniel, Daniel figured he might just let him. He didn't have the stomach for electrocuting anyone today.

"I used to live here."

"Must have been a long time ago."

"It was. I was just a little kid then."

The man's demeanor softened. "Do things look much different?"

"No. They pretty much look exactly the same." It seemed like an impossibility, but it was true.

"Would you like to come in? Have a look around? We've done some remodeling in the kitchen and bathrooms, but we haven't changed things all that much."

Daniel thought about it. It might be good to wander the old rooms and halls. There used to be a piano in the big living room, and elite osteomancers and their families would come over for Victory Day parties. There was a backyard pool and a barbecue pit. Maybe Daniel would find something there to fill the empty picture frame.

"That's kind of you," Daniel said. "But I should go home."

The party was Em's idea, and she had to shame Daniel into coming. Moth threatened him with physical harm unless he showed up. The venue was Cassandra's house.

Daniel arrived with a bottle of tequila in a paper bag, and four bars of really good chocolate for Em. It wasn't from San Francisco, but she forgave him for that.

He found things in full swing. It was a small gathering—just Sam and Em and Jo and Moth and Cassandra—but it was loud, with Moth generating the boisterousness of a soccer team celebrating a World Cup victory.

"Jerk face!" Moth hollered, bear-hugging Daniel and carrying him from the threshold to the middle of the living room. "You're late. I was about to go looking for you with my party fist."

Daniel handed him the bottle. "This is booze. Drink this and calm down."

"I will," Moth bellowed. "I will drink this and calm down."

Sitting on the couch, protectively close to Sam, Em laughed, not at Moth, but at Daniel's wince.

"She's in the kitchen," Sam said. He alone knew how uncomfortable Daniel was coming here. Sam was the only one Daniel had told about Cassandra killing his mother.

"Right," Daniel said, steeling himself. It was only eight steps to the kitchen, but it was a long eight steps.

Cassandra was pulling a tray of tamales from the oven. Her shoulders stiffened when Daniel entered.

She set the tray down on the stovetop and turned around.

Over the years, Daniel had seen almost every kind of expression on her face when she looked at him. Anger. Exasperation. Hurt. Love. This was the first time he'd seen fear. She knew he wouldn't harm her physically, but there were worse kinds of harm.

"I didn't plan a speech," he said. "Because you know how it is. You can map out a job to every last detail, but in the end, things always go to shit and you just have to improvise."

"Well, I did plan a speech. Do you want to hear it?"

"No."

"Okay." She prodded some tamales with a spatula.

"I don't know what to say. I can't say thank you for killing my mother."

"No. I don't suppose anyone could."

"But Cassandra?"

"Yeah?"

"It's a pretty fucked-up world, isn't it?"

She put down the spatula, and they embraced in front of the stove, where the food she'd prepared to celebrate the recovery of the Hierarch's golem and Daniel's son gave off delicious aromas.

Later, Daniel stood out on the lawn, watching the reflected moon dance in the canal waters. Laughter leaked from the house, mostly Moth's, but also Sam's and Em's and Jo's, and even Cassandra's. His boat bumped against the curb of the canal.

"Hey." Sam came out of the house and joined Daniel. "Moth is making margaritas. You better claim one before they're gone."

Daniel tried to inspect Sam without revealing he was doing so. The new golem body was still thin and pale, and Sam moved in it uncertainly, as if he were walking on ice.

"How are you feeling?"

"Everything feels weird," Sam said. "Then again, everything *is* weird, so I guess that's to be expected. So stop looking at me like I'm a bomb about to go off. I'm okay."

"Okay." There was a fresh burst of laughter from the house. "You should go back inside. I'll be there in a bit."

"Yeah? Then why's your suitcase in the trunk of your boat?"

"How'd you know it's back there?"

Sam shook his head, as if Daniel should have known better. Which he should have. "Cassandra lifted your keys and snuck out to check."

Daniel dug into his jacket pocket.

"They're there," Sam said. "She snuck them back, of course."

"Of course."

"So, where are you going?"

"Don't know."

Daniel had run away from his father's house when the Hierarch came to feed on magic. He'd run away with Sam to keep him from hungry osteomancers. Those had been the right decisions. And it was the right decision now, not to escape anything, but to lure away anyone who would come after him. To keep the Northern Hierarch and Cynara away from his friends. To make sure when she was grown, Ethelinda wouldn't seek revenge on the people Daniel loved.

"I have an idea for you, Daniel." Sam held out his hand for the keys. "Leave tomorrow if you want. But tonight, stay here. Stay here, not as the mastermind of a criminal band. Not directing things. Not leading us all into dark places. Just stay here. Enjoy some light and laughter. Have some margaritas."

Sam kept his hand out. Daniel gave him the keys, and Sam retrieved Daniel's suitcase from the trunk.

As they went back to the house, a trace of light streaked across the sky.

Sam saw it, too.

"I've spotted a lot of those the last few nights," he said. "I've decided it's Annabel Stokes."

Daniel smiled. "A firedrake powered by healing magic. That's magic too good to believe in."

"Maybe," said Sam, holding the front door open for him. "But if it's true? Then what a world this could be."

ACKNOWLEDGMENTS

My thanks go first to my wife and best friend, Lisa Will, for making my life possible and fun. And a great heaping pile of thanks to the team at Tor Books, an incomplete roster of which includes Patrick Nielsen Hayden, Miriam Weinberg, Patty Garcia, Leah Withers, Theresa DeLucci, Irene Gallo, and so many other people who did the thousands of things it takes to turn a manuscript into a book that you can find on store bookshelves.

Thank you, booksellers of all types, for practicing your profession with love and dedication to books and reading. And particular thanks to Mysterious Galaxy, my home store.

I'm grateful to Cliff Nielsen for his wonderful cover art, and to Caitlin Blasdell for her expert agenting.

Thanks to Joe Skilton and Terry Tyson, real magicians who generously gave me advice on sleight of hand. If I got things wrong, it's my fault, not theirs.

I owe a lot of gratitude to bloggers, reviewers, fellow authors, and folks on social media for showing interest in my work. The encouragement is very much appreciated. So, too, is the support I receive from so many awesome friends, including Deb Coates, Sarah Prineas, and Jenn Reese. And a special thanks to

Elise Matthiesen, who sent me a pendant with a piece of stego-don bone.

And finally, a shout out to my officemates Dozer and Amelia. I love them, but they are a little bit horrible. They are dogs.